PRAISE FOR DANA MARTON

"In *Secret Soldier*, Dana Marton introduces an irresistible couple who take the reader on a fast-paced, unforgettable military adventure."

RT Book Review on *Secret Soldier*

FORCED
DISAPPEARANCE

ALSO BY DANA MARTON

FORCED
DISAPPEARANCE
DANA MARTON

Montlake
Romance

Published by Montlake Romance, Seattle

www.apub.com

Amazon, the Amazon logo, and Montlake Romance are trademarks of Amazon.com, Inc., or its affiliates.

ISBN-13: 9781477826058
ISBN-10: 147782605X

Cover design by Marc J. Cohen
Library of Congress Control Number: 2014909531

Printed in the United States of America

I'd like to dedicate this book to my wonderful readers, who are with me book after book and are a constant source of friendship and support on Facebook: Ramona Kersch Kekstadt, Jenn Nixon, Sue Chatterjee, Dotty Graves, Deb Posey Chudzinksi, Ellen Viars, Janet Vaulard, Deb Burchfield, Mary Gooding, Stacy Brown, Amanda Scott, Mandy Pederick, Margaret Sholders, and all my other wonderful reader friends.

Chapter 1

ONE OF THESE DAYS, THEY WERE GOING TO KILL THE STUPID MONKEY. GLENN Danning squinted against the Venezuelan sun, watching through the gap-toothed windowpanes as the half-dozen soldiers in the compound's courtyard took turns throwing their knives.

The monkey darted toward the cement block wall that separated the courtyard from the jungle, scrambling toward the top where the yellow, blue, and red Venezuelan flag danced in the breeze, but a rope mercilessly yanked the animal back toward his cage.

Army barracks surrounded the space on three sides, a gated opening and guard shack closing off the fourth. Five beat-up military trucks and a Jeep were parked inside, the rest of the dusty courtyard empty, used for morning and evening formation for the soldiers and as a hangout place when they were on break.

The monkey darted around, but once a knife was in motion, he froze and covered his eyes, as if he was in some kind of circus act. That seemed to amuse the men to no end. They laughed, taunting the animal for his cowardice.

Their attacks were halfhearted at best. If they killed their sole source of entertainment, they'd have nothing to look forward to in their day other than mind-numbing guard duty.

Tied hand and foot to the wooden chair in the middle of the interrogation room, Glenn suspected the reason he still lived was pretty much the same.

He drew his gaze from the window to check the clock over the metal door just as the door opened.

The small garrison's commanding officer was late.

"Trouble with room service this morning?" Glenn joked, and went on despite the decidedly unamused look on the man's face. "Me too. To tell you the truth, I've been in better hotels."

He tried to read the man's eyes. The commander had never been late before.

Did someone from the US embassy show up finally? Glenn had been memorizing schedules and making friends with one of the guards, planning to escape on his own. But if help was here . . .

"If you have a scheduling conflict"—he smiled at the commander— "we can just postpone. I'm pretty flexible time wise, actually."

The commander's eyes remained cold, humor clearly wasted on the bastard. Since Glenn didn't crack jokes to entertain his captor, he wasn't too heartbroken. He joked around to keep his own spirits up. He needed whatever mental boost he could get in this place. *Bleak* was the word, everything hard cement and equally hard metal.

Even with several of the small windowpanes broken out and air moving through, the stench of sweat, blood, and urine filled the room—the least of his discomforts, for sure. He filled his lungs, bracing himself for the coming festivities.

The commander, around five foot seven in his army boots, his green uniform still crisp this early in the day, leaned his riding crop against the wall by the door and paused to pick his teeth with his fingernail. Then he dropped his hand to his side and sucked air through his yellow teeth before he said, "You talk, filthy American spy, or I kill you right now."

After four full weeks of bloody torture, neither of them took the words too seriously. Once Glenn had survived the first, unbearable, days, the two of them had settled into a routine. The bastard huffed and puffed, tossing threats, while Glenn protested his innocence, then passed out when the pain turned too ugly.

Unfortunately, the commander had learned his prisoner's limits fast. At the beginning, they were done in half an hour, then Glenn would come to in his cell, every inch of his body hurting. But by now the commander knew exactly what and how much his prisoner could handle. Their torture sessions could easily last half a day.

"We could skip today," Glenn suggested cheerfully. "What's the point of being boss if you can't play hooky now and then? You go have some fun. Hell, you look like you could use it. I won't tell anybody."

The man didn't react as he pushed over the wooden cart that held his instruments. With a cold look, he skipped over the pliers and the metal spikes and grabbed a handful of electrodes. He pressed them onto Glenn's forehead and neck, then turned on the nasty little device that delivered the electric shocks. He skipped the lower settings altogether and went straight to ten.

Oh shit.

Glenn braced himself in the wooden chair.

The air crackled a second before unbearable pain sliced through him, as if he'd been cut in two by a giant ax. The stomach-turning smell of burned flesh filled his nose. His muscles turned painfully rigid, his joints popped, audible over the buzz of the machine.

He'd dislocated his shoulder the last time they'd gone to level nine, the highest setting they'd flirted with until now. At this stage, his best hope was not to break his own bones when he convulsed, or bite off his tongue and choke on the blood.

His peripheral vision narrowed, the room dimming. *Hello, darkness, my old friend.* But before he could pass out, the commander flipped off the switch, and Glenn slumped forward in the chair, only his restraints holding him in place.

The pain, unfortunately, did not leave with the electric current. He could barely breathe as the man strode to the door and picked up his riding crop, shouting in heavily-accented English as he approached again.

"You are American spy! You are enemy of the Bolivarian Republic of Venezuela. Why did you come here? Who sent you? You tell me names!" With each sentence, he smacked the riding crop against the side of his boot for emphasis.

"Inocente." Glenn pushed the single word through clenched teeth, his jaw muscles still contracted.

If he thought responding in the man's native language would help him, he had another thing coming. The riding crop lashed across his face the next second, missing his right eye by a fraction of an inch, sending blood squirting as it broke his skin.

The air stuck in his lungs. He clenched his jaw even harder, doing his best to block out the pain, forcing his brain to think.

Something did happen this morning.

The new level of violence went beyond the routine interrogation he'd become used to, had trained himself to bear day after day.

Maybe the US embassy *had* tracked him down and demanded him back. Maybe today was the commander's last chance to get anything out of him. Glenn braced himself, hope giving him strength. If he had to survive only this one last day, he could handle anything.

Or not, he thought two hours later—a bloody, broken mess— sitting only because he was tied in that position. His tormentor tossed the bloody pliers he'd used to yank out a toenail, then strode out of the room with a curse.

The commander took breaks as regular as a union worker, for which Glenn was profoundly grateful. The brief reprieves gave him a chance to recuperate.

His bladder was full, pressing painfully against his bruised kidneys. His captors didn't allow him use of the facilities while in interrogation, the humiliation part of the effort to break him. So he did what he'd been forced to do daily in here—released his muscles. Warm urine trickled down his leg to the cement floor, adding to the stench around him.

Don't think about it. Don't feel. Don't break.

He closed his eyes and went away in his mind, the only thing he had control over.

Slowly, a picture formed. He stood on his favorite golf course at Myrtle Beach: sunshine, birds, endless green, the ocean. He soaked that in for a minute, before pain blasted through the stained-glass window images of his imagination.

He drew a deep breath, kept his eyes closed, and went to his engineering lab. Working on a problem might occupy his mind more thoroughly. But even that didn't work today. So he went back to her.

Miranda Soto, the first girl who'd ever let him see her naked. That kind of thing left an impression on a guy. Scientific fact: a situation in which a naked woman wouldn't lift a man's spirits did not exist.

They'd both gone to MIT at seventeen to study engineering. He'd been a total nerd. He didn't notice things if they didn't have pulleys and levers and cranks. But he'd noticed *her*. She'd bested him in their very first class, on the very first project.

On the next project they'd been partners. They'd spent a lot of time together, designing the engineering of an energy-neutral palm house for the Boston Public Garden. He'd developed a serious fondness for her mind, for her long, dark hair, for her breasts. He might have become obsessed with the breasts, in particular. He'd asked her if he could touch them.

She'd looked like she was going to deck him. "For experimental reasons," he'd said. "I've never done this. I want to know how it works." Her eyes narrowed. And then she'd unbuttoned her shirt and said, "Sure."

They began an eighteen-month enthusiastic study of life sciences, human sexuality, in specific. She'd been his best friend. His first lover. She'd made him feel like a man.

A smile tugged at Glenn's lips. She'd made him feel a lot of things. And then she'd left him.

He opened his eyes. *That* part had not been happy.

He turned his head to the window, toward the slightest of breezes coming in. A new batch of soldiers were having a smoke, leaving the monkey alone for the time being. The animal winked at Glenn, his only other talent beyond covering his eyes. He never winked at anyone else, only the prisoner when they caught each other's glance through the window now and then. Maybe Winky was smart enough to know that they were sharing the same fate.

Glenn looked from the monkey to the men. *Something strange there.* The men's uniforms were cleaner than usual, their hair in order. And the courtyard had been swept at one point during the interrogation. Some kind of a tropical fruit tree grew outside the wall and dropped fruit inside the compound. The ones Winky could reach, he ate. The rest were left to rot where they fell. But someone had cleaned them away today.

Why the change?

Somebody was definitely coming. Someone the commander wanted to impress.

But the hope Glenn had been working up crashed and died the next second when a new thought pushed to the surface. The commander wouldn't care about impressing visitors from the US embassy. He hated Americans, considered them all capitalist pigs.

The only reason to release Glenn would be to make nice with the US. In which case, the last minute bloody torture would be counterproductive. If Venezuela decided to return their prisoner, they would have let Glenn wash this morning, given him clean clothes, gotten him into as good a shape as possible so they could deny torture.

But if the Americans weren't coming, then who?

A cold shiver ran down his spine despite the heat. Losing the last bit of hope hurt more than the electric shocks, more than the whip. He swore. It didn't make him feel any better.

Think.

The visitor had to be someone who'd be pleased by the torture, by the prisoner's busted face. The commander's superior officer? That would explain the renewed vigor in questioning. The commander would be hard-pressed to show results.

Speaking of the devil . . . Even as Glenn watched, the man appeared in a doorway outside and began barking commands at his men in the courtyard. The soldiers jumped to attention and ran to do his bidding while the commander disappeared back into the building.

He strode into the interrogation room a minute later. *Break over.* He cranked the machine. "Who are your connections? Tell me their names."

And the pain began all over again.

"You are a spy. Why are you here?"

Glenn's body twisted. *Make it up. Confess*, his brain screamed.

Maybe they'd trade him. But that hinged on the US having a Venezuelan spy in custody and being willing to make the trade. Glenn, an ordinary businessman, wasn't exactly a valuable asset. Chances were, a confession would make his situation worse, not better. If he faked being a spy, the commander would push even harder to get classified government information out of him.

The machine hummed louder, then a second later, a fresh wave of agony hit. When darkness slowly moved in to claim Glenn, the commander turned off the switch and gave him a few minutes to breathe, to revive, to anticipate the next onslaught of pain. The bastard smiled as he waited. He did enjoy his nasty little game.

"This has to run up your electric bill." Glenn used the last of his strength to speak. "What do you say we give energy conservation a nod and quit for today?"

The man narrowed his cold eyes, instant displeasure replacing his smile. He didn't like being talked back to. "I broke many men. I broke them fast. Why don't you break, American?"

"I guess I wasn't made to break," Glenn lied, even as he at last teetered on the ragged edge of his breaking point.

He turned his head toward the light of the window and the slight breeze. The soldiers were moving the trucks around. He hadn't even heard the motors start up. They weren't leaving, just pulling the vehicles to the other side of the courtyard.

They were clearing the area in front of the cement brick wall. Now that the trucks weren't blocking his line of sight, Glenn could fully see the wall for the first time, the cement chinked all over the place.

Bullet holes? The courtyard was too narrow for target shooting, but even as he thought that, his brain produced the answer. *Firing squad.*

He swallowed hard. *Dead men tell no tales.*

Maybe the commander didn't want whoever was coming to talk with the prisoner. Maybe he wasn't supposed to interrogate Glenn as hard as he had. Maybe he didn't want to admit that he'd been wrong and their captive wasn't a spy.

With Glenn dead, the commander could spin the story any way he wanted. He could tell his superiors that the prisoner *had* been a spy, but had been shot while trying to escape—whatever he had to say to cover up his mistake of detaining and torturing a US citizen.

Glenn's attention snapped back to the room as adrenaline rushed through him. His slow-moving plans for the friendly guard were never going to happen. No time for that. Not much time left for anything. So he did the first thing he could think of: made his body go rigid, rolled his eyes back in his head, and faked a seizure.

The commander threw something at him. Then, after a minute, he called for his soldiers, who dragged Glenn to his windowless cell and tossed him in.

For long minutes, he lay there in the darkness and just wheezed in cool, dank air, gave his body a chance to recover from the torture. How long before they'd drag him outside? An hour or two tops. They'd want him revived enough so he could stand for the firing squad.

Cold panic clawed its way up his spine.

Don't think about it. Don't feel. Don't break.

He went to Miranda, to her sweet lips and creamy skin. The way he felt buried in her body to the hilt, his nose nestled in her soft hair that always smelled like the honey shampoo some of the chemistry students mixed up in the lab and sold for beer money. As mad and betrayed as he'd felt all these years for her leaving, out of his entire life, she was still his best memory.

Glenn didn't open his eyes until he was sure the men were gone and no longer watching him through the narrow slat in the door. Slowly, he unfolded his battered fingers and ran his thumb over the electrode he'd ripped off and palmed while faking the seizure. The two-inch copper rod was going to save his life, he decided.

He ignored the pain that rippled through him as he stood and moved toward the strip of light under the door. He felt for the old-fashioned lock, bent the end of the thin copper rod, and inserted it into the small opening, listened as he turned his makeshift key. Nothing. He repositioned the rod and turned it again. And again.

His ears strained for the click of freedom as much as for footsteps outside, knowing the soldiers could come for him at any second. But he didn't hear anything.

He pulled out the rod, reworked the end so the bent part was two millimeters longer. Then he tried the lock again, and this time something caught with a small, metallic click.

He pocketed the piece of metal as he straightened, then opened the door a fraction of an inch and listened. Silence in the hallway. He peeked out into the long, gray corridor. Nobody in sight.

Left or right?

The soldiers usually dragged him left for interrogation. He limped in the opposite direction.

At the end of the hallway, he had a choice to either step out to the courtyard or go upstairs. Since a dozen soldiers milled around outside now, Glenn limped up the stairs and ended up on the flat roof. *High ground. So far so good.* He could see the full extent of the compound for the first time.

Six military barracks, all built from cement blocks, formed two courtyards. In addition to the soldiers outside, he could see others through the windows in the buildings.

To the east, a majestic dam stood in the distance. *Guri Dam?* Had they brought him that far south? He squinted, trying to remember the Venezuelan map.

Guri Dam was on the other side of the country from Caracas, where he'd been grabbed in the night a month ago. A definite setback. At this stage, he'd have an easier time reaching the Brazilian border than the US embassy in Caracas.

He looked to the south, toward Brazil. He could see some sort of shantytown—probably the *campamento* he'd heard the soldiers talk about, then a lake, which had to be Lake Guri. The small military installation was probably here to protect the dam.

Keeping low, he moved to the edge of the roof where the building backed up to the jungle. Twenty, possibly twenty-five, feet to the ground.

Maybe he could jump without breaking anything.

Then what? He flexed his swollen, bleeding toes, grit his teeth against the pain. No shoes; he'd lost those in the interrogation room during his first week here. But even if his feet weren't already damaged, he couldn't walk through the jungle barefoot.

Okay, what else?

Hurry!

With a parting glance at the forest, he limped to the other side of the roof and focused on the paved road outside the garrison. He needed a car.

The big army trucks in the courtyard would be too slow, but the smaller military Jeep just inside the gate had potential. He wasn't against grand theft auto under the circumstances.

He retraced his own bloody footprints to the stairs, stopping to listen at the top. Boots slapped against the floor somewhere farther down the hallway, coming closer and closer. Step by silent step Glenn stole down the stairs to intercept the man.

When the soldier was within reach, Glenn popped out of the staircase and elbowed the surprised man in the face, knocking him out, and grabbed the rifle before it could fall to the floor with a clatter.

Quick. He had to clear out before somebody else came.

He slung the weapon over his shoulder before grabbing the guy, ignoring the riot of pain in his muscles as he half carried, half dragged the soldier up to the roof.

He yanked off the man's boots first. They would have been too small even if Glenn's feet weren't swollen beyond recognition, so he tossed them aside, focusing on the positive—the rest of the uniform would fit.

He shoved his own filthy shirt into the man's mouth, then used his threadbare pants to secure the gag in place, tying the pant legs behind the soldier's head.

He kicked off his wet underwear and dragged on the uniform that would have been too small a month ago, but now hung on his emaciated body. The pants were loose, but he couldn't keep the soldier's belt. He needed that to tie the guy's hands and feet together behind his back. The soldier would work himself loose eventually, but hopefully not before Glenn was a good distance away.

Time to go.

He pulled the green canvas hat deep over his face and hurried down the stairs, stopped at the door that led outside. *Showtime.* He stepped into the courtyard.

His heart beat double speed. The rifle made him feel better, but it wouldn't hold the soldiers off too long. His best bet for survival was to stay unnoticed.

The men hurried about their business, preparing for whoever was coming. All armed, all in better shape than Glenn.

No time to hesitate. No time to think up a better plan.

Glenn pushed forward and kept his gait even and strong, ignoring the pain in his feet. He walked with purpose, a man who belonged here. He headed toward the Jeep, adjusting his hat, partly so his uplifted arm would cover his face, and partly so if the soldiers looked at him, their attention would be drawn to the motion on top and miss the fact that Glenn was barefoot and bleeding.

A dozen more steps. He stared straight ahead. And then the stupid monkey screeched.

The rebar cage Winky was tied to stood maybe a dozen feet to Glenn's right. His step faltered. He turned toward the animal, kept his head down, and moved forward. *One second. Two. Three. Four. Five.* He reached the cage. He sliced the rope with the knife he'd lifted off the soldier he'd knocked out. Then he grabbed the end of the rope, turned, and led Winky toward the Jeep.

"Qué pasa?" one of the soldiers called after him. *What's going on?*

Glenn jerked his head toward the main building where he suspected the commander would have his quarters. The gesture should say he was acting on orders. He hurried to the Jeep, the monkey jumping into the back as if he knew his freedom was at hand.

Except another soldier called out, louder and with more authority than the first. "Alto!" *Stop!*

Like hell. Glenn jumped behind the wheel and turned the key in the ignition. He stepped hard on the gas, blinking to clear the stars he saw from the pain in his feet.

"Hang on," he called back to the monkey as the Jeep burst through the wooden gate, slivers flying in every which direction, soldiers shouting and running to catch up.

Twenty yards. Fifty. A hundred. The Jeep nearly reached the main road by the time the first bullets slammed into the back. Glenn turned onto the highway he'd seen from the roof, southward toward the Brazilian border, and kept the gas pedal floored. Winky screeched endlessly in the back, covering his eyes.

"We're as good as gone, amigo," Glenn tried his best to sound reassuring while he drove like mad. "We're halfway to freedom, buddy."

Okay, maybe a little less than halfway.

They hadn't gone a mile before he spotted a military convoy coming head on.

Despicably bad timing. "Looks like the commander's visitors are here."

He glanced back at the trucks roaring after him from the compound. He couldn't go forward and he couldn't go back.

He had one rifle, and a monkey for backup who couldn't stand the sight of violence.

So Glenn yanked the wheel to the right, veered off the road sharply, and crashed into the jungle.

Chapter 2

SHE SHOULD HAVE BEEN SITTING IN MILITARY PRISON. SHE WOULD HAVE PRE-ferred it.

Instead, Miranda Soto was starting a new job at the Civilian Personnel Recovery Unit, CPRU, a new government agency she'd never heard of before she'd been contacted by retired US Army general Eugene Roberts.

She didn't want the job. Alas, she'd spent half her adult life in the army, and when a general asked, nobody said, *Thanks, but no thanks, sir.*

Miranda exited the Washington, D.C., parking garage across the street from her new workplace, stopped at the food cart, and grabbed a bottle of iced coffee. She walked to the corner to cross the street, saw the vet sitting on the grass, dog tags hanging outside his camouflage shirt, one hand held stiffly at his side, sandy hair way past regulation length. He was probably only ten years older than she was, but he looked old enough to be her father. Being homeless did that to people.

He certainly put her worries about her new job into perspective.

She detoured his way and handed him her unopened bottle. "Afghanistan or Iraq?"

"Fallujah." He had that bleak look in his eyes she knew only too well, had his own demons like Miranda had hers.

She reached into her pocket and gave him a small card. "I volunteer at a veterans' assistance agency in the evenings, if you want to stop by. We have free pizza usually." She dug into her wallet and pulled out what bills she had, close to fifty bucks.

He hesitated. "That's too much."

"I just got a new job. First day. Let's celebrate."

He offered a rusty grin. "I'll toast you with a hamburger."

"Make it a double-decker. I'll see you at Vet Services?"

"They got more girls as cute as you?" he asked with a new spark in his blue eyes.

She thought of the volunteers, mostly retired ladies. "In spades."

"I'll check it out." He looked like he might mean that instead of just saying the words to get her off his back. "You better get going. Don't want to be late on your first day."

She hurried on with a quick wave, crossed the street, and strode into a giant block of a government building that swallowed her whole. Elaine Fisher, CPRU office manager, was waiting for her at security.

"I hope you'll like our little department." Elaine, all smiles, led Miranda to the elevators. "General Roberts is testifying at a congressional hearing. He won't be in today, but he's looking forward to meeting you in person tomorrow."

She was in her mid-forties, roughly fifteen years older and maybe half an inch shorter than Miranda, her reddish-brown hair gathered in a clip at her nape. "Is this what you did before?"

"Something similar. Personnel Recovery."

Personnel Recovery searched for military when they went missing. CPRU, her new employer, was the civilian counterpart.

Elaine tucked her ID card into the pocket of her pink shirt, which matched her flower-patterned silk skirt. She pressed the last button, which had a capital B next to it. "It'll be helpful to have another investigator. With about fifteen million Americans traveling overseas each year, we have no shortage of people who need our help."

Seemed like a big job. Large areas of the world were dangerous, due to political and military upheavals, and dangerous to Americans specifically.

"I thought the US embassies took care of US citizens who got into trouble abroad." The job had come about so suddenly, Miranda still had more questions than answers.

"Nominally. The embassies don't have the right investigative personnel. We do," Elaine said with pride as they exited the elevator at the basement level.

A staircase stood at the end of the hallway, leading down. Elaine moved down the steps, and Miranda followed. Apparently, the basement had a basement. Maybe they had security down here, and she needed to get her ID card before they could go up to the offices.

They turned at the bottom of the stairs—the bunker-like, gray cement hallway stretching a hundred feet forward before coming to an abrupt dead end. Elaine opened the single door under the staircase with a proud tilt of her chin.

Miranda blinked. *Under the stairs. Harry freaking Potter.*

"This is my little empire." Elaine gestured to the largest desk in the room, just inside the entrance. A row of baby pictures covered the half partition that defined her space. "My first grandbaby. Girl." She beamed.

"Very pretty." Miranda thought of the photo in her wallet, Matthew sitting at the kitchen table, bouncing Abby on his knee. Not something she'd ever display. She couldn't handle questions. Her losses were her own; they didn't belong in the workplace.

Hell, *she* didn't belong in the workplace, not here. She didn't want to fail again. But when a general asked . . .

Following Elaine, she moved farther into the cavernous office space, curious why she'd been selected, how much the people here knew about her past. Not everything. They wouldn't want her if they did.

A dozen desks sat pushed against the walls in a haphazard pattern, only one in use, by a man who didn't even look up from his laptop as they stepped in. Black, tall, wide-shouldered, he sat in the far corner, the wall behind him covered with a hundred or so headshots, people of every shape and race.

A row of doors stood to the right, most of them open. One door led to a break room, another door to file storage. Past that, Miranda noted a meeting room and three offices. Only one office was occupied at the moment.

Miranda noted the woman inside, lost in a phone conversation. "Where are the rest of the people?"

"Most of the investigators are out on cases. Bjorn, the IT guy, is on vacation. He'll be back tomorrow." Elaine led her to a desk and picked up a manila folder, then handed it to her. "This should have your login ID, passwords, security badge. Everything you need."

Miranda scanned the contents, a dozen printouts and a badge. Not a fancy badge like the CIA or FBI would have, just a laminated card, more like a press pass. The badge had her photo, then her name, followed by "INVESTIGATOR" in capital letters, then the logo of the Department of Defense, and some brief text about her working with the authorization of the United States of America.

She set down the folder and reached for the large cardboard box occupying her chair.

"That's your starter kit." Elaine fussed. "Laptop, cell phone, and so on. You'll have to sign for everything. The paperwork is all in there too. I'll come back and collect it later. Oh, you have a coffee mug in the box too. Coffee's in the break room. If you need something we don't have in the vending machine here, the cafeteria is on the third floor. I'll take you up for lunch. Word of warning, if guys from the other departments make rude bodily noises, just ignore." She rolled her eyes. "Civilian Personnel Recovery Unit is our new name. Originally, we were the Foreign Recovery Team."

Miranda flashed a questioning look.

"FRT."

If there was an intelligent comment to that, Miranda failed to find it.

"You'll meet the other investigators as they return from assignment." Elaine nodded toward the man in the corner and her eyes turned dreamy for a moment. "I'll introduce you to Milo once he's off the phone. He just got back. He's heading out again. We had two new cases come in this morning."

Elaine drew her gaze from the man to Miranda with effort. "I'll let you settle in. When you're ready, come over and I'll take you into Karin's office. Karin Kovacs supervises the investigators."

She hurried back to her desk where the phone was ringing, while Miranda turned on her new laptop and signed into her CPRU email. She had mail already, a confidentiality agreement, access codes to various law enforcement databases, office emergency procedures, other useful documents and links.

She spent maybe fifteen minutes scanning them, then decided she could go through them in detail later. Right now, she was anxious to learn more about her new job, so she closed the laptop and headed to Elaine's desk. "I'm ready."

"Cup of coffee first?" the woman offered as she stood.

Okay, maybe some fortification would be good. "Sure."

Milo was in the break room, his jaw set tightly as if he hadn't smiled in years. Like Elaine, he looked to be in his mid-forties. Elaine introduced him, flushing a little.

He examined Miranda, somber eyes scanning her like an X-ray machine. "Welcome to the Island of Misfit Toys. What have you done to be put here?"

Nothing to share over the water cooler. She wasn't even sure if the general knew the full reason behind her dishonorable discharge from the army. "What did the others do?"

Milo shrugged. "We have a couple of ex-CIA agents whose identities have been compromised, and a few burned-out FBI investigators. Some of us have been transferred here as punishment. It's the Last Chance Ranch." He gave a wry grin. "We have some ex-military. PTSD galore. First time I accidentally knocked over a chair, half the unit hit the deck." He caught himself. "No offense."

"None taken."

Milo gave her a parting nod and strode back to his desk.

"Why is *he* here?" Miranda asked Elaine as she gulped some coffee. "What's with the pictures above his desk?"

Elaine put a hand to her chest. "He was part of the FBI team that sorted clues prior to nine-eleven. He put together a report, warning of imminent attacks. When he approached the CIA, they ignored him. The agency and the bureau never combined their notes. He thinks he should have done more."

Okay. Wow. Miranda looked at him through the open door. She lived with guilt every day of her life, but she had a feeling it didn't even compare to what Milo must be feeling.

Elaine cast another longing glance toward him. "He keeps pictures of the targets he recovered. He's determined to save one life for each that was lost in the attacks he couldn't prevent."

"That's thousands."

"When Milo says he will, you can believe him. He was shot in the neck last year. Doctor said he wasn't going to make it. He was back to work two weeks later." The words brimmed with admiration. "He refuses to die until his mission is finished."

Her new place of employment was a mental ward, Miranda thought. But far from finding the thought troubling, she relaxed for the first time since she'd walked through the door. She might just fit in.

She finished her coffee and rinsed her mug, left it on the tray next to the others. "Let's go see the boss."

"So what did *you* do to be put here?" Elaine asked on their way over. "You forgot to say."

Miranda glanced at Milo as they passed his desk. Maybe everyone here had a past as dark as hers. Yet the words were still difficult to speak, cold and hard in her mouth like bullets, regretted the second they flew. "I killed a man."

Elaine didn't bat an eyelash. "Haven't we all." She stopped in front of Karin Kovacs's office, knocked on the door, then opened it. "Miranda Soto is here to see you." Then she flashed Miranda an encouraging smile before she walked away.

Okay, weirdest workplace ever. Miranda drew a deep breath, ready to meet her new boss at last.

Tall, pale, wearing a strict charcoal-gray suit, the boss was trim and fit. Her blonde locks were fabulous enough for a shampoo commercial, falling in a perfect straight line to the middle of her back, making Miranda conscious of her short-chopped, no-glamour brown hair that she'd cut for convenience in the army and hadn't figured out what to do with since. Karin Kovacs had no smiles for her as she invited her in with a brisk gesture. Their introduction was even brisker. She didn't seem like the type to waste time on pleasantries.

"Any questions so far?"

"Where do I pick up my service weapon?"

"No service weapons. Every country has different weapons restrictions."

Miranda digested that information. All right. She'd been trained in hand-to-hand combat in the army.

Karin held her gaze, assessing. "I understand you left the army because you shot someone you weren't supposed to. Friendly fire?"

"Something like that," she lied, relieved that Karin didn't know everything.

"We're not going to have any accidents here."

"No, ma'am."

A brisk nod. "Any other questions?"

Miranda glanced at Milo through the open office door. "When do I meet my partner?" She was used to working in teams. She liked having someone to watch her back if things went south. Which, sooner or later, they did on every job, in her experience.

"No partners," Karin informed her matter-of-factly. "Keep in mind that CPRU has no authority to do anything in any of the countries you'll be visiting. You'll be a guest. They have their own law enforcement to fight crime. You'll be there with their permission and at the discretion of their goodwill. In fact, your very presence will imply that we think they can't handle the job, so the work is best done delicately. We can't send an entire team."

Right. "So basically, go in, find the target, and get out without stepping on any toes."

"Keeping a low profile is key. Think of it this way, it's like one of those prime-time crime shows, except our investigators work without a team, deal with hostile cultures and foreign government bureaucracy, and investigate in remote regions where Internet and cell phone reception might not exist, without access to modern lab equipment and the usual amenities." She sounded almost as if she was trying to discourage the new recruit.

Which, of course, had the opposite effect on Miranda. She smiled at last. "CSI: Sahara Desert?"

"Without the authority or the equipment. You'll be spending most of your life on the road, investigating in remote areas, probably living in miserable circumstances. For minimal pay." She watched Miranda dispassionately as she paused. "I usually meet our recruits before they come in for training. Normally, I'm the one who hires the investigators."

Okay, that explained the reserved reception. Miranda shifted on the chair. So why had the general taken an interest in her personally? He'd stepped on Karin's territory. *Great.* Her boss hated her already, and she'd barely started.

"Elaine said two new cases came in today." She wanted to prove, to Karin and to herself, that her mind was on the job, in the right place.

"One LR, one BR. Milo is taking the Live Retrieval. LRs get priority. The Body Retrieval will have to wait." She slid a folder over to Miranda. "This is what a case looks like when it comes in. Basic parameters."

But Miranda didn't hear the last words. She was staring at the photo stapled to the inside of the folder and the name written under it. In a dazed rush, she read the summary sheet. Glenn Danning. Last seen in Caracas, Venezuela, on the fifteenth of March.

Body Retrieval.

Her heart twisted inside her chest. God, she hadn't seen him in ten years. *Four weeks!* "Why did the case come in so late?"

"Mr. Danning was on vacation in Venezuela and not checking in frequently, the family didn't immediately realize that he was missing. And then they tried to find him with their private resources first."

Of course, they would. Gloria wouldn't want publicity. She was old money, from an era when prominent families kept their private lives private. She could afford the best help money could buy and handle the search for her son without the press.

Miranda cleared her throat, a million disjointed thoughts flying through her mind. "I know him."

Karin's eyes narrowed. "Personally? How well?"

"We went to college together. MIT. Could I work on his case? Please."

She hadn't been sure about the job. Part of her was scared of it, what it would do to her, the memories and nightmares it might bring back. But now she held her breath for Karin's response. She needed to bring Glenn back, even if in a box. She owed him that much. Once, a lifetime ago, they'd been good friends. *Lovers.*

Karin raised a strict eyebrow. "We need to go through our protocols first. And training."

"I can read through the protocols on the plane. I had two years with Personnel Recovery in the army. I know how it's done. He's a friend. If it's just a body recovery . . ." She hated saying the words, wouldn't think of that until she had confirmation. "I can't really mess it up, can I? But if he's still alive, every day counts. I know him. I know how he thinks. I'd be the best person to track him."

Her new boss assessed her, tapped her pen on the desk, then laid it down. "I'll check with the general." She picked up her phone and sent a text.

Then Karin pulled a three-inch-thick folder from her desk drawer and plopped it in front of Miranda. "I have some time this morning. Might as well start bringing you up to speed."

Karin ran through a couple of past and current cases, explaining the kind of incidents they handled, the type of protocols they used, and the available resources.

A full hour passed before Karin's phone pinged. She glanced at the screen, then looked back at Miranda, her face emotionless. "All right. If you think you're ready, Glenn Danning is your first case."

A test, Miranda thought. If she failed, Karin had the perfect excuse to let her go.

An hour ago, she would have been fine with that. Not anymore. She was going to bring Glenn back, one way or the other. She was *not* going to fail here.

Chapter 3

HE WAS GOING TO DIE IN THE MIDDLE OF THE VENEZUELAN JUNGLE, WITHOUT his family ever knowing what had become of him. Despite the muggy heat, shivers ran through Glenn as he lay at the foot of a smooth-barked tree on a bed of rotting leaves. He had no shelter, no way to reach the outside world. His Jeep was stuck in the thick vegetation less than a hundred feet from the main road, at least two-dozen miles behind him.

"Let me know if you spot a pizza joint," he called up to the monkey above him in the trees. For some reason, Winky had followed him instead of running off when freed.

Glenn listened to the sounds of the jungle, a symphony of birds and bugs. He hadn't heard the soldiers behind them since that morning. Maybe they'd given up.

They probably thought the jungle would kill him. He hated to make them right, but he was pretty much tapped out. He closed his eyes, trying to ignore the pain.

He'd cleaned his feet in a creek he'd come across at one point, wrapped them in banana leaves that he stuffed with moss for cushioning. The makeshift shoes kept his wounds protected from dirt, albeit too late.

His feet were infected, he had a fever, and he was starving. "One quick nap, then we'll get going," he promised the monkey.

But instead of sleep, his brain filled with images: the commander, the torture . . . Miranda, because he'd been using the memory of her to disassociate from the present. Except now his fever-addled brain remembered only her leaving, discarding him. Ripping his heart out. Not a woman to trust, obviously. He'd been completely naïve and unguarded with her. He hadn't made that same mistake since.

First he'd loved her, then he'd hated her. His mind filled with scenes of fights that never happened, of him telling her exactly what he thought of her. She screamed that she couldn't care less about him. And she buzzed.

Glenn opened his eyes. No, the jungle was buzzing. Or was the sound in his head?

Winky screeched up in the tree, jumping around, clearly agitated. Glenn sat up. Maybe he wasn't hallucinating the noise. What was it?

He struggled to his feet and followed the sound as the buzzing grew louder and louder.

Roadwork?

That'd mean a road. Hope and excitement lent him strength. He lurched forward. But instead of a road crew, once he fought his way through the vegetation that resisted him at every step, he found a sizable logging operation. He crouched behind one of the denser bushes as he watched.

A dozen men worked the heavy machinery that cut the trees and stripped them of their branches, then stacked the logs onto a trailer. They weren't nearly as interesting as the twenty-gallon water container and several coolers—presumably filled with food—on the opposite end of the clearing.

He wanted to run for the buffet. Hunger pushed him forward, urging for a blind dash. But even fever-brained, he knew to be cautious. He stayed in cover.

Would the men turn him over to the police, suspicious of a foreigner who couldn't explain what he was doing here? He couldn't exactly say that he was on the run from the military, who thought he was a foreign spy.

Illegal loggers, on the other hand, wouldn't be so keen on contacting law enforcement. But they weren't keen on witnesses either. They might just shoot him.

His empty stomach cramped with hunger. The loggers had food and water. If he could regain his strength, he might yet beat the fever. If they would help . . .

Except, the dozen burly guys standing between him and the coolers looked rather discouraging. Several carried weapons. Against the dangers of the jungle? Or against anyone who might happen by?

Food and water. Within reach.

He sat back on his heels. Winky dropped to the ground next to him. Not near enough to touch, but close enough to indicate a certain level of trust and camaraderie. A good start, but Glenn needed a favor.

You never knew till you asked. "I could use some distraction."

The monkey winked at him.

Chapter 4

"THIS IS NOT WHAT WE ASKED FOR," TYLER DANNING SAID. GLENN'S younger brother stood at the head of the twenty-foot tiger maple executive conference table at Danning Enterprises, flanked by Gloria Danning, his mother, on one side, and Cesar Montilla, the company vice president, on the other.

The privately held company owned one of Baltimore's most prominent high-rises and had its offices on the top floors, while renting out the rest to other businesses. The executive conference room featured a wall of windows overlooking the city. Apparently, making parts for oil rigs brought in good money.

"Why isn't the FBI handling this?" Tyler demanded.

Miranda turned fully toward him, away from the view. "Because it's not their job. It's mine."

She'd met Tyler ten years ago, when Glenn had dragged her home for a Danning family Thanksgiving. Tyler had been a lanky high school senior at the time. Now he was a pissed-off corporate executive, clearly used to power. He had the same facial structure as Glenn, but while Glenn had inherited Gloria's lighter coloring, Tyler had their father's darker features.

Miranda imagined he intimidated a lot of people. Since she'd faced down insurgents with AK-47s, a self-important suit didn't exactly make her quake. She met his disapproving gaze head on. "Do you have any idea who would benefit from your brother's disappearance?"

Tyler scoffed.

"Who stands to inherit his company shares?" she clarified.

And Gloria burst out with, "Don't be ridiculous!"

Cesar moved next to Gloria and patted her hand on the table. They were about the same age and had been friends for decades. His daughter, Victoria, had been married to Glenn, briefly, until their divorce five years ago, according to the files.

Miranda would have liked to know more about that, but the current stage of the investigation didn't warrant digging into the topic. She waited for Tyler to answer her question.

"In the event of my brother's death, his shares would be divided between Gloria and me equally," Tyler said after a long moment. Even her two sons called Gloria by her given name.

The powerful matriarch had aged in the decade since she'd warned Miranda away from her older son in no uncertain terms. She'd acted like the queen of the castle, which, unarguably, she'd been. Even now, she was as much a grand dame as ever, with perfectly coiffed hair, her still slim figure wrapped in blue silk. She wore the famous Danning pearls. But her mouth was bracketed by lines, worry sitting in her gray eyes. She was a mother who'd lost her child. Miranda couldn't even resent her. She could relate.

She observed the power trio of Danning Enterprises as they glared at her from the other side of the table. The number one question, the one an impartial investigator would ask, was: Did any of the three have anything to do with Glenn's disappearance?

Glenn was an engineer at heart. He wasn't given to flights of fancy. He'd never been irresponsible, certainly not enough to wander off on some adventure and neglect to tell his family. That left foul play. But at whose hands?

Tyler kept huffing and puffing. "We've employed a team of private investigators for the past several weeks. They came back empty-handed. You seriously mean to go after my brother alone?"

She hadn't been enough for them ten years ago, and she wasn't enough for them now. Nothing changed. Okay, not entirely true. This time, their rejection didn't hurt.

The last time, she'd been in love with Glenn. Even if she'd told herself she wasn't, to make leaving easier. She'd never, for a moment since that time, acknowledged how much she missed him.

And now here they were again.

Miranda kept her demeanor polite. "The sooner you give me all the information you have, the sooner I can get started. Are you aware of your brother having any enemies?"

Tyler and Gloria looked appalled and offended at the suggestion.

But Cesar Montilla said, "He's head of one of the largest privately held companies in the country. We push out competitors. We hire and fire hundreds of employees each year, let vendors go if they don't live up to our expectations. Environmental groups protest us because we work in the oil industry, even if ninety percent of our products have to do with safety. Hard feelings are unavoidable in any business."

Gloria's lips flattened. "I want the FBI. This is a travesty. What is the CIA doing? And why can't we have a SEAL team go after him? That's what they're for. My father was a United States senator, for heaven's sake."

Miranda met her gaze. "We can't send the Navy SEALs into Caracas for the same reason we don't have Venezuelan army troops in New York City when a Venezuelan tourist disappears. NYPD investigates crime in New York. The Caracas police investigate crime in Caracas."

"Well, the Caracas police are good for nothing," Gloria snapped. But she nodded at Tyler, and he strode out of the room, annoyance showing in every stride.

Gloria clasped her hands on the top of the table. "Just, please, bring my son back. That's all I'm asking." She hesitated. "If I offended you, before, I'm sorry."

She looked like she meant it. A day for miracles.

"We have such big plans for him. He's going to follow his grandfather's path to the Senate." Her eyes softened. "He could do so much good for so many people. You have to bring him back."

Miranda nodded. "I'm going to do my best." Their falling-out had happened a decade ago. She was working a case here, and she was going to give it everything she had, because that was the way she worked.

"When was the last time you heard from him?" She knew the answer from the files, but as an investigator, her job was to look for inconsistencies in people's stories.

Cesar cleared his throat. "He sent an email to his secretary on March first, around eight p.m. Just checking in."

That matched the files. Miranda had a copy of the email, nothing suspicious, Glenn saying he hoped everything was going well at the office and reminding the secretary to contact him if needed.

Before Miranda could ask anything else, Tyler returned with a stack of papers. "This is all we have." He dropped the pile onto the table in front of her. "These are all the reports from the previous investigators, and all the documents we provided them."

"Including a list of companies you've recently taken over and employees fired?"

Tyler gave a curt nod.

She asked questions for another three hours, but didn't find much to go on. His family obviously loved Glenn. His ex-wife had remarried, happily, lived in New York with three kids by her new husband. Glenn had received no threats prior to his disappearance. He had not, they all insisted, participated in anything remotely criminal.

Yet every time Miranda asked for specifics about his vacation, the energy in the room shifted. *Something there,* she thought. But no matter how hard she pushed, the three people in the room stuck to their story.

When the time came to leave for the airport, Cesar Montilla showed her out, walking with her to the bank of elevators. He'd founded the company with Oscar Danning right after they'd finished college. They'd been like brothers.

The man had to be at least fifty, but he looked younger, had plenty of energy in his steps to complement his swarthy good looks. He aged like a movie star, the graying at his temples making him look only more handsome.

He remained somber as they walked. "I think Glenn . . . something bad might have happened to him. Of course, Gloria doesn't want to face the possibility." He pressed his narrow lips together. "When the boy married my only daughter, my Victoria—" He paused. "But even after the divorce, Glenn was like a son to me." He gave a pained sigh.

He shook his head, his shoulders drooping. "I think the best thing would be to have him declared dead, if you can't find any proof for the opposite. Gloria has problems with her heart. The prolonged stress of not knowing is killing her, whether she shows it or not. The uncertainty has to stop. She needs to be allowed to grieve and move on to acceptance."

The thought that Glenn might have had an accident or been killed spread like an ache in Miranda's chest. Yet, as an investigator, she had to be realistic. *Body Retrieval.* She hated the term already. *We'll see about that.*

She stepped onto the elevator, but held the door open. "Do you still have contacts in Venezuela?"

According to her file, Cesar had been born there, relocated to the US for his education, then decided to stay and take up US citizenship.

His expression darkened. "My family had holdings in the oil business. In 1976, while I was studying here, the government nationalized the oil industry, confiscated our properties and wells." He cleared his throat. "My father committed suicide. My mother died of a broken heart the year after. I have not been back since her funeral. I am American."

"So no contacts?"

"None."

Miranda nodded. She could understand why he wouldn't be a fan of the current Venezuelan government.

She glanced toward the glass doors of the meeting room where Tyler and Gloria were talking, their faces tense, as if they were fighting over something.

Those two had the most to gain financially from Glenn's death, but she couldn't picture either of them going against family. And yet . . . they *did* wait a good long time before asking the government for help. And they *were* hiding something.

But sticking around here to find out what they were concealing seemed a less effective course of action than going to where Glenn had disappeared and trying to track him there. Time was of the essence.

Miranda drove to the airport, then took the fourteen-hour flight to Caracas—with a brief layover in Mexico City—and had time to sleep as well as review the case materials one more time.

She didn't push away the memories that rushed her. Anything she knew about Glenn could be helpful to the investigation. She lay back in her seat and closed her eyes, went back to the days she hadn't allowed herself to think about in the past ten years.

Glenn had been such a geek when she'd met him. Brilliant. Absentminded, yet with ingrained manners. He'd be solving problems in his head, not even knowing what hallway he was walking down, but opening doors for girls on reflex. Unfailingly polite, but barely looking at the opposite sex.

Then he'd looked at her.

"Do you think I could—" He'd hesitated, the two of them alone late at night in the lab.

She'd been working on a scientific paper for publication, and she'd thought he was about to ask whether she'd be willing to add his name to the credits. He *had* contributed.

Instead, he'd said, "Would you mind if I touched your breasts?"

She'd almost smacked him with a dial caliper. Why did he have to be like the fraternity idiots who bugged her?

But he'd seemed so pained and earnest. "For experimental reasons. I've never done this. I want to know how it works."

Okay, she'd understood that. She'd had the same interest in the mechanics of sex, and the same lack of data that could be called remotely empirical.

So data gathering they did. That night, and for many nights after.

The plane's engines a dull hum around her, suddenly it seemed no time had passed at all, and she could remember everything, the sensations, his scent, his voice that had a way of sending tingles through her.

Body Retrieval. The words sliced into her like bayonets.

Her eyes popped open. *No.*

She filled her lungs. "All right, Glenn," she whispered under her breath. "Please, be alive. I'm coming."

———

Elaine had booked her into an inexpensive tourist hotel in the vicinity of the Marriott, where Glenn had a room for his stay. Perfectly sufficient, since Miranda didn't plan on spending a lot of time in her room. She cleaned up, then headed out. She drove through the crowded city, to the police headquarters on Calle la Lagunita.

While she'd been in the air, Elaine had made an appointment for Miranda with the police captain. Captain Ferdinand Renzo—a man in his mid-fifties, stocky as a powder keg, his thinning hair in an optimistic comb-over, his lips topped with a jaunty mustache—received her in his utilitarian office. He wore a green dress uniform decorated with a plethora of colorful medals.

To impress her?

She'd be impressed if he had some solid clues for her, Miranda thought as she greeted him.

"Señorita Soto, welcome to Venezuela!" He gave a smarmy smile as wide as his lips would stretch, and pumped her hand with a little too much enthusiasm. "Please. Take a seat."

"Thank you, Captain."

"I'm glad you came so I can assure you in person that Mr. Danning is perfectly well." He puffed out his chest, looking thoroughly pleased.

"He is?" Excitement buzzed through her. "Did he return to his hotel?" She hadn't gone to the Marriott yet. She wanted to check in with the police first. Why hadn't anybody called her?

"We believe he's taken a private yacht to the islands. Venezuela offers magnificent opportunities for fun and relaxation, but tourists, they don't want to miss Aruba and Bonaire. You know how Americans travel. A different country every day. No slowdown, eh? No siesta in your country? Maybe you can get rest and relaxation while you're here. Caracas is the most wonderful country in the world."

"About Mr. Danning—"

"You must go up in the Teleférico. We have the largest cable car in the world." The captain brimmed with pride. "You can see everything from up there. You'll be gliding along with the angels."

He patted his mustache. "I'll assign an escort to you, so you will not be inconvenienced in any way. You will be taken to our Museo de Arte Contemporáneo. And you must see the Catedral Metropolitana de Caracas."

"Do you know what island Mr. Danning is on exactly?"

He kept the smile. "I cannot be sure." He shrugged. "I'm sure Mr. Danning will go home in due time. He's having too much fun. That is all."

"Do you have the name of the yacht he rented? The name of the rental company?"

"I'm not certain. But there is nothing to worry about, Señorita Soto. Tourists, they move around. They get drunk, they fall in love with a pretty girl, lose track of time. People in Venezuela have fun."

He was pushing the happy, all-is-well vibe so hard it made her head hurt.

"Do you have *any* tangible proof that Mr. Danning is still alive?"

"Of course he is." The smile stayed, but the look in his eyes hardened.

"What actual proof is there? If somebody has seen him, I'd like to talk to that person. How do I know that he hasn't been kidnapped or killed?"

The man's smile disappeared in a flash. "Our investigators have investigated."

"And what have they found?"

"They found that there's nothing to worry about, Señorita Soto. Venezuela is a very safe country. Foreign tourists don't disappear here."

In the interest of preserving goodwill, she didn't point out that Glenn Danning obviously had. "If you don't mind, I'll ask around."

"Mr. Danning is fine. He's on vacation." His voice held force now, all humor gone from his face.

She drew a slow breath. She couldn't afford to make local law enforcement an enemy on day one. Since a significant amount of the country's revenue came from tourism, their reluctance to admit any problems was understandable. In hindsight, suggesting that Glenn might have been killed here was probably not the best approach.

"I'm sure Mr. Danning is well and enjoying your beautiful country, as you said. I just need to catch up with him for a moment so his family can stop worrying."

The man watched her for a long second before he nodded. "Very well. One of my officers will assist you."

Someone to keep an eye on her and stop her from discovering anything that would reflect poorly on the country. "That won't be necessary."

"I insist." He reached for the phone, but the door opened before he could have dialed, and the most gorgeous man Miranda had ever seen stepped inside.

He was about six inches taller than she, midnight hair, midnight eyes, even teeth shining out of his tanned face. His smile was positively dazzling, his shoulders wide, his waist trim. *Bad-boy sheriff.*

The newcomer swept his dark gaze over her, then he nodded to the captain, who suddenly looked like he had indigestion.

The captain stood. "Excuse me, señorita."

He stomped to the door and stepped outside with the man. She could hear a muffled argument, the voices too low to make out any words, especially with her rusty Spanish.

At least a dozen minutes passed before the men came back in. She noted the barely visible bulge under the new guy's dark suit, a firearm in a shoulder holster. A detective?

She received an answer to her question the next second.

"Señorita Miranda Soto, may I introduce Señor Roberto Falcón, investigator. Señor Falcón will be your escort while you are in Caracas."

The captain was smiling again, but she had the distinct feeling Falcón hadn't been his pick. If not his, then whose? Probably somebody higher up the chain of command. News of her presence here seemed to have spread through the ranks pretty fast.

As much as they downplayed it, the disappearance of an American millionaire had to be a big deal. They weren't going to be able to sweep something like this under the rug. The story would come out sooner or later, and if Glenn *had* been murdered, it *would* hurt tourism, possibly even trade. Other major corporations might be more reluctant to send their employees to Caracas, less likely to set up offices here.

Unlike the captain's, Falcón's smiles seemed genuine as he escorted her out.

"I'm very glad to make your acquaintance, señorita. Where would you like to go first?" He gave her his full attention and then some, all smiles, all smooth gentlemanly manners, his dark gaze never leaving her face.

All that dazzling male perfection threw her off stride for a moment, not that she was going to show it. She squared her shoulders. "The Marriott is the last place Danning was seen alive."

"Why don't I drive? My car has a siren. Very useful for cutting through Caracas traffic," he suggested.

She wasn't crazy about a babysitter, but sirens would be nice. And Falcón had authority in the city. If he asked the questions, they might actually get answers. Having him on her side could turn out to be a good thing. "I would appreciate that, Señor Falcón."

"Please, call me Roberto."

When he smiled like that, she felt honest-to-goodness flutters she didn't want to deal with. "Miranda."

The smile widened as he stared at her. "You are so beautiful, you could be Venezuelan."

She was pretty sure that was a compliment. "The captain seems to think Mr. Danning might have taken a boat to the islands," she said as they got into his car.

He drove a black Mercedes instead of a police cruiser, the siren built into the dashboard up front by the window. *Pretty fancy car.* He must be fairly high up the food chain himself. Maybe that bode well for her. Maybe she'd been assigned the best of the best, the Caracas police wanting to show off.

The motor purred to life under his hand. "He's been missing for a month from what I understand?"

"Yes." She was relieved that Roberto was familiar with the case. "Have you investigated his disappearance?"

"I only received the case files last night."

After Elaine had called down to make appointments for her? "May I see them?"

"Of course. I'm here to assist you in any way I can. I'll make sure you receive full copies."

"Muchas gracias." So far, she couldn't complain about cooperation. "So you're with the Cuerpo de Investigaciones Científicas, Penales y Criminalísticas?"

He flashed an approving look. "You've done your homework."

She liked to do things right. She'd spent an hour or so on the plane researching Venezuelan law enforcement, split across various police agencies, which seemed pretty chaotic to her American sensibilities.

In addition to the Cuerpo de Investigaciones, they had the newly founded National Police. The National Guard was also part of law enforcement, reporting to the Ministry of Defense. Then DISIP, Venezuela's CIA.

Each of the country's twenty-three states also had its own police force. Law enforcement had vast overlaps and blind spots—a decentralized mess wrought with corruption, as far as she could tell at first glance, but she wasn't going to worry about that until she had to. For now, she had to deal with only Caracas.

"Where do you think Danning is?" she asked.

He didn't hesitate. He gave it to her straight. "Dead."

She filled her lungs.

Body Retrieval. That seemed to be the consensus—except for the police captain, who sounded like he worked for the tourist board. Her heart tripped. Glenn and she hadn't been close in years. And even back when they'd been together, she'd known that they were all wrong for each other. She'd been the one to end the relationship.

But she *had* missed the friendship. She wanted to find him alive. She *needed* to find him alive. Maybe *because* she'd left him. She owed him something. If she found him, it'd be one debt in her life she could consider paid. God knew, she could do precious little about the others.

"If he was alive," Roberto said, "there would have been some indication. A ransom note if he'd been kidnapped. I'm afraid something bad has happened to him."

At least, Roberto wasn't scared of hard answers, she thought, and said, "The captain seems convinced of the opposite."

He flashed a sardonic smile. "The captain is proud of his city and the job his men do here. He's not going to admit to crime against tourists without a body. And even then, he's likely to say Danning had too much to drink, tripped, and broke his neck when he fell."

"What do you think happened?"

He thought for a moment. "Danning has a large fortune in the US. He's been rich all his life. A man like that doesn't run off to be poor. If we're looking at murder, the two most basic reasons are love or money."

She'd considered both on the plane. "He's not attached at the moment. He has an ex-wife, but they divorced amicably five years ago. I don't see her putting a hit on him suddenly." Especially since Victoria was wealthy in her own right, happily married with kids.

"Which leaves money. As you said, he's worth millions. People have killed for less."

"Or he could have been the victim of random violence in Caracas." Her least favorite option. Random crime was always the most difficult to investigate.

Roberto nodded, then pulled over since they'd arrived at the Marriott. A flash of his badge and they were interviewing hotel management in minutes. His smooth translating made sure that all her questions were answered.

He even gained them access to Glenn's room, which was little help, considering that several guests had stayed there since. But they found the housekeeper who'd cleaned the room after Glenn, a nervous immigrant from Guyana.

"Everything was normal while señor was here. He wasn't messy," the girl said in rapid Spanish. "But he left his things behind. He didn't come back."

On their way back down from the room, Miranda asked to see the manager again.

"What happened to Mr. Danning's belongings?"

"Just clothes. One of the investigators the family sent returned them to the United States."

She wished they'd told her. There might have been a clue there, although the private eyes had found nothing, apparently, or it would have been included in their reports. Still, she made a mental note to call the family when she returned to her hotel.

"Where to next?" Roberto asked once they were in the elevator, on their way down.

She pulled up Glenn's bank statement on her phone. "His credit card was last charged the day he disappeared. No boat rental charges. He last used the card at a restaurant. I'd like to retrace his steps."

"As you wish." Roberto held the door open for her.

Then he drove her to all the places Glenn visited on March first. Lunch in the industrial district, coffee in a little coffee shop on the edge of an upscale housing development. Nothing on the main tourist drag.

"Why don't you let me invite you to lunch, and we can get to know each other a little better?" Roberto suggested when they headed off to the restaurant where Glenn had dinner.

She had no idea if he was flirting or just being a Latin male. The culture—including what was considered professional and what wasn't, how men and women related to each other—was different here.

First and foremost, she didn't want to give offense. She was hungry. Lunch sounded reasonable at two p.m. And the truth was, she wouldn't have minded learning more about him.

They found the restaurant, in the business district, without trouble: Especiero—a modern space with a gleaming open kitchen. Miranda showed Glenn's photo to the waitstaff. The hostess and one of the waiters remembered him, but both said he left without incident.

After a pleasant meal, on their way out, Miranda stopped to talk to a beggar by the curb who was missing both ears. She tried not to stare as she flashed the photo and asked the man in her best broken Spanish whether he'd seen the person in the picture. The beggar shook his head. Miranda dropped a few bolívars into his tin cup anyway.

"That's pretty useless," Roberto commented as he held his car's door open for her. Since he had a special sticker on the windshield, he'd been able to pull over right in front of the restaurant and park by the curb. "The beggars rotate around."

He seemed to be right. Even as Miranda slipped in on the passenger side, the man she'd just talked to tucked his cardboard sign under his arm and shuffled away.

"What do you think happened to his ears?"

"Probably a conflict with one of the crime lords who run the slums."

"Do you think Glenn could have ended up in the slums? Kidnapped?"

"You would have received a ransom note by now. Slum violence usually stays in the slums. Danning's disappearance has none of the earmarks. We have no indication that he went anywhere near the lawless areas."

"How lawless?"

"Cops don't go in there. If the government wants something, they do a military-style invasion, with troops. The level of violence . . ." He shrugged. "Venezuela has one tenth of the population of the US and twenty thousand violent deaths every year. In the slums, if you can't afford a gun and you have business to take care of, you can rent one. No rules, no laws."

Didn't sound like a place she particularly wanted to visit, unless she found clues that led there. She couldn't imagine Glenn having any business in the "lawless areas," as Roberto had put it.

She scrolled through the files on her phone. Where had Glenn been between lunch and dinner? Did the person he'd met arrange for his disappearance?

He'd never made it back to his rental at the parking garage on the corner, according to the files. Glenn's silver Audi S4 had been eventually found on level two by the rental agency. According to the private investigators the family hired, they'd watched the security footage already and seen no sign of Glenn returning from his dinner.

"I'd like to go to the garage next," she told Roberto. "And I'd like access to the security footage for March first." She wanted to see for herself what there was to see.

"I'll set that up." He pulled into traffic, then drove to the end of the block and into the brand-new four-storey parking garage.

She noted the automatic gate, no attendants on duty who could have witnessed any wrongdoing.

Roberto drove up to the second level as slowly as possible, giving her a chance to notice all the details. Like any parking garage, the structure was dim and grim, plenty of places for someone to hide for an ambush. Except, supposedly, security video showed no such thing. Glenn had disappeared before he made it this far.

How?

Miranda was still trying to figure that out when Roberto dropped her off at her hotel a little after four p.m. Rain had begun to fall, but just barely, nothing like the torrential downpour of the rainy season that she knew to be coming shortly. She hoped to be home with Glenn by the time that hit.

For a moment, she wondered what he was like now. Still as nerdy? Still as inquisitive a lover? A long-forgotten memory flashed into her mind, the two of them at Menemsha Beach on Martha's Vineyard, where he'd taken her for a long weekend, making love in the ocean in the middle of the night because he'd wanted to experiment with water.

She pushed the stray images away, as she always had. They felt like a betrayal of Matthew.

"I could come up for some coffee and we could discuss the investigation," Roberto offered with a sexy smile, his dark gaze holding hers.

Oh. Miranda blinked. It'd been a long time since anyone had looked at her like that. Part of her appreciated the attention, but mostly she wasn't sure if she was ready. Matthew, Glenn, Roberto— too many men in her head.

Yet . . . a quick affair with a hot guy who wanted her. *What was wrong with that?* Once she went back to the US, they'd never see each other again. They would be consenting adults, having a moment of fun. It wouldn't really affect the investigation in any way. He wasn't a suspect, and he wasn't a coworker, not really.

But she found herself shaking her head. "I'm pretty tired from the long flight. I'm going to grab a little extra sleep."

He gave a disappointed nod, but didn't push, which she appreciated. They said goodbye, and she went upstairs, worked through her files, trying to decide what to do the next day.

She thought about the restaurant in the business district where Glenn had had dinner, the last place anyone remembered seeing him. Where had he gone from there? Why didn't he go back to his car?

She closed her eyes to visualize him coming out of the restaurant after a good meal. She tried to picture him as the man in the files, but his image kept reverting in her mind to the Glenn she'd known in college, so she went with it.

In the movie in her mind, he stepped outside, pausing to loosen his tie against the heat.

She opened her eyes. Who wore a tie on vacation? Yet, the wait staff at the restaurant had given a full description that included a charcoal-gray suit and an olive-green tie and shirt. The restaurant was nice, but not so fancy that someone would put on a suit and tie if he wasn't wearing them already. She made a mental note of the anomaly, then closed her eyes again.

He turned toward the parking garage, but never made it to his car. And nobody had seen anything suspicious. She wracked her brain, then gave up an hour later when she became so desperate she was considering alien abduction.

Put yourself in the spot. She needed to be there. She needed to be in the same spot, at the same time. Glenn had disappeared around eight in the evening. She glanced at her phone, which showed seven p.m.

She drove back, parked in the same parking structure as Glenn, on the second floor.

She walked down the stairs and out to the street, turning toward the restaurant. The rain had stopped; everything smelled fresh and glistened. A different crowd filled the street, and young people out partying had replaced professionals going about their business. She noted every shop she passed—all closed this time of the night. She decided that interviewing the shop owners wasn't a priority for now.

Traffic bustled on the busy four-lane road, even at this late hour. Somebody had to have seen something, but she had no way to identify who'd been driving by here that night.

She didn't see any traffic cameras, no cameras above the doors of the small shops either. Surveillance wasn't at US levels yet in Caracas.

At the restaurant she turned around and walked back toward the parking garage, watching the stores, watching traffic again. If there was a clue to be had here, she was determined to find it.

Her gaze caught on the beggar settling in front of the parking garage—the same earless man she'd given money to earlier in the day. He must have rotated back to this street again.

She walked over to him. "Perdóneme," she began, then went on in her best broken Spanish. "Do you know others who work on this corner?"

The man shook his tin cup.

She dropped a couple of bolívars into it. "I'm still looking for this man." She showed him the printout of Glenn's photo, then reclaimed it long enough to scribble the hotel and her name on the bottom. She handed it over. She could print another copy for herself. "You bring me someone who saw this man, sí?" She searched her wallet and pulled a bill, held it up. "I pay you one hundred US dollars."

The man gave a toothless grin that didn't reach his eyes. The eyes said he was thinking about knocking her off the curb, into traffic, and grabbing the bill. "Juan will help." He leaned forward.

She stepped back and tucked the money away. "Thank you, Juan. Find whoever was sitting here a month ago, around this time in the evening. You bring him to me, sí?"

Chapter 5

ROBERTO, ALL SUAVE CHARM AND SMILES, WAITED FOR MIRANDA IN THE lobby when she came down in the morning, impatient to make progress today.

He looked her over and gave an appreciative whistle.

She couldn't help a smile. She was used to not being noticed as a woman at work, litigation had taken that out of US workplaces. Which was pretty much for the better. But Roberto's easygoing charm wasn't offensive.

"Good morning."

"A morning spent with a beautiful woman cannot be bad," he declared, then said after a small pause, "We have a meeting scheduled with the parking garage security."

"Thank you, Roberto."

He handed her the slim folder he was holding. "Danning's case file."

His ready assistance kept taking her by surprise. She scanned the two-dozen pages of printouts, everything in Spanish. Looked like basic case parameters and a handful of interviews. "Thank you. I might need help with translation later."

"I'm at your service."

Roberto held the door open for her as they exited the lobby. He wore a sharp, dark suit, similar to the one he'd worn the day before. Same look, same helpful attitude. Yet she couldn't shake the feeling that he'd been assigned to her more so to keep an eye on her than to help her investigate.

Once again, his gleaming black Mercedes waited by the curb, but they barely took two steps toward it when Juan, the homeless guy, rushed up to them, tugging a scruffy friend in tow.

"Señorita!" Juan kept his head down and his back bent, giving Roberto a wide berth. "Señorita, un momento."

Roberto moved swiftly to put himself between her and the men, but she put a hand on his arm. "It's okay. I was expecting them."

He raised a dark eyebrow. But, after a moment, he stood down with a nod.

She stepped closer to the men. "What is it, Juan?"

"Rami saw your friend." Juan tugged the younger man forward.

Rami looked like a trash truck had run him over. Or like he'd slept in the back of a trash truck, his clothes stained and ripped beyond recognition.

She pulled out a new printout she kept ready in her pocket, hope sending a rush of adrenaline through her. "Have you seen this man?"

Smelling as if he'd taken his breakfast in liquid form, the guy waffled, his small brown eyes narrowing as he watched her with a calculating expression.

Oh, for heaven's sake. She reached into her pocket and handed him a handful of bolívars.

Rami smiled, half his teeth yellow and chipped, the other half black and rotten. "Sí, señorita. I saw him at the parking garage."

Maybe. "What was he wearing?"

The man closed his eyes for a second, drawing his brows together. Then his eyes popped open. "Rich suit. Green shirt."

Okay. So maybe he *had* seen Glenn. "Was he heading toward the garage or away from it?" If the man had seen Glenn heading to the restaurant, he would be of little help. Glenn had disappeared on his way back to his car.

Rami sucked a rotten black tooth. "He was walking toward me."

Excitement jumped inside her. "Toward the corner?"

"Sí."

"Did he go into the parking garage?" she rushed to ask.

"No, señorita." The man cast a flat glance toward Roberto, obviously not a fan of police. "A car stopped and two men got out. They took him."

"Did they look friendly? Or did they have guns? How much do you remember?"

"Guns, sí." He looked at Roberto again.

Roberto, mindful that he was impeding progress, stepped back and gave the man some space.

"Were they police?" Miranda asked under her breath.

But Rami shook his head.

"Then what?" She reached into her pocket for more money, held it while the man evaluated whether the bills would be worth the trouble he might get into for speaking.

But after a brief consideration, he whispered, "National Guard." Then he grabbed the money and booked the hell out of there, ducking between pedestrians and disappearing around the corner the next second.

Juan stayed, but stood back, poised to flee, his eyes on Roberto. With the police sticker on his car, everybody knew who Roberto was.

"Juan is good help, sí?"

"Sí." She pulled a hundred dollars from her wallet and handed the money over. The information she'd gained was worth it.

Juan scampered off after his friend without another word.

She looked after them, a million more questions flying through her head, but those men wouldn't have the answers. No matter. She'd find more answers somewhere else. She'd already found more than the private investigators had. She grinned. *Progress.*

"National Guard?" Roberto rubbed his chin. "Do you still want to go to the parking garage security firm?" He walked her to his car and opened the passenger-side door for her.

She sat in. "What do you know about the National Guard?"

"They have over thirty thousand officers and the most comprehensive law-enforcement system in the country. Compare that to the Cuerpo de Investigaciones Científicas with eight thousand, or the National Police with less than three thousand." He slid behind the wheel.

"Why would they take Danning?"

"He could have been busted for drugs, prostitution, any number of things. Tourists are not always on their best behavior when they travel."

The Glenn she knew hadn't been interested in drugs or prostitutes, but she hadn't seen him in the last decade. People changed. Could he change that much? She shook her head, waiting for more as Roberto pulled away from the curb.

"As sad as it makes me, we cannot count out corruption," he said after a while.

"You mean they could have picked him up because he's a rich American, then trumped up some charge in the hopes that he would pay them off to make it all go away?"

Roberto shrugged. "Every country has corruption, has people in power who are as bad as the criminals, sí?"

Sadly, she couldn't contradict him. She'd seen plenty of bad behavior from people who should have known better. She thought that over for a while. "But why didn't he simply pay? He has money."

Roberto's gaze cut to her, sharpened. "What was he doing here?"

"A simple vacation. He was a tourist."

Roberto raised an eyebrow.

Yeah, she wasn't a hundred percent sure either. Glenn hadn't done anything touristy, as far as she could tell. He'd been wearing a suit and tie when he'd disappeared.

"I assume the National Guard has a command center in Caracas?" She considered the new direction her investigation was taking. "Could we go there next, please?"

"Regional Command Five is a few blocks from here."

He stayed silent for the rest of the ride, lost in thought, his forehead furrowed.

"You will find him," he pronounced as he pulled up to the guardhouse and gate that led to the National Guard headquarters.

"How do you know?"

Roberto held up his badge to the guardhouse window. "You are a good investigator."

He pulled up in front of a square building that looked gray and imposing, decidedly military in flavor. He checked them in at reception with his badge and requested to talk with the colonel.

She expected a runaround, to be told to come back next week. But, after a couple of phone calls, they were escorted by a young guardsman farther into the building.

Everyone they passed wore the National Guard uniform, either in dark green or green camouflage. The guardsmen paid them scant attention. Their escort led Miranda and Roberto down a long corridor to a utilitarian waiting room in the back, where they were seated.

She smiled at Roberto. "Thanks."

"I want to find Señor Danning as much as you do," he said pleasantly. "I'm not that different from the police captain. I don't want tourists to think of my country as a dangerous destination. I'm here to help."

Maybe. She had her doubts about him, whether he'd been sent to obfuscate her investigation as well as to keep an eye on her and report back to the captain. But so far Roberto truly seemed to be on her side. And his badge did come in handy.

As far as partners went, she couldn't complain. She felt pretty optimistic as they waited.

The door opened in a few minutes and a gaunt, older man appeared, in full uniform. His crooked lips stretched into an instant smile, upsetting the balance of his bushy, white mustache.

"Welcome, Señorita Soto." The colonel greeted her first, then Roberto. "Señor Falcón." He gestured them into his lair, toward the two chairs facing his desk. "How can I help you?"

She scanned the large office as they sat. Two bookshelves and half a dozen filing cabinets lined the walls to the side. The wall behind the desk displayed several regional maps.

Miranda pulled Glenn's photo from her pocket and laid it on the desk. "I'm looking for Glenn Danning, a United States citizen. He disappeared here in Caracas on March first. I understand that he was arrested by the National Guard."

The sprawling desk held an older model computer, a stack of loose papers, and a pile of green folders. She tried to scan the tabs without being too obvious, but the labels seemed to be code words, except for the one on top. The top folder was marked "Transport Log" in Spanish.

The colonel caught her looking and pushed the folders aside. He picked up Glenn's photo, examined it, then lifted his gaze to hers, his expression unchanged. "Your information is incorrect."

Okay, here came the stonewalling. She'd expected it. "Can I ask if you keep an arrest log?"

"Certainly, señorita."

"Could you double-check for March first? Just in case." She smiled. "Then if he's not there, I can cross this off my list of things to check and move on to the next item. I'd really appreciate the help."

The man turned to the outdated computer in front of him, his eyes on the small, gray monitor that extended a foot in the back. His fingers picked out the keys on the keyboard one by one.

When the computer beeped, he turned the bulky monitor toward her. "See for yourself."

She ran down the list of names. A Hitler Ramírez, a Mussolini Contreras, a Kennedy Briceño, and two Elvises, among other names of historical figures and pop cultural icons, made her do a double take. Apparently, Venezuelan naming conventions leaned toward the famous and exotic instead of the traditional.

But the name she'd hoped to see wasn't there.

"Perhaps he was processed on the following day?" Since he'd been picked up in the evening, after dinner.

The colonel began another search. He didn't turn the monitor back toward him, so she could watch. He was running a general search for "Danning, Glenn" for all dates. She didn't understand the full error message when it popped up in the middle of the screen, but she did understand the most important word: *ilocalizable*. Unable to locate.

The man leaned back in his chair. "I'm sorry, señorita. I wish I could help. We value tourists. My job is to keep everyone safe. Perhaps Mr. Danning left the country to continue his vacation in Brazil or on one of the islands?"

She held back a groan. The islands seemed to be everyone's hobbyhorse, pushing the problems outside the borders. But before she could ask the colonel why Glenn would have decided to travel on without his luggage, without checking out of his hotel, a knock on the door interrupted them.

When a guardsman stepped inside, the colonel strode over to talk to him. They exchanged words in hushed, rapid Spanish.

Her language skills weren't good enough to catch any of it, but Roberto watched them closely, even leaning toward them a little. Maybe he would share with her later.

She half turned, as if still looking at the computer screen, but reached for the stack of folders on the desk and opened the one on top, the transport log. She surreptitiously snapped a picture with her phone then turned the page and snapped another photo, but she didn't get to page three. She had to close the folder and turn back as the colonel headed back to them.

"Is there anything else I can do for you, señorita?" He stepped back behind his desk.

Tell me the truth. But since the National Guard refused to acknowledge ever having seen Glenn, she couldn't do much here for now. She thanked the man for his help, then walked out with Roberto.

"Did you catch any of what he was talking about with the guardsman?"

"An issue with some upcoming military parade."

All right, so they weren't going to gain much useful information here today. She'd just have to push on another front. She was going to find Glenn—wherever he was, whatever shape he was in. She refused to think that she might be too late.

"I think I'd like to see those parking garage security videos, after all," she told Roberto as they drove out of the guarded parking lot.

"Not a problem."

And it wasn't. In less than half an hour, they were sitting in a small meeting room at Salazar Security Services.

Miranda watched the grainy footage on a wall monitor. Her heart rate picked up as Glenn stepped out of his rental car, tall, wide-shouldered, confident, and impeccably dressed. He looked very different from how she remembered him. Instead of an endearing nerd, he looked every inch the successful businessman.

He checked his phone on his way to the elevator, his posture relaxed. He didn't look like he was expecting trouble. The camera outside the building recorded him walking down the sidewalk toward the restaurant. He didn't meet anyone, at least not within camera range.

He returned an hour later, on his phone again as he walked. He was sending a message. That had to be his last communication, the email to his secretary.

He shoved the phone into his pocket when he finished, then he passed out of range of the first outside camera. Between that moment and when the second camera could have picked him up, he disappeared.

The car with the men who'd picked him up, according to Rami, hadn't been recorded. Almost as if they'd known the exact spot to pull over to avoid surveillance.

"Could you please rewind?"

The security manager obliged her without a word.

She watched the footage again, this time looking at the traffic. "There," she pointed at an unmarked black van, excitement surging through her.

Traffic flowed. The cars that appeared on the first exterior camera moved into the view of the second a moment later. But there was a delay with the van. It must have stopped for a couple of seconds in the blind spot between the two cameras.

She leaned forward. "Can you enlarge that?"

The manager did. Sadly, the image was too grainy to make out the faces in the front, or the license plate.

"It doesn't look like an official National Guard vehicle," Roberto observed.

"Could be an undercover car."

"Could be," he agreed. Then he added, "The colonel had no record of Danning in the system."

"It's possible that a couple of guardsmen picked him up to extort money, as you said. Off the books."

Roberto didn't respond.

She stared at the frozen image on the screen. Glenn had been taken by whoever was in the black van. Possibly the National Guard, who handily denied everything. She had no authority to conduct a search of their building complex in Caracas. She had no authority to request any documents.

This is what a dead end looked like, she thought, and wanted to kick the table leg in frustration. Instead, she asked the manager to save a still shot of the van and send it to her phone, which the man did without argument. Once again, she had a strong suspicion that she wouldn't have seen anywhere near this level of cooperation without Roberto being present.

On the way down in the elevator, he asked her to lunch again. She agreed, insisting that they'd go back to Especiero.

But she didn't find any new clues at the restaurant, no matter how carefully she observed the place and how many questions she asked the waitstaff.

After lunch, she talked Roberto into staking out the corner by the parking garage and talking to every single panhandler within view, which ate up the rest of the day. She was hoping for more information, more detail, but nobody seemed to know anything, not even for money, and neither Juan nor Rami had come back.

When Roberto returned her to the hotel at last, he asked to come up for a chat once again.

"I'm really tired."

He raised a dark eyebrow. "There's someone else." His sexy lips pulled into a pout. "You're a beautiful, intelligent woman. He's a lucky man."

"I've recently lost my husband." She rolled the tightening muscles in her shoulders. Probably nobody else would think that two years ago was *recently*, but that was how she felt. Matthew, Abby, then the army incident—the last two years had been rough. Romance wasn't on her radar. Not even, if she wanted to be honest with herself, no-strings-attached sex with a stranger.

"I'm sorry," she said, then fled to the elevators, leaving Roberto staring after her.

After a long, hot shower relaxed her, Miranda ordered room service and downloaded the day's photos from her phone to her laptop while she ate. As she'd suspected, the picture of the black van was unusable, no matter how much she played with contrast and brightness.

The photos she took of the National Guard transportation log weren't much better quality. She'd held the phone at the wrong angle.

But maybe with some expert help . . .

She attached her three image files to an email and sent them to Bjorn, the in-house IT specialist at CPRU. *Let's see what the guy is made of. Time for a test.*

Next she called Tyler Danning. After she identified herself, she began with an apology, "I'm sorry for calling this late."

"Have you found my brother?"

She hesitated, then plowed ahead with the thought that had been swirling around in her head all day. "Are you familiar with the term *forced disappearance*?"

"I'm sorry?"

"It's an international human rights term for when someone is secretly kidnapped or imprisoned by a state or by someone with state authorization."

A pause on the other end, then, "You mean like the CIA?"

"I meant the Venezuelan government."

"But why?"

"Usually it's done to place the abducted person outside of the law. If the government wants to question or even kill a member of the opposition or a foreign national with impunity, they make the person disappear. Then they claim no knowledge of the person's whereabouts, so they can do whatever they mean to do in secret."

Another long pause on the line. "It sounds like a spy novel."

Maybe. But— "Can you think of any reason why the Venezuelan government would be interested in your brother?"

"Absolutely not."

Frustration tightened her jaw. "Your brother's life could depend on me having all available information."

She could hear the deep breath Tyler drew before he came back with, "His disappearance has nothing to do with why he went there. People disappear in foreign countries all the time. Just find him."

"I think he came here to do business." His credit card had been used mostly in the industrial district and the business district, he'd been dressed for business, there was no record of him doing anything touristy. "Was he meeting heads of oil companies here? Why? Trying to sell them your products? For a collaboration?"

"That kind of information getting out and reaching the competition would kill the entire project," Tyler snapped on the other end. "I'd appreciate it if you didn't repeat anything like that."

"Is the project worth more than your brother's life?" she pushed back, running out of patience.

"Look," Tyler snarled, "the Venezuelan government is paranoid about US businesses interfering in their country. They think the US is trying to overthrow their government so US energy conglomerates can get their hands on Venezuelan oil. The energy industry is government controlled down there. The last thing they want is capitalist foreign companies grabbing their natural resources."

A picture was beginning to emerge in Miranda's head. "But if Glenn traveled as a tourist, how would the government know that he was here on a business trip?"

"They wouldn't," Tyler assured her with a dramatic sigh. "He set up his appointments very carefully. This was just a scouting trip, putting feelers out. Nobody knew why he went to Caracas except for executive-level management here at home, and the three people he was meeting there."

"Do you have their names?"

"I contacted them already. The meetings had gone smoothly. Nothing unusual. None of them even knew that Glenn disappeared, until I called."

"I want names, Tyler."

"They stuck their necks out to meet with us. I don't want to cause trouble for them."

Maybe he was being thoughtful, or maybe he thought the project could be still salvaged. She couldn't say he wasn't right to be cautious. She did have Roberto shadowing her every step.

After a few more questions, including asking about Glenn's returned personal effects, and receiving only the vaguest of answers, Miranda ended the call and, swallowing her frustration with the lack of progress, went to bed.

She slept restlessly, all her old nightmares coming back—Matthew dying on the battlefield, Abby, the other little girl, then herself, pulling the trigger. She woke to her laptop pinging at eight a.m., grateful for the end of the gruesome movie reel in her brain.

She rubbed a hand over her face, shook the last of the images from her head, then focused on the screen. Incoming email from Bjorn. He sent back her three photos digitally enhanced.

Miranda brought up the van photo. Still unusable.

The transport log from the National Guard popped up on her screen next. She scanned the first page, ran down the names. Another odd list: Bieber Gonzales, Leonardo Ruiz, a couple of Josés, an odd mixture of traditional and celebrity names. The second page was more of the same.

Except for the very last line.

The last person they identified only as Prisoner #786. Next to that, the transport log had one printed word: Guri. After that, somebody had handwritten *Strictly Confidential*.

She touched her fingertip to that last line on her screen. Prisoner #786 had been transported to Guri under heavy guard on March second. Excitement surged through her.

Prisoner #786 had to be Glenn.

She dressed in a hurry, packed her suitcase, and sailed downstairs.

Roberto was waiting for her in the lobby, leaning against the reception desk and flirting with the young woman behind it.

The smile slid off his face as he glanced at Miranda and the suitcase she was dragging. "Are you leaving?"

"Just the hotel." She stepped up to the counter to check out. "I want to see more of your beautiful country. How do you feel about visiting the Guri Dam?"

He raised an eyebrow. "The dam is close to seven hundred kilometers from here."

Sounded doable. "What does that mean in drive time?"

"Over ten hours, depending on road conditions."

"I can go alone. I don't want to waste your time."

"Nonsense. I promised to help." He reached up to rub his chin as he watched her. "Why don't you walk back to the restaurant and have breakfast. I'll grab an overnight bag for myself. I'll be back by the time you're finished."

She hesitated. She was pretty sure he'd been assigned to her to keep an eye on her. But he *was* helpful, knew the language better than she did, definitely knew the roads better. He had a badge that could come in handy with getting answers at Guri. He hadn't tried to impede her investigation yet. She could find no reason to refuse him.

She let her face relax into a smile. "All right. Breakfast would be great." She paused for a second. "You wouldn't know by any chance if there's a National Guard outpost at Guri, would you?"

He had this look on his face, as if he was impressed with her for some reason. "Just a small outpost. The dam provides more than a third of the country's power needs. It's a strategic installation."

Meaning, any damage to it would be a national security threat, so it needed protection. "I thought Venezuela was big on oil and gas."

"The more hydroelectric energy we make for our own consumption, the more of the oil and the gas we can sell on the international market."

That made sense.

While she had breakfast, she brought up the map again on her laptop and zoomed in as much as possible, using satellite images to scan Guri Lake and the dam. The area didn't look like much, as far as population went, maybe a hundred houses altogether.

She kept coming back to the same small compound over and over. That had to be the National Guard outpost.

Once she found Glenn, she could contact the home office and the US government could exert pressure on the Venezuelan government to have him released. She refused to think of the alternative, that the only thing she'd find at Guri would be Glenn's body.

Chapter 6

GLENN WASN'T AT GURI.

The commander denied any knowledge of him. While Falcon went off to make some phone calls, the commander personally escorted Miranda through the compound to show her that no Americans were being held there. He let her go wherever she wanted, seemingly a man with nothing to hide, yet the way he watched her made her skin crawl.

His men, on the other hand, gave her wide berth, avoiding eye contact as if instructed. If she tried to question them, they claimed not to know English, or not to understand her Spanish accent.

Every instinct she had said that the whole garrison was lying.

"What do you think?" Roberto asked as they left the outpost. "Back to Caracas?"

"No. I'm sure Glenn was here."

"He's not here now."

"Which means they either killed him or he escaped." She thought for a minute. "If he was killed, I'm not going to find him without cadaver dogs and a CSI team." Her heart twisted. She pushed any thought of defeat away and looked up and down the road, her gaze settling on the dam.

Other than Guri Dam and the lake there wasn't much here—forests and mountains in the distance. Most of the country's population seemed to be concentrated in the north, the central and southern states kind of a no-man's-land, save a few cities and towns here and there. "If he escaped, where did he go?"

"Toward the nearest airport?"

"They'd be looking for him at the airports. He'd know that. How far are we from Brazil?"

Roberto shrugged. "Another six hundred kilometers. The only major road between here and there is Route 10. It goes to Santa Elena de Uairén, right on the border."

"Let's try that first. If we can't find anyone who's seen him, we'll come back here." She headed back to their car.

Roberto had traded his Mercedes for an older-model military Jeep before they left Caracas, a choice she hadn't been crazy about at the time, since the Jeep didn't have air-conditioning, but she now approved wholeheartedly. The all-terrain tires and high clearance would serve them well if the road got any worse.

They got into the car at the same time, but Roberto didn't start the engine. Instead, he looked at her, then he reached for the glove compartment, retrieved a handgun, and handed it to her. "We'll be cutting through the jungle," he said simply.

She checked the magazine. Full. She stared at the gun in her hand for a second, then at him. She hadn't expected this kind of vote of confidence. Maybe she'd misjudged the man. Maybe she didn't need to be so wary around him. "Thanks."

He nodded, then drove a few hundred feet and stopped at the town's store for more food and water. While Roberto shopped, she showed Glenn's photo around. The locals wouldn't say anything. They probably didn't want to risk the commander's ire.

Roberto drove about fifty miles before they reached the next batch of houses, a dozen huts haphazardly lined up by the side of the road. Again, Miranda showed the photo around, but nobody had seen Glenn.

"Are you sure?" she asked the middle-aged man with missing bottom teeth who seemed to be the small community's leader.

The man brushed off his simple peasant clothes. "I can only tell you what I told the soldiers, señorita. I did not see that man. He didn't come here."

Her heart rate picked up. "You told the soldiers that?"

"Sí."

"When?"

He paled and stepped back. "I can't tell you no more, señorita. No gringo here. You go now. I don't want trouble." He made a shooing motion toward her and Roberto, then turned and hurried away.

She grinned.

Roberto raised an eyebrow. "You think he's lying?"

"No. But if the soldiers were looking for Glenn, that means he escaped. There's a good chance he's still alive." The first piece of good news she'd gained since she'd arrived in the country.

———

By tomorrow this time, he'd be out of danger, Glenn thought as he limped into Santa Elena de Uairén, keeping an eye out for soldiers. A whole week passed since he'd come across the illegal logging operation in the forest. Hiding in the back of one of the trucks, stealing food and water at night, had worked out better than he'd expected.

The loggers had cut across to Route 10 under Guri Lake, then drove south through Canaima National Park. They weren't cutting, so Glenn figured they were scouting new territory. He'd jumped off when they turned north again two days later. Then he'd walked and come across an indigenous village. Just in time. If he hadn't found the witchdoctor, he would have probably lost his right foot to gangrene.

He was just recovering his full strength. If he had to limp all the way to Brazil, then so be it. He had the map and the clothes he'd lifted off the loggers, even a decent pair of boots. He was ready.

He glanced back. No sign of Winky. The monkey had followed him all this time, even bringing him fruit from the forest every once in a while. But it seemed the animal drew the line at entering the city.

Glenn shook his head. You knew you spent too much time in the jungle when your best friend was a monkey.

He moved forward. He needed supplies for his trip across the border.

Once in Brazil, he'd head to Boa Vista—about a hundred and thirty miles from Santa Elena, according to the map. He could hitch a ride on the road. He wasn't wanted in Brazil, he wouldn't have to hide in the woods and make his own way. He could take transportation from Boa Vista to the US embassy in Rio and request a new passport, then fly home to Baltimore.

Glenn pulled his floppy green hat low over his face as he walked through the maze of huts on the outskirts of the city. He did nothing to draw attention to himself and soon reached a more affluent area with houses, then the main drag with shops.

Santa Elena was the closest settlement to the border, a fairly large town from what he could see. They had to have police.

Did the local officers have his picture? He was less than ten miles from safety. As long as nobody recognized him.

He kept his head down as he crossed the road, nearly tripping over his own battered feet in surprise when a voice called out his name.

"Glenn! Glenn Danning!"

—

Oh. The past hit her with a force of a tank, and Miranda felt blown over.

She moved toward him. *Glenn.*

He was not the geeky college student she remembered—and he didn't resemble the image on the grainy parking garage video either—but he *was* Glenn. Her lungs struggled for breath as memories rushed her, feelings she'd long forgotten.

She should have looked him up long before now. They could have been friends again.

He'd lost weight. His face was gaunt. He walked with a limp. No more expensive business suit, he was dressed like a native, poised to run before recognition dawned on his face.

"*Jesus.* Don't yell my name. Miranda?" He narrowed his eyes as he stared at her. "What are you doing here?"

Okay, the voice was him, exactly the same, floating through her, bringing back a million more memories. She shoved them all aside and for a second just luxuriated in sweet relief.

"I came to take you back home." Impulse pushed her to hug him but, okay, she was here in an official capacity, and he seemed keen to keep some distance between them.

Why wasn't *he* more excited? "What's wrong?"

The way he kept his head down and kept glancing around reminded her of Oreo, an abused dog her aunt had adopted when she'd been a kid. No matter how much love that dog received, she always acted like she was expecting a kick.

The Glenn she remembered had a meticulously ordered way about him and confidence that came from his mental abilities and family background. Now he looked scruffy and uncertain.

"What happened to you at Guri?"

He looked ready to flee.

"Wait," she said. There'd be time for questions later. Step one was to reassure him. "The United States government sent me to return you to US soil. I'm here to save you." She grinned.

He didn't return her enthusiasm. He frowned as he checked up and down the street once again, his steel-gray eyes confused and wary. "You came with the army?"

"I'm not with the army anymore. I came with a local investigator."

While she'd been showing Glenn's photo around on the streets, Roberto had gone to the lodge to book them rooms. They'd slept in the car on the side of the road for a few hours last night, but they needed more rest, a shower, and something to eat.

She smiled at Glenn. "We've driven across the whole country."

But Glenn wasn't listening. Keeping his head low, he hurried away from her, half running, half limping toward a narrow side street.

She caught up with him. Put a hand on his arm. "I'm on assignment here to take you back."

He shrugged her off and kept going, his eyes filled with alarm. "You can't trust the locals."

"I know." She had no intention of taking Glenn to Roberto. "Come on."

He hesitated. "Where are we going?"

"Finding you a safe place to stay until I can come back and get you." Her mind raced. She could spend the rest of the day pretending to search for Glenn, give up, tell Roberto she's come to believe the colonel was right and Glenn had moved on to Brazil. Thank Roberto for his help, tell him she was moving her investigation across the border. Make a production out of having Roberto take her to the local airport, and fly away. Then rent a car in Brazil and come back for Glenn. "I can come back for you in twenty-four hours."

"I have my own plans."

"Trust me."

He stopped at last in the shadow of a coffee shop's doorway. Stared at her.

She stared back. She'd found him. Bruised and battered, but *alive.*

He reached out, touched the end of her short hair with caution, his eyes never leaving her face for a second. He breathed in and out slowly. "It's hard to believe that you're here."

The tightness that had squeezed her chest since she'd found out that he was missing eased. But beyond feeling ridiculously happy that he was found and safe, she felt some small sense of relief for herself too. She'd found him. In just three days. *Mission accomplished.* Maybe she *was* cut out for the job. Maybe she wasn't too messed up. Maybe she could still do this.

In some odd way, in finding him, she felt as if she found herself too, a little.

She'd think about that later. Right now she needed to think about him. "As soon as you're safely stashed away somewhere, I'll call your family. They've been worried about you."

A police car rolled down the street, slowly, as if looking for someone. Glenn tucked his chin in and turned into the coffee shop, cut through it, among the tables, heading to the back exit. She hurried after him.

They burst out into an alley and ran.

Or rather, she did. He couldn't keep up.

She slowed. "Are you injured?"

He shrugged, and her heart twisted.

"When was the last time you ate?"

"Three days ago."

She wished she had some food on her. She matched her steps to his and they hurried out of the alley, down another street, and another.

"Cops," he hissed, skidding to a halt.

Okay, she saw them, another blue car cruising.

Glenn turned back, and they cut through an empty lot, came out on one of the wider streets. She glanced around. They'd be too out in the open here. She wanted to find an abandoned store or a boarded-up house where Glenn could hide for a day. Not on a busy street like this though. They needed to check more side streets.

She headed toward the nearest turnoff with Glenn, but couldn't see the type of place she was looking for. She did spot a small eatery, however. Nobody would look at them twice in a hole-in-the-wall place like this.

"Come on." She hurried forward. "I'm treating you to a meal." They should be safe. Roberto was making arrangements on the city's main drag at the tourist lodge.

Glenn's jaw tightened. He looked like he was going to argue, but hunger won out and he went with her. "We'll have to be fast."

The smell of frying meat hit them as they stepped inside, the place a single large room, mostly locals around the tables. Her heart twisted as she watched Glenn swallow repeatedly. "Hey, we have time for a bite." She smiled.

They went to the back and took a table in the corner. She ordered soup for the both of them. He'd better start with something light.

He kept looking at other people eating, then glancing to the door. He'd been abused, badly, she thought, and silently cursed the Guri commander. "I have a lot of questions."

"Not here."

She nodded. They'd have time. She had found Glenn. Alive. She grinned. Right now she just wanted him to relax and eat, but before their soup arrived, Roberto strode in, and her euphoria dimmed.

Roberto hurried toward them, a too-wide smile on his face. "Señor Danning?"

Glenn's entire body stiffened. He cast a quick glance around, half lifting from his chair, ready to run for it, but Roberto was next to them in seconds.

He lifted his hands, palms out, in the common gesture of no-harm-intended. He flashed Miranda an impressed smile before turning to Glenn again. "We've been looking for you. I'm glad we've found you at last."

Glenn checked him over. Miranda knew the exact moment he spotted the concealed weapon. His face tightened.

Roberto dropped into the chair on Miranda's other side, boxing her into the corner, his eyes on Glenn. "Tell us what happened."

Unease put Miranda on alert. How was it possible that Roberto strolled into the same off-the-beaten-path eatery as they had, several blocks from where she'd left him?

Glenn glared. "Your National Guard kidnapped me. They accused me of being a spy." He kept his voice low so nobody beyond their table would hear.

Roberto leaned back in his seat, watching him carefully. "Why?"

"Finding that out is second on my to-do list, right below getting out of this damned country."

"We'll drive up to Caracas, then fly back to the US," Miranda put in. Would Roberto let them? She wanted badly for him to be what he seemed, a helpful partner interested in justice.

"I'd rather go to Brazil." Glenn looked pointedly at Roberto. "I don't trust anyone in this country."

Miranda put a hand on his. However this played out, she *was* going to get Glenn back home. "Just trust me."

But even as she said that, armed guardsmen rushed into the restaurant and headed straight toward them. *Oh shit.*

Glenn ran for the back door, cursing, and was gone in two seconds, Roberto darting after him. Miranda was only a few steps behind them. "No! Wait!"

"Alto! Alto!" Half a dozen rifles pointed at her.

She froze, anger steaming through her. "Okay. Don't shoot."

She raised her hands into the air and bent forward as if to drop to her knees in surrender. But instead, she grabbed a chair and threw it at the soldiers, then sprinted through the back door as shots flew by her.

She burst outside. Came to a screeching halt. *Oh, hell.* More guardsmen waited out back.

She slammed her back against the door so their buddies couldn't follow her, reached for her weapon, and pointed it straight at Roberto's head as he was slapping handcuffs on Glenn, looking pretty satisfied with himself.

"Let him go," she demanded. "Put your weapons down."

But instead of telling his men to obey, Roberto smiled at her.

"I will shoot." She meant it. She had a dozen bullets and only seven men against her. She had a fair chance.

The door banged against her back, but she held steady, bracing herself with her feet. The nearest soldier grabbed for her. She moved her aim from Roberto and shot at her attacker.

Nothing happened.

She squeezed the trigger again. Yet no matter how many times she tried, the weapon didn't fire. Fear shot through her then.

She threw the gun at the man with a curse. She'd been surprised that Roberto would give her a weapon. Of course, if he'd fixed it so it wouldn't work . . . But why give her a weapon at all? She cursed again as she understood at last. GPS locator—probably in a hollow bullet. That was how he'd found her.

The soldiers behind her burst through the door at last, propelling her forward, into the hands of men waiting for her. She knocked two down, flipped the third. But the rest rushed her all at once and overpowered her.

One of the soldiers grabbed her and twisted her arm behind her back to hold her in place as she struggled.

"Get your hands off me! I'm here under the full protection of the United States government. I have a badge."

Her credentials didn't impress the guy. He didn't budge an inch.

Roberto handed Glenn over to another batch of soldiers. The men shoved him over to a waiting army truck, the back canvas covered. They boosted him up.

"Roberto!" Miranda struggled. "You can't do this. This is an illegal arrest."

He kept his expression shuttered as he walked over. "Sorry, señorita. I wish this could have ended differently, but we don't tolerate spies in our country, the same way you don't tolerate them in yours."

As he patted her down and took her phone, wallet, and badge, she felt nothing but outrage. "I'm not a spy, for heaven's sake, and neither is Glenn Danning!"

His face remained emotionless as he held out handcuffs for her.

The soldier let her go. There were guardsmen all around, all armed. Glenn was already in the back of the truck. *No way to escape.*

She held her hands out for the cuffs as she seethed. She needed to go with Glenn. She wasn't letting him out of her sight.

"Are you even with the police?" she asked Roberto.

Roberto's smile held a twinge of regret. He held her hands for a second after he cuffed her. "DISIP."

Dirección de los Servicios de Inteligencia y Prevención—the Venezuelan equivalent of the CIA. Because for some idiotic reason they thought Glenn was a spy. She grit her teeth.

"Listen, you're making a big mistake here," she called back as one of the men began shoving her toward the back of the truck.

"We call it apprehension and recovery." Roberto nodded to the soldiers, and they hoisted her into the truck without ceremony.

Four soldiers came up behind her, pushing the prisoners to the back while they sat closer to the tailgate. The green canvas flap dropped down, closing them in. Someone shouted orders outside, then the engine revved and the truck lurched forward.

Shit, shit, shit, dammit!

One dark thought after another flew through her head as she began to fully understand their situation. They were branded as spies. The Venezuelan government was going to deny all knowledge of her disappearance as they'd denied Glenn's. The only way for Venezuela to come out of this without an international incident was for both of them to disappear without a trace.

They were as good as dead.

Cold sweat rolled down her spine. She caught Glenn's gaze as he sat on the wooden bench across from her, his entire body rigid, his face flushed with fury.

"We have to escape," she mouthed.

He didn't bother to keep his voice down as he responded. "I would have been out of the country by morning if you hadn't shown up." His gaze boiled with anger.

Oh, he was mad at *her*.

As if to underscore that, he said, "Stay the hell away from me."

All right, so he didn't want to be friends again.

Chapter 7

SHE'D CHANGED. GLENN DIDN'T LIKE IT.

She'd cut her hair. Why would she do that? She'd had lovely hair, silky soft waves tumbling down to her butt. For school and the engineering lab she'd always worn it in a thick braid so it wouldn't get in the way. But at night with him . . . He'd loved the sight of all that dark hair spread out on the pillow. He'd loved *her*. Not that it'd mattered to her.

Why would she show up in his life now to mess him up all over again? His mind had a hard time catching up with the fact that she was here.

Hot fury pumped through Glenn's veins. After surviving the torture, the fever, the illegal loggers, the trip through the jungle, he'd been less than ten miles from freedom . . . His jaw clenched so tightly, his teeth ground against each other.

Miranda.

She sat in the back of the truck opposite him. *Why now? After all these years . . .*

He was mad as hell, yet couldn't take his eyes off her, comparing every little detail to his memories, trying to reconcile this new Miranda with the old. Her body was different. More compact, with more muscle. She'd moved with a controlled strength that showed her army training. Wearing a simple shirt with khaki cargo pants, she had the whole Lara Croft thing going, her head held high, unbowed in captivity.

He had a flashback to their video-gaming days and he almost, *almost*, softened toward her a little.

"Break. Out." She carefully mouthed the two words at him.

She was *not* going to tell him what to do. He glared and mouthed back, "You're not in charge." He was going to break out because he wanted to break out. He wasn't going back to Guri for more torture. *Fuck the commander.*

But before he had time to come up with a plan, Miranda Pain-in-the-Ass Soto parted her knees and dropped her cuffed, fisted hands between her legs where the soldiers wouldn't see them, then unfolded three fingers on her right hand while holding his gaze. *Three.* She closed one finger. *Two.* Closed another one. *One.* Only her index finger was extended.

A countdown. He had one second to figure out what they were doing. Then she gave a final nod and attacked with lightning speed.

She slammed her elbow into the face of the soldier next to her, hard enough to break his nose and knock him off his seat, then she threw herself on the second man as he shouted, "Alto! Alto!"

She yelled at Glenn. "Hurry!"

He was fighting, doing his level best to mirror what she did. He didn't have her skills, but he did have some extra weight to throw into his punches.

By the time he immobilized his first guy, she already had her cuffed hands wrapped around the last man's throat, choking consciousness out of him as the truck rattled down the road.

The lightning attack lasted less than a minute.

Jesus. The sudden, violent rush of effort stole the air from Glenn's lungs. He kneeled in the bottom of the truck, breathing hard, staring at her. All four soldiers were incapacitated, lying partially on top of each other.

He'd gotten one; she'd gotten three, her face flushed from the fight.

His old video-gaming nerd self would have had a boner by now. The more mature Glenn was . . . All right, turned on, dammit, as he watched her, her chest heaving while she tried to catch her breath next to him.

"Let's grab what we can." She was moving again already, reaching into the shirt pocket of one of the knocked-out soldiers. She pulled out a small key.

How did she know the guy had it? Apparently, she'd paid more attention than Glenn had.

"Hands," she ordered. "Hurry up."

He held out his wrists and was free the next second, then he took the key and unlocked her cuffs in turn, hating the red circles on her pale skin.

She paid no attention to her injury. She grabbed a pistol and shoved it into the waistband of her pants for easy access, then took the water canteens off two of the men and clipped them onto her belt. Glenn did the same with the other two.

She grabbed a knife. So did he. They both grabbed hats. Then as he patted down the last guy, he found a lighter and half a pack of cigarettes. He pocketed those. He had a feeling they were heading back to the forest where fire might come in handy.

The jungle was torturous in its own way, but Glenn preferred it to the commander.

When Miranda picked up a rifle, so did he. Then she moved to the tailgate and made room for him next to her, in front of the closed canvas flaps. "On three again," she said. "One, two, three."

She pushed the canvas aside on the last word and opened fire on the military Jeep that followed the truck for extra security. The Jeep swerved, then slowed before the driver straightened it, his passengers returning fire.

At the noise of the gunfight, the driver of the transport truck slammed on the breaks, realizing something had gone terribly wrong in the back. The sudden lurch nearly tossed Miranda and Glenn off the truck. Glenn careened to correct, but Miranda shoved him.

"Jump!" She pushed him straight into the path of the oncoming bullets.

He lost his rifle as he tumbled to the ground, had no time to pick it up. Above him, Miranda kept shooting non-stop, kept the soldiers pinned down in the Jeep long enough for Glenn to make a mad dash toward the forest.

He ran like hell, certain about only two things: they were going to die, and Miranda Soto was raving mad.

He didn't look back until he was in cover behind a tree, then he pulled his pistol and shot blindly at whoever was still moving. Only Roberto was alive in the Jeep, his head pulled down behind the dashboard as he shot at them.

The two men from the cab of the transport truck were jumping to the ground with their rifles to enter the fray. Glenn fired to hold them back, trying to provide Miranda with some cover. His heart beat hard enough to break through his ribcage. He had zero gun skills. Didn't she know that?!

She showed plenty of skill as she dropped to the ground at last, shooting backwards as she dashed toward him. "Go! Go! Go!"

He didn't need any further encouragement. He ran like hell.

She caught up with him pretty fast, tucked her gun away, shouting over the sound of gunfire. "They're shooting blind. They can't see us. Keep going."

He put every ounce of energy he had into moving forward, not that the going was easy. More like an obstacle course: bushes and trees, rocks and exposed roots in their way. One wrong step, and a fall could mean being skewered by a broken bamboo shaft or a branch.

Then an endless patch of thorny bushes slowed them further yet.

"We have to reach the border," he gasped as he fought his way through the heavy undergrowth. "Boa Vista is just on the other side. We can get transport from there to Rio."

"The border will be under lockdown before we can reach it."

"Then we cut through the jungle. Go the long way around."

"This is the start of the rainy season. It's rained every day since I've been here. Soon the rain will start and won't stop for weeks. We can't walk over a hundred miles through heavy jungle without a machete. Not through mudslides and flooding rivers."

He grunted. She always thought she had a better solution to everything. As company president, he wasn't used to his decisions being questioned at every turn. Even more annoying was the fact that she was right. Not that he was ready to concede.

He bent a thick, thorny branch out of the way. "We'd be safer in Brazil." She couldn't argue with that.

Of course, she did. "We can't cross the border through the jungle in the rainy season. And if we take the road, we'll be caught before we get anywhere near freedom. And even if we reach the Brazilian border, they aren't going to let us in without papers. The border guards will be notified to watch out for criminal fugitives. Instead of asylum, chances are we'd be returned to Roberto."

Glenn pushed forward, then stopped when he realized he had the knife he'd taken off one of the soldiers. He pulled it from his belt and began hacking away the vines and branches. A machete would have been better, but he was making more progress than when he'd been tearing at the vegetation with his bare hands.

But as soon as Miranda realized what he was doing, she put a hand on his shoulder. "Don't. You're going to leave a trail a blind man could follow."

Oh, here we go, Miss Know-It-All Smarty-Pants. He'd forgotten that his roommate in college used to call her Hermione.

The fact that she was right was just an extra layer of irk frosting on Glenn's layer cake of pissed-off. He was sick and tired of her being right. It was particularly annoying that part of him was impressed by how fast she could think under pressure.

"Are you suggesting that we sit out the rainy season in the jungle?" He went back to using his bare hands to bend branches out of the way.

"First, let's get away from the men behind us. When we can do it safely, we'll sneak back into the city and hitch a ride on a plane."

He glanced back. "There's an airport here?" Why hadn't he thought of that? Probably because they were in the middle of nowhere. "How big is Santa Elena?" He'd pictured it as a small town in the middle of the jungle.

"Almost thirty thousand people."

Leave it to her to know exactly.

"I pay attention to detail when I work a case," she said. "If I didn't, I wouldn't have found you."

"In which case, I wouldn't have been caught," he pointed out, then felt like a jerk when the expression on her face changed. She looked as if he'd just kicked her.

He turned away from her and refocused on the undergrowth he needed to fight through, hoping he wasn't touching anything poisonous. "How do we walk into the city without getting caught?" Everyone would be looking for them now.

She didn't respond immediately. Good to know she didn't have an instant response to every question.

But only a minute or two passed before she said, "Through the slums. People who live there are not the type to call the cops, even if they see some raggedy foreigners. And we're not going to run into a patrolling officer. The cops don't go into the slums unless there's a coordinated takedown going on and they have considerable backup."

"How are you an expert on slums?" He kept pushing forward.

"Roberto told me some things."

"I bet he did."

"Listen."

He turned.

She held up a hand to bid him to silence.

He strained his ears. "What is it?" he whispered after a long moment.

"Nothing. I haven't heard anyone behind us for a while. I think we lost them."

He listened again. She was right. Nothing but the birds and the bugs. His shoulders relaxed. "I know where the bad section of the city is. I walked through it this morning. Let's circle around and find our way into Santa Elena through the slums then." He paused. "Even if we cut through the slums without trouble, the airport will be guarded."

"We'll figure out something." She scanned him from head to toe before her gaze returned to his. "Are you all right?"

"You?" She had a bloody scratch on her face, probably from a branch. He wanted to wipe the dried drops, but didn't reach out.

She held his gaze. "We should go."

"Yeah." He had the crazy impulse to push her up against the nearest tree and kiss her.

He put his carnal urges down to dehydration. They were definitely not going there. Ever again.

He moved past her, spotted an animal trail that headed in the right general direction. "Let's try this."

She fell in step behind him. "Maybe it'll take us to a road that goes into town."

But their plan didn't go as smoothly as that. They circled back to the road, but every time they tried to leave the woods, they saw guardsmen. The few roads that led into town were riddled with checkpoints. The National Guard had the outskirts of the city covered.

"We could spend the night in the woods," Glenn suggested as they pulled behind a stand of bamboo, well out of sight. To keep walking after dark was simply too dangerous. They wouldn't see where they were stepping. "Maybe we'll have better luck tomorrow."

"You think you can handle a night in the jungle?"

His manly pride bristled, but he couldn't fault her for the question. He'd been a total nerd the last time they'd seen each other, barely a step above the pocket-protector geeks. He'd changed. He wasn't the same clueless kid who'd fallen for the first pretty girl who liked engineering, and then let her rip his heart out and hack it into pieces. "I can handle anything you can handle."

A couple of seconds ticked by before she nodded. "It'll be dark in an hour. Let's find a campsite."

They began moving again, away from the road and deeper into the forest, scanning their surroundings, struggling for at least half an hour before he spotted a small clearing at last.

"There." He pointed. "Trees close enough to each other to build a platform to sleep on."

"And not much undergrowth for snakes to hide in," she added as she assessed the spot.

"Plenty of bushes all around, so people can't see the light of our fire unless they are right on top of us," he finished listing the advantages.

She raised her eyebrows in surprise. "You've done this before?"

"How did you think I made it this far from Guri?" He'd survived more than one night alone in the woods, on the run, sick.

"How did you?"

He pulled out his knife. "Stowed away with illegal loggers, then walked through the jungle." When she looked skeptical, he bit back a smile. Miranda Soto had a lot to learn about him.

To further prove that he could take care of himself without her help, he moved over to the nearest stand of bamboo that would make the bulk of their bedding and began hacking away at the sturdy stalks. She joined to help.

Okay, so maybe she was faster with the knife than he was. She moved with the assurance of a woman who knew how to use a weapon. He couldn't help thinking, once again, how much she'd changed all around. But the biggest difference was in her eyes.

The softness he remembered was gone. As was the easy smile from her full lips. Result of the years she'd spent in the army?

If she hadn't left him, maybe he could have prevented whatever stole that carefree girl right out of her. But even as he thought that, he shook his head. Hell, she didn't look like she needed a protector. She could probably take him if she really put her mind to it.

She proved her strength by carrying an armload of bamboo over to their selected campsite. He cut some more, then gathered it up and followed her over, sat on a rock as he watched her cut the bamboo stalks to the right size with her knife.

She eyed their clothing. "We're going to need rope."

The idea of letting her cut her shirt up into strips held a certain appeal. A crystal-clear image of her naked body flashed into his mind, sending an unexpected rush of heat to his groin. *No.* He was a full-grown man now, a man who'd seen a thing or two in the world, not a hormone-driven college kid. He was not going to fall under her spell again.

"I'll make some rope." He'd learned a lot during the days he was recuperating from his foot infection in that indigenous village under the witchdoctor's tutelage.

He drew a bamboo stalk over his knee and pressed his knife into the end, splitting the shaft lengthwise. Then he took one half and cut it into quarters. Next, he took a quarter and cut that in half, then halved that, until he had a strip of bamboo maybe half an inch thick.

When he had the entire bamboo stalk cut down to narrow strips, he picked them up and walked over to the nearest tree, looped the handful of strips over the tree trunk and pulled back and forth, alternating his hands in a sawing motion to break down the fiber a little, making the strands less stiff. The whole process required maybe fifteen minutes.

By then, she had the rest of the bamboo stalks set up, so they tied everything together and created a sleeping platform three feet or so off the ground, keeping sound building principles in mind.

She tested the structure. "More lateral support here?"

"I was thinking of braces at a forty-five-degree angle."

She laughed.

"What?"

She shook her head. "Two engineers constructing a stick bed."

He grinned at her. "We're probably overthinking it."

"You think?"

So they settled for the simple design, something that would serve for a night, but wouldn't necessarily stand the test of time and reflect modern building codes. When they were done, they tested it once again, together, sitting on opposite ends. The platform held their combined weight without trouble.

"Not a design I'd patent, but it'll do," he said as an orange bird burst into song above them, a pleasant, trilling sound. He lay back to listen. His battered body appreciated being vertical.

The heat of the day abated to a bearable level. The jungle was a green cocoon around them.

Suddenly, he felt oddly relaxed and happy, something that had eluded him in his cushy life back home lately. Strange that he would find his zen now, in the middle of the woods with barely the basic necessities, facing all kinds of danger.

The bird gifted them with one last trill, then flew away, an orange feather floating down and landing on Glenn's chin.

He blew it off. "You know how to make a roof?"

"And walls, and bridges, and irrigation systems. Given the proper materials. Just not from palm leaves." She looked up at the darkening sky. "Of course, it'll probably rain overnight."

"It's called a rainforest for a reason." He scanned the tree canopy. "And a roof will keep the bugs and snakes that fall out of the trees from landing on top of us." Another thing he'd learned during his trek through the jungle.

She shrugged.

He bit back a smile. Ten years ago, she would have run screaming for the hills at the mention of snakes and bugs. He supposed she'd faced that and worse in the army. She'd toughened up. A pretty amazing package of brains, beauty, and strength. He gave up resisting being impressed by her.

He sat up. "Let's start by looking for some large leaves."

He checked around, hoping for some banana palms. He couldn't see any of those, but did see some kind of other plant with leaves that were as large as a combo platter at an average US restaurant. "I'll make the roof, you go and find firewood."

"Deal."

"It might take a while. Finding dry wood in a rainforest is about as easy as it sounds."

"I'll manage." She took one of the canteens, her knife, and her gun.

"Don't go too far," he called after her. He didn't want to get separated.

But she stayed within shouting distance. While he worked at jerry-rigging a semi-decent roof over the bamboo platform, he could hear her moving around in the woods, walking around the campsite in a wide circle, branches snapping.

Somehow she managed to return with an armload of wood and even a handful of smaller branches for kindling.

"Were you in Iraq all this time?" he asked as they worked on stacking the logs in a teepee-shaped formation. For tinder, he used half the cigarettes he'd gotten off one of the soldiers.

"At the beginning," she said, blowing on the tinder once he lit it. "After the troop drawdown began, I joined Personnel Recovery. PR looks for soldiers and DOD contractors who disappear in an operational environment."

He shoved the burning tinder in the middle of the kindling and watched the small sticks catch on fire. "I'm not a soldier or a DOD contractor," he observed as he watched her, on her knees, bending toward the fire to blow, her firm behind sticking up in the air, making his palms itch.

"I left the army," she said between two puffs.

"Why?"

Instead of answering, she sat back on her heels. "We have nothing to eat."

"We won't starve until morning. Once the sun comes up, we'll find a way to sneak into town and get food there." They could trade one of their weapons in the slums.

He stood and kicked some half-rotten leaves back from the flames, clearing a foot-wide perimeter. No sense in risking that their shelter would catch on fire while they slept.

Security measures taken, he sat back down. "So if the army didn't send you, who did?"

"CPRU. Civilian Personnel Recovery Unit. It's something new the government is trying, offering similar protection to civilians as the army offers to soldiers." She watched him over the flames as the forest grew dark around them. "How do you think the Venezuelan government found out that you were in Caracas on business?"

"I came for a vacation."

Her forehead furrowed into an impatient frown. "For better or worse, we depend on each other for survival. We need to watch each other's backs so we can get out of here. This is probably not the best time to start lying to each other."

Yeah, maybe not. "I came to see if Danning Enterprises might be able to loosen the chokehold the government has on the local oil industry."

"And the National Guard didn't like it?"

"Somebody didn't like it. Barely a handful of people knew what I was doing here."

"Who do you think let something slip?"

"Not the people I was meeting. They wanted this. They contacted me. And they'd get into just as much trouble."

"Someone at your company?"

"Only my brother, mother, and Cesar knew."

The fire was fully going at last, just large enough to give them warmth if they sat right next to it, but not so big that it would give them away, although he didn't think anyone would be looking for them at night.

The jungle was a dangerous place even when a person could see. Leaches, poisonous plants, parasites, too many poisonous things to step on, too many sharp branches to scratch or cut the skin and start a hell of an infection.

He'd developed a healthy respect for the rainforest over the past few days. That respect had kept him alive. He could only hope his luck would hold a little while longer.

He pushed to his feet and used the light of the fire to pile some bamboo leaves on their sleeping platform. He was beginning to get used to roughing it. His bed in the indigenous village hadn't been much better. "Is life like this when you're deployed?"

"Not really. I was Iraq, not Vietnam. Desert. But mostly we slept on the base."

The idea of her in danger bothered him. "Were you injured?"

She shook her head.

"Did you lose any friends?"

She stared into the fire. "Everybody lost friends." She paused, then said in a softer voice, "I lost my husband."

That had him sitting back down. "You were married."

The news hit him harder than it should have. What did he expect, that she would be sitting around all this time, regretting that she'd left him? He hated the sudden jealous streak. It wasn't like him.

"I'm sorry for your loss." He watched her from across the fire, understanding now what had put the shadows into her eyes. "When?"

"Two years ago."

He tried to fill in the gaps. "Were you deployed together?"

"He was in Afghanistan. Both of our tours were just ending. I didn't reenlist. I wanted to be with my daughter."

He stared. "You have a daughter?"

"Abby." She closed her eyes. Cleared her throat. "I lost her last year. She was six." Grief shimmered in the air around her.

He sat stunned, unsure what to say, trying to process all that she'd revealed in the past few minutes.

She didn't wait for him to recover. She pushed to her feet and strode over to their bamboo platform. "We better get some sleep."

"Yeah," he said, because he couldn't find better words, the last of the anger and resentment he'd held toward her over the years evaporating. He wanted to go after her and gather her against him, except he wasn't sure if he'd be welcome. It'd been a long time since they'd been friends.

He waited a few minutes, giving her some privacy, then banked the fire and walked over to the platform, lay down next to her, giving her as much space as he could. Their makeshift bed was fairly narrow, not much more than an inch or two between them as they both lay on their backs, their arms under their heads.

"I'm sorry," he said again. He couldn't even imagine that kind of loss. His father had died a couple of years back, but he'd had lung cancer. They'd known for a long time that the end was coming, had time to prepare for it, had a chance to say goodbye.

She turned on her side, away from him. "Good night."

He was good with numbers, angles, engineering principles, business—a lot of things, really. But not with emotions. The strange mix of feelings that swirled inside him threw him off balance. There were things he wanted to say, should have said, but all that came out was, "Good night, Miranda."

A bird screeched in the night a few yards away. As a soft rain began to fall, drumming on the palm leaves over their heads, the bugs sought shelter and quieted.

His body was heavy with fatigue, but despite his exhaustion, Glenn couldn't sleep. He stayed awake long after Miranda's breathing evened, after the fire burned down. When the chill of the night crept into their shelter, he moved closer and took her into his arms, spooning her from behind.

Her army-honed body felt different from what he remembered. He'd loved how she felt back when they'd been lovers, but he couldn't say he liked the new Miranda any less—all strength and sinuous muscle. He inhaled her familiar scent and acknowledged the testosterone surge her nearness elicited. He considered himself an intellectual, but deep down he was just a Neanderthal whose basic instinct was to comfort her—with sex. Not an appropriate course of action. They hadn't had a relationship like that for a long time.

He closed his eyes and for a moment he pretended that she was the old Miranda. *His* Miranda. He rested his chin on the top of her head, tucking himself around her as tightly as possible. For the moment, he had precious little to give, only his warmth, so he gave that to her.

Chapter 8

SO THE NEW GLENN WAS DEFINITELY NOT LIKE THE OLD GLENN, MIRANDA thought as she woke in his arms at dawn, pressed against his wide chest, soaking up the heat of his hard body.

He'd been a nerdy engineering student. Okay, they'd both been pretty socially awkward. She'd had braces. He'd had thick, horned-rimmed glasses. They met in Engineering Principles 101, bonded over receiving the two highest grades at midterms.

They'd become study buddies first, then lovers after a few months and a lot of awkward kisses and groping sessions in dark corners. It had been the first time for the both of them.

"Good morning." His rusty voice in her ear interrupted her trip down memory lane.

As soon as he pulled away from her and rolled onto his back, she missed his heat. Ridiculous. She didn't need him. She briskly shoved herself away from the platform. "Fire?"

He sat up and stretched. "We should dry off."

The makeshift roof had kept most of the night rain off them, but their clothes were damp.

She dragged out the dry wood they'd stored under the platform, then grabbed a couple of cigarettes for tinder and started a fire while Glenn got up and took off his shirt.

He shook off the leaves that had stuck to it, and a couple of inch-long ants. She brushed off her own shirt, grateful to see that the ants had left her alone. She blew on the fledgling fire, then looked up at him.

He was stretching with his back to her, his arms above his head as he bent at the waist to the right first, then to the left.

Holy mother. The new and improved Glenn had a body that could have been in one of those firemen pinup calendars. Impressive cords of muscles flexed under his skin.

"What do you do?" she blurted.

He turned, cocking an eyebrow. "I manage the family company."

"No, I meant . . ." His sculpted chest distracted her, the faint smattering of hair that started below his bellybutton and led into the pants that were a size too large for him, held up only by what looked like a bamboo rope belt. The waistband sat below his hips and revealed enough for her to know he wasn't wearing underwear.

She snapped her gaze back to his. "You look different. Do you do sports?" Back in the day they used to make fun of the hotshot football players. If he told her he'd turned into a jock since, she might just faint into the fire.

He shrugged. "I swim. The pool is a good place to think. I don't have to pay much attention, just stay in my lane and keep going."

"You didn't used to be sporty."

"The better health, the fewer sick days, the less time away from the company."

Of course. All very logical, very much like him. Nothing geeky about his swimmer's body, though—flat abs, great pecs, wide shoulders.

He stepped forward. "Are you okay? We should find some food."

Her expression was probably off, but not from hunger.

She looked away from him, tossing another handful of branches on the fire, and the flames grew. He came closer to hold his shirt up to the heat. She shifted forward so her clothes would dry too. She definitely wasn't stripping.

The sky was still dim, but the fire provided enough light to illuminate more than the impressive outline of his body. She could do little but stare at the puckered scars that marred his skin, the rows of burn marks along his collarbones.

She swallowed, anger rising swiftly. "How badly did they hurt you?"

He shook out his shirt one more time, then shrugged into it, sat across the fire from her. His mouth tightened as he looked toward his feet. "No permanent damage."

"What about the burns? I'm sure they still hurt."

His expression darkened. "Sometimes the commander smoked cigars. He liked using me for an ashtray."

Her stomach clenched. He was half a head taller and nearly twice as wide in the shoulders, yet she felt her protective instincts take over. She'd been a soldier, her job to keep America and Americans safe. She doubted that instinct would ever go away. She wanted to . . . What? Hug him? *Maybe.*

She wished she could have come sooner. Her heart twisted at the thought of what he'd been through in the past few weeks.

She drew a deep breath. Regrets were a waste of time. She was here now. She was going to do whatever it took to get them back to the US safely. She popped to her feet with a new burst of energy. "We should get going."

"Right." He brightened at the prospect of leaving the forest behind. "Let's do this before the soldiers get all caffeinated."

She groaned. "Don't bring up coffee."

"Remember the wickedly strong espresso in the main hall at MIT?"

She threw a stick at him. "Sadist." Then she kicked dirt on the fire while he packed up, laughing at her.

As they moved out, a monkey screeched in the trees above them, so close it startled her.

Glenn looked up. "Winky?"

"Who?" She followed his gaze.

"My old buddy. We were POWs together. He followed me when I escaped." Glenn grinned. "He goes off, then comes back. I have no idea how he finds me."

"He probably thinks you're part of his tribe." She shook her head. "He came with you from Guri?"

"He was caged in the courtyard, target practice for the soldiers. I couldn't leave him."

Okay, that was the Glenn she knew, the one with the big heart. She felt herself softening, so she picked up her pace.

They walked a full hour, Winky following them, jumping from tree to tree, before they reached the end of the woods. Only a dirt road separated them from the nearest houses, little more than hovels, on the edge of the city. Not a difficult distance, but two guardsmen sat in a military SUV a few hundred feet to their right. Roberto had the city on lockdown.

Miranda gestured toward the men with her head. Glenn nodded, and they silently retreated a hundred feet.

"We'll go around them, then try again in a little while," she said. The authorities couldn't have enough people to circle the entire city, could they?

He followed when she moved on.

They didn't talk much. Better not to be overheard if there were soldiers in the woods. And the going required their full attention. They had to watch where they stepped, what they grabbed.

Since they were moving as quietly as possible, they heard the people up ahead before the people could have heard them. Miranda raised her right hand, her fist in line with her ear.

Though he'd never been in the military, Glenn seemed to get the signal because he immediately stopped.

She turned back and mouthed, "Soldiers."

Even as he nodded, they heard laughter and a woman's voice, too faint to make out what she was saying.

They crept forward slowly, carefully, crouching in the cover of a thick stand of bushes once they reached the path. Twenty or so tourists were walking through the woods, escorted by two guardsmen. The tourists wore backpacks, looking prepared for a full day of hiking.

"Are you going up in the plane to see Angel Falls tomorrow?" a tall, aristocratic-looking woman asked in a British accent.

Her partner, a pudgy, red-headed fellow, shook his head. "I think I'll stay back at lodgings to download the photos and sort through them a bit." He was snapping pictures even as he spoke.

"Do you think the guards are necessary?" the woman asked.

The man shrugged as he moved on. "They're worried about the two fugitives the tour guide told us about this morning. Better safe than sorry."

The guards trailed behind them, bringing up the rear.

Miranda flashed Glenn a questioning look. If there were guardsmen with the tourists, then they had to be all over the city. How many National Guards had Roberto called into Santa Elena?

Her stomach growled. Glenn had to be hungry too. She looked after the small group as they disappeared from sight on the winding path. The nearest food was in those backpacks. And maybe a phone too. If she could call Elaine at the office, they might yet be saved. The general could enter some kind of diplomatic negotiations if he had proof that two US citizens were here under duress.

She nodded after the tour group and whispered, "Breakfast and phone."

Glenn's lips stretched into a grin.

God, that grin could do things to her. She swallowed. *Could.* As in the past. Definitely not now.

They followed the group at a distance. The monkey screeched now and then, but the sound wasn't out of place, blending in with birdcalls. Nobody turned back to investigate.

The tourists fawned over every new plant, snapped photos of every leaf and bug. Miranda kept close to them, but out of sight. At some point, the group would have to stop to eat and relieve themselves, if nothing else. Sooner or later, those backpacks would come off and be set on the ground. And a clever hand reaching out from the bushes might come up with something useful then. She just had to wait.

So they did, for two full hours, before the boisterous group stopped at last in the middle of a clearing. Backpacks did drop to the ground, but nowhere near where one could be raided.

The tour guide stood on a stump to gain everyone's attention.

"We have the third-highest woody bamboo diversity in Latin America." He spoke in English with a soft accent, beaming with pride. "About ten genera and sixty species. Among our states, the southern states have the greatest diversity of woody bamboo."

One of the tourists raised a hand as if in school. "Could you tell us more about the different species?" he asked in a heavy German accent.

"Certainly." The man on the stump smiled even wider. "Most of the bamboo are *Myriocladus* or *Chusquea*. The rest are from the genera *Rhipidocladum*, *Atractantha*, *Guadua*, *Arthrostylidium*, *Neurolepis*, *Elytrostachys*, *Merostachys*, and *Aulonemia*." His chest puffed out. "We have more *Guadua* diversity than any other country except Brazil."

An excited twitter ran through the group. Miranda flashed Glenn an unimpressed look. Apparently, they'd run into botanists on holiday.

"Does bamboo play a major role in the economy?" a young woman wanted to know, her lilting accent decidedly French.

"Unfortunately, no. Not yet," the guide answered. "Other than the bamboo spoons and bowls and other souvenirs you see in the gift shops, our bamboo resources are underutilized. But the government is conducting studies on how we could better use bamboo as a natural resource."

He paused before he went on. "Of course, the indigenous people and the peasants build houses from it. It's also used for drying racks for tobacco. But bamboo-based organic textiles are becoming popular. And bamboo flooring is catching on. Unlike hardwood, bamboo is an easily replenished resource."

He went on about that for another twenty minutes before the group moved on. His last words were, "I'll point out species and genera as we go."

Oh, jeez, let's get the party started, Miranda thought. But the tourists looked positively titillated, while she and Glenn exchanged snarky expressions. Back at MIT, there'd been a friendly rivalry between the engineering and life sciences departments. They'd enjoyed outdoing each other in the Nerd Olympics.

The tourists soon came into an enormous stand of bamboo. They followed a man-made path, but off the beaten track, the stalks grew too close to each other. In places, Miranda and Glenn could barely squeeze through.

When forward movement became impossible, they waited until the group progressed far enough ahead, then they fought their way to the path and followed behind, out of sight.

Another two hours passed by the time the group stopped again, on the other side of the endless stand of bamboo, where a zip-line course waited for them in the trees. Miranda and Glenn went around them, stayed in cover as the tourists dropped their backpacks, climbed a rope ladder to a large platform twenty feet off the ground, then to a second platform twenty feet above that, then a third platform twenty feet higher yet.

While they lined up for their next thrilling experience, the two guardsmen stayed on the ground.

"I distract the guards, you grab some food and a cell phone," Miranda whispered to Glenn.

"I'll distract the guards."

Seriously? He needed to exert his male dominance now? She rolled her eyes and skirted the clearing, moving as close to the bags as possible. Then she waited until she heard some stomping and branches cracking across the clearing in the woods.

The guardsmen grabbed their rifles and ran toward the sound.

She waited until they disappeared into the bushes before she sprinted forward. *One second.* In the first bag she found a large, empty Ziploc bag with crumbs, probably the remains of somebody's breakfast.

Nobody was going to miss an empty bag. She grabbed it. *Two seconds.* She looked for opened bags of food—pretzels, nuts, bite-size nutrition bars, raisins—and grabbed a handful from each, dumping her loot into the empty bag. At least half a minute ticked by, but by the end she had at least two pounds' worth of trail mix, and in such a way that nobody would miss anything.

She was elbow deep into a fancy black backpack when a tourist—the young Frenchwoman—climbed down the rope ladder and nearly caught her.

Heart pumping, Miranda jumped behind the tree, the trunk at least three feet wide, enough to hide her.

She peeked toward the bags. *Oh, man.* The flap on the fancy black backpack lay open. She hadn't closed it. She pulled back into cover since the woman was heading straight toward the pile.

Would she notice?

Would she stay down here?

Miranda held her breath. If the woman stayed and the guardsmen came back . . . They'd notice her. If not immediately, then when the rest of the botanists returned to the ground and began milling around. She could stay on the opposite side of the tree from one person. It'd be impossible with twenty people spreading out.

Shit.

Think!

Were the guardsmen authorized to shoot on sight, or had they been ordered to bring the fugitives back? Either way, she suspected the end result would be very similar.

The woman sat on the pile of backpacks and drank deeply from her water bottle, even as Miranda could hear voices in the bushes where the guardsmen had disappeared. The voices grew louder as the seconds ticked on. The men were coming back.

She glanced toward the woods. If she ran now, the woman would see her. She'd probably scream. The guardsmen would be after Miranda the next second. Poised to flee, she pulled out her weapon, hoping Glenn was smart enough to run in the opposite direction and save himself once gunfire erupted.

But the Frenchwoman stashed away her drink at last and hurried back to the ladder, climbing back up with agility.

The guardsmen were still shouting to each other in the bushes. So the second the French tourist was on the first platform, Miranda dashed back to the backpacks. She wanted a cell phone, desperately.

She closed the bag she'd left open earlier, then searched the outer pockets. Nothing there, but she found a phone in the second bag she checked. As she tugged it out, her sleeve caught on the zipper of a pink hygiene kit. Would the owner notice if it went missing? Possibly not until she got back to the hostel. Most likely, she would think it had fallen out during her trek through the jungle.

Miranda grabbed the kit and dashed back into the cover of the woods, not a moment too soon. The guardsmen were returning, all muddied up and swearing, talking about a stupid monkey.

She hurried back to Glenn, feeling a hundred percent better about their chances.

They had food and they had a phone. They were as good as saved.

———

He grinned when he saw her with the food and the phone. He looked as if he was considering picking her up and swinging her around. "Well done."

She took a small, precautionary step back. "You provided good distraction," she admitted grudgingly.

While the tourists zip-lined above, squealing, she shoved some trail mix into her mouth, then handed the bag to Glenn. Then she checked the phone. Full battery. Maybe, just maybe, luck was on their side for once.

She held her breath, hoping nobody would choose this moment to call the phone and bring attention to them. But she needn't have worried. The first thing the phone did was pop a message up on the screen: *No Service.*

———

Glenn dropped the phone on the path so the tourists would find it on their way back and the owner would think it had simply fallen out of his bag. Without service, a phone wasn't much use. They should have figured. Most US cell phone companies barely covered the continental US, let alone the South American jungle.

He and Miranda needed a phone from someone local, a phone that actually worked here.

Knowing now that the population had been notified about fugitives and how strict security was, they decided to spend another day in the woods to strategize and consider their options.

After the great snack heist, they spent the rest of the afternoon searching for water to refill their old-fashioned aluminum canteens; then they boiled the water back at their campsite to sterilize it. They had food, water, and shelter—better than nothing.

Glenn picked through their newfound toiletry bag while Miranda put fresh leaves on their sleeping platform since last night's bedding was full of bugs that had moved in during the day.

The pink plastic bag held one bar of soap in a matching pink plastic case, a toothbrush, toothpaste, a razor, a comb, nail clippers, a handful of cotton balls, and a six-pack of flavored condoms—strawberry.

Okay, that brought back some college memories of discovering sex and really, really liking it, liking it more than engineering. They might have been inexperienced, but both he and Miranda had curious minds, which turned out to be as much as an advantage in bed as it'd been in the class room. When faced with something unknown, they both believed in extensive experimenting and testing. Including nearly the entire contents of an X-rated novelty store one semester.

He held up the pack. "Somebody was hoping to get lucky while on vacation."

She rolled her eyes. "Botanists. They're all floozies."

He grinned at the old college joke. A couple of girls in the dorm room next to Miranda's had used the botany department lab to mix up herbal aphrodisiacs. They successfully sold a whole variety of love potions on the campus black market. But not as successfully as some of the guys in the department, who were always mixing things that could be smoked.

Miranda scanned the six-pack. "Those could come in handy. We used to get them in our army emergency pack. You can collect and transport water in them. Close to half a gallon, actually. Or use one to hold a wound dressing in place, keep dirt out, and make the dressing waterproof."

He cocked an eyebrow. "Okay. I have to say, my mind went to a different place entirely."

She snorted as she shook her head, a half smile twisting her full lips. "One of those will keep your tinder and matches dry in a place like this, or if you have to wade through water."

She went back to working on their bed. "And condoms burn if you have no tinder. A onetime use, so preferably to be avoided. You can use them to make a slingshot and hunt. You can use them to prevent moisture or sand from getting into the barrel of your weapon." She finished with the bamboo leaf bedding and wiped her hands on her pants as she turned toward him.

"Okay." He dropped the condoms back into the bag and took out the toothpaste instead. "We'll save them. Not that I plan on spending a lot more time in the jungle. We'll find a way into the city tomorrow."

He snapped off a foot-long, half-inch-wide branch from a fibrous brush, cleaned it, broke it in half, then gave half to Miranda. Then he squeezed some toothpaste on the end and proceeded to brush his teeth. She followed his example, finished first, and went to bed.

Glenn banked the fire before he joined her on the sleeping platform.

She scooted to the edge to give him room. "I'd like to make more progress tomorrow than we made today." She sounded frustrated.

She would be. She'd always been a type A personality. They both were. Not in things like sports, but they had been driven about grades and projects. For him, that eventually translated to competing in business.

Night fell around them, the birds in the trees quieting, the bugs starting up their serenade, taking second shift.

"Your file said you're divorced," she said out of the blue.

He didn't want to think about Victoria. "Ancient history."

"What was she like?"

"Harvard Law School. Blonde and tall. Ambitious. She's Cesar's daughter. I've known her forever. We've always moved in the same circles. My mother and Cesar both pushed a union since we were kids."

She turned toward him, the bamboo-leaf bedding rustling under them. "Like an arranged marriage?"

"Not like that." But not blinding love, either. "We were good friends. We respected each other. She worked for the company and knew it inside out. Marrying her had been the logical thing to do. We agreed to give it a try."

Miranda hesitated a moment before saying, "She was the right woman for where you were going, in a way I wasn't."

He stilled. "What are you talking about?"

"I wasn't the right woman for where you were going. That's what your mother told me when you took me home for Thanksgiving."

He swore under his breath. "Don't blame your running away on my mother."

"Not what I meant. I knew that I didn't fit even without her telling me. Believe me. The chauffeur who picked us up at the airport, then the maids, and then the cook clued me in. Different worlds."

She'd left him because she couldn't deal with her insecurities. Of all the stupid things to do—

"You're just as good as anyone else. Money doesn't make a person better."

"Believe me, that's not what Gloria thought. She looked at me as she would have looked at termite damage." A threat to basic structure.

He stayed silent for a long moment. "I'm sorry if that's how you felt. You should have told me."

"Then what? You would have talked to her, and maybe she would have pretended harder that she was happy to see me with the heir to the Danning fortune."

He shifted. "Just as a quick reminder: it's the twenty-first century in America, not eighteenth-century England."

"Yet the heir married an heiress. I assume Cesar owns plenty of company stock since he started the business with your father."

"Twenty-five percent," he murmured. Then asked a few moments later, "Is that why you left me? The money bothered you that much?"

"I left because my scholarship ran out at MIT. The army promised to pay me to finish my engineering degree. They did."

"I told you I would pay the rest of your tuition."

"And I told you I wasn't for sale."

He didn't want to think about the fight they'd had about that, her deliberately misunderstanding his gesture. She'd chosen not to accept his help.

He'd hated the decision back then, and he hated it now. But he gave credit where credit was due. "You wanted to do it on your own and you did it. Got your degree. Rose in the ranks. Found an exciting career after the army. So now you have everything you ever wanted."

———

Miranda thought of the empty, one-bedroom apartment she was renting in D.C. She thought of Matthew and Abby, and her heart squeezed painfully. "I have nothing."

She felt Glenn's fingers brushing against her in the dark, then taking her hand.

"I'm sorry about your family."

Not going to talk about it. "Why did you get divorced?" She diverted.

He thought before he answered. "I'm not sure if we were ever in love. Not enough, in any case. We were friends, we had mutual admiration, lust—we were young and healthy. We made great business partners. She worked at the company. I knew I could trust her with anything."

He paused, and she waited him out.

"We grew apart. Neither of us spent a lot of time at home. I had a couple of projects that were at a stage where I had to travel a lot. She met someone else and asked me for a divorce. I agreed."

"How very amicable."

"No sense in throwing a fit over it."

That sounded cold. And she knew he wasn't a cold person. She hated to think that maybe because she'd rejected him, he hadn't been able to trust the next person, hadn't been able to give himself fully. He had his pride. Maybe he'd decided not to put himself in a spot where he could be hurt again. Which would have been a shame, because he was a great guy who deserved happiness.

He'd been a good friend to her. She wished they could go back to that. "I'm sorry it didn't work out," she said, letting him hold her hand.

And after a moment, he asked, "Were you very much in love with Matthew?"

"Yes." Not as much as she'd been in love with Glenn in college, but nothing matched first love, she supposed. Their first explosion of passion had been a mythical thing.

She *did* love Matthew, even if they hadn't been able to spend as much time together as they'd wanted to. Their deployments had kept them apart for most of their marriage. She'd hoped that would change eventually, but that day had never come. They missed what could have been.

He turned to his side to face her, rustling the bamboo bedding. "Was your daughter sick? Abby?"

The question startled her, but then she remembered his younger brother who had had leukemia and passed away at ten or eleven. She pressed her lips together. Gloria had already lost a child. And now she thought she'd lost Glenn. Even if Miranda had still carried some resentment toward the woman, she would have let it go in this moment. She never thought she was like Gloria in any way, but they did have losing a child in common.

She drew a slow breath, conscious that Glenn was still waiting for her answer. "Abby was kidnapped. Killed." The words scraped against her throat as if they had claws.

He pulled her into his arms without notice, his chin coming to rest on the top of her head, the gesture making her want to cry for some reason, even as he said, "I'm sorry. You don't have to talk about it."

Good, because she was pretty much incapable of that. Her losses were her own. She didn't discuss them with anyone, ever.

His warmth and strength wrapped all around her and offered precious comfort. This was the friendship that she'd missed. Matthew had been gone by the time she lost Abby, so she'd borne that burden alone.

And she'd been alone since, for the most part.

She'd dated twice since she'd been widowed, but it never felt right. Glenn's embrace was familiar and somehow easier to give in to. She snuggled against him. Tilted her head up so she could look into his eyes, as much as she could in the darkness. "Thanks."

"For what?"

"For being the kind of guy that you are."

"A preppy mama's-boy nerd?"

She winced. She might have said that when she'd broken up with him. "I didn't mean it. I was mad and embarrassed because I had to leave college. And I hated that your mother was right about me. We would have never fit long term. I wasn't what you needed."

"It would have been nice if the two of you let me decide that for myself," he said mildly.

She relaxed against him. "I missed this," she said on a sigh, without meaning to, without knowing what she meant exactly.

But before she could take it back, Glenn dipped his head and brushed his lips against hers.

Chapter 9

MEMORIES HIT GLENN SO HARD, THEY NEARLY KNOCKED HIM OFF THE SLEEP-
ing platform. Good thing he had Miranda to hang on to.

He wasn't sure how he'd meant the kiss. She was distressed and
his head simply dipped into the familiar gesture. He'd meant to
comfort, he supposed, but the second he pressed his lips against
hers, instant lust raced through him.

He felt like a horny eighteen-year-old, wanting to plow forward
with abandon, without restraint. But since he had the control of a
man now, he exercised some much-needed restraint and brushed
his lips against hers slowly.

Don't scare her.

He kissed the groove in the middle of her bottom lip, then
the corners, one after the other. He wanted to taste her next, so
he rubbed his nose against hers in a long-forgotten gesture, and
nudged her until she opened her mouth to him.

He was already hard against her, his erection nestled against
the V of her legs. He only got harder when his tongue swept inside
to fully taste her.

After a moment of hesitation, her fingers dug into his hair. She didn't play coy, didn't hold back. She never had, one of the things he'd loved about her. With Miranda, what you saw was what you got, and it was plenty: a keen mind, a warm heart, and unbridled passion.

At the moment, he was most interested in the unbridled passion part.

His hand slid down to cover her butt. She had a lot more muscle definition in interesting places than she used to have. He wanted to discover her anew, learn every inch of her all over again. He shifted so he was half on top of her.

Her hand slid up his chest, but not to push him away. She ran her fingers over his pecs. "You're not as nerdy as I remembered."

He gave a bark of a laugh. "I'll take that as a compliment."

He could barely make out her face in the light of the glowing embers of the fire, but he saw her lips stretch into a smile.

She held his gaze. "Funny how everything comes right back after all these years."

"I hardly think we're old enough for memory loss." But he knew what she meant. Just now, he felt almost as if the past ten years had never happened.

"It's just the circumstances." She gave a soft sigh. "Adrenaline rush. We're thrust together in a survival situation, dependent on each other."

He paused. Watched her. "Sounds like you're trying to talk yourself out of something here."

"Maybe I am."

He eased his hand from her butt to her lower back with regret. As far as he was concerned, using one condom now would have left plenty for other emergency survival purposes, but he didn't want to pressure her. "Sorry if I pushed."

"You didn't. I'm just saying, under the circumstances, we might not be exercising our best judgment."

His body vehemently disagreed. But he wasn't going to argue with her. He hadn't really recovered yet from her exploding back into his life again.

He moved off her and lay back next to her, his body twitching with disappointment. He had no idea what he was doing here with her like this. But he couldn't pretend that nothing had happened.

"How do you feel about giving a try to figuring things out once we're back in D.C.? We'll be back in a couple of days. We'll sneak into Santa Elena tomorrow, then onto an airplane." He paused, his ardor cooling as he remembered their predicament, the fact that they weren't out of the woods yet, literally or proverbially. "You really think we can manage sneaking on a plane without security catching us?"

She took a long time answering. "We'll have to. As far as Roberto and DISIP are concerned, we're capitalist spies in a communist country. They'll make us disappear forever, faster than you can say, 'Hail to the commander.'"

———

Miranda ate a couple of handfuls of trail mix for breakfast, sharing some with Winky, who dropped by in the early morning to serve as their alarm clock, jumping on their makeshift roof and scaring the bejesus out of her.

"Do that again, and no more breakfast," she warned.

The animal shoved a pretzel into his mouth and winked at her.

"Hey, your monkey is flirting with me," she called back to Glenn.

"Don't get too excited. He used to do that whenever I was in the torture chamber. Maybe he winks at people he thinks are doomed." Glenn climbed down one of the trees that supported their sleeping platform. He'd hidden her rifle up in the branches. They couldn't take that into the city without drawing attention.

All through their morning preparations, they talked about their options and what they needed to do, neither of them mentioning the kiss they'd shared the night before.

Well, if Glenn could forget about it, she certainly wasn't going to bring it up, not even if her lips tingled every time she looked at him.

She kicked dirt over the fire. "Let's go."

They'd agreed to once again follow the road from the woods until they found a break in perimeter security. Except, what if they couldn't find a break? They hadn't so far.

"How did you keep hidden for all that time before I found you?" she asked as they headed out.

"I spent most of the time in the back of a giant logging truck."

If only that could work here. She shook her head. "Even if we see trucks on the road, we can't get on unless one stops and the driver walks away long enough for us to come out of the woods and hide in the back. Without being seen by the perimeter guards."

Glenn grunted his agreement as he jumped over a fallen log full of termites. She vaulted over right behind him. The monkey stopped to snack. They plodded forward, watching out for danger. Winky caught up after a while, screeching his support in the trees above them.

Glenn swatted at the little black flies that buzzed around his head. "How about the tourists?"

She'd already thought about that. "We can't join them. The guide would know we weren't with the group. Twenty people are not so many that two extra wouldn't stick out. Even if we didn't look like this."

Their clothes were wrinkled and dirty. They definitely looked like they'd spent the last couple of nights in the jungle and not at the nearest tourist hostel.

Glenn slowed his steps as he turned to her. "Do you think the tourists we saw yesterday walked all the way from the city?"

"I doubt it." *Oh.* She grinned. God, she could have kissed him all over again. Excitement leaped to life. "I bet a bus brings them to the edge of the jungle."

"Let's find out." Glenn changed course immediately, picking up pace as he hurried toward the path where they'd seen the tourists the day before.

They found what they were looking for in about an hour, but the path stood silent. Either today's tour group had already passed through here or they hadn't arrived yet.

Glenn and Miranda stayed in the cover of the woods, following the path toward the city, until they reached the end of the forest and found a dirt parking lot with two tour buses, one dark blue and the other one red, already waiting there.

The shot of hope was more than welcome. Almost as good as coffee.

"You're a genius," she whispered to Glenn and gave his hand a quick squeeze.

"I spent years trying to tell you that," he deadpanned, making her smile.

Which she appreciated, since her body was buzzing with nerves. If they messed this up, they might not get another chance. They needed to come up with a workable plan for getting on one of those buses.

Obviously, the tourists were on their jungle trek already, unlikely to return for hours and hours with their assigned guards. The bus drivers, who stood between the vehicles smoking and joking around with each other, presented a problem, however.

Her Spanish wasn't great, but she could make out the gist of the jib-jab. Sounded like the taller was one telling a mother-in-law joke. The men both laughed when he finished.

Miranda flashed a *now what* look to Glenn. Yesterday's distraction trick wouldn't work here. The drivers wouldn't go into the woods to investigate some strange noise. If anything, they'd get into their vehicles.

Glenn scanned the clearing and the men. "We could take them," he said under his breath.

She stared. Okay, that was so unlike Glenn. But maybe not unlike the new Glenn. He definitely had survival instincts and all kinds of strengths.

She didn't want to think about how much she liked that.

Right. So they could take the drivers. Take the drivers' uniforms. But then what? Drive an empty bus back into town? That'd be suspicious. And the guardsmen at the checkpoint would likely have her and Glenn's pictures. They'd be recognized if they tried to return out in the open.

She scanned the two vehicles again, carefully, inch by inch. "What if we got under one of the buses and hung on?"

Glenn considered. "As a last resort. Looks pretty dangerous."

Yeah. The road that led from the parking lot was a dirt road, uneven and full of rocks. They could get brushed off and flattened under one of the back tires.

She discarded that idea for the moment and moved on to the next. She eyed the luggage compartments on the side of the blue bus that stood the closest to them. From what they'd seen the day before, the tourists had small backpacks for their daytrip. Small enough to pile in the back of the bus and in the overhead luggage compartments. It seemed unlikely that they'd be stored under the bus for a short trip.

"Storage," she whispered, even as her shoulders tensed. The small space wouldn't have been her first choice, or even second.

Glenn narrowed his eyes as he scanned the bottom part of the bus. "Wouldn't they be locked?"

The compartments were tightly closed, except . . . Was there a small gap in the door on the last one? She looked closer. Maybe it had a broken lock.

Glenn whispered next to her ear, his warm breath fanning her neck. "How do we get in without getting noticed?"

She ignored the tingles. "From behind."

The buses faced the forest. With the drivers chatting in front, if she and Glenn approached on the road from the city side, they wouldn't be seen.

Unless the drivers moved. Or, unless another bus came.

"Are you sure?" Glenn asked.

She knew what he meant. Once they entered the city, if things didn't work out, they might not be able to return to the jungle through perimeter security. Once they were inside the loop, they could become trapped there.

She filled her lungs. "It's a chance we have to take."

They pulled back and, staying in the woods, skirted the parking lot, walked back along the road, then left the cover of the trees and hurried forward in a crouch, keeping the vehicles between themselves and the drivers.

Glenn reached the blue bus first, tilted the compartment door up without trouble and let her climb in, then came in after her. She swallowed her unease as she shifted to the back to accommodate his large frame. There'd better not be a poisonous snake or a giant spider hiding in there with them.

Once Glenn closed the flap, they were enveloped in nearly complete darkness, other than the narrow strip of light that edged the door. They both remained silent. They could hear the guards talking, which meant the guards would hear them.

God, she hated small, dark places. Every muscle in her body clenched.

Half an hour passed before she leaned toward his ear to whisper, "Maybe we got in too early."

"We might not have been able to slip in later," he whispered back.

He was right. If the drivers walked around or moved to a different spot, approaching the compartment unseen might have become impossible.

An hour passed, then two. Miranda tried to sleep, but she was too wired and the sheet of metal under her too uncomfortable. To distract herself from the dark memories that tried to muscle their way into her head, she shared the rest of the remaining trail mix in her pocket with Glenn. They ate in silence, then drank sparingly. The bus might not head back into Santa Elena for hours yet, and they couldn't go to the bathroom.

She tried to breathe slowly, evenly, but anxiety crept into her chest little by little. *No big deal*, she told herself. Nobody was chasing them; nobody was shooting at them. They just had to stay still and quiet. They weren't in any real danger. Yet the stupid anxiety spread, squeezed her lungs tighter and tighter.

By the fourth hour, the walls began closing in on her. The men talking outside in a foreign language, the heat, the darkness, and the small space . . . Cold sweat ran down her back. Her entire body was tense, from her toes to the top of her head. She shifted, trying to relax.

Glenn put his hand on her arm. "What is it?" he asked under his breath.

She didn't want to talk about it. *Oh hell.*

"I was captured once when I was deployed in Iraq," she whispered.

Maybe talking would distract her from the crushing sense of claustrophobia. Dialogue would keep her firmly in the here and now, keep the past from pushing into the present. "We were on patrol, going through burned-out houses to make sure nobody was hiding there, setting up an ambush for a convoy that was supposed to come through later in the day."

He reached up to touch her face, his fingers gentle, cupping the curve of her jaw, anchoring her to him. That helped.

"Anyway, I found some teenagers in there, smoking, a couple of boys. I was herding them out, not realizing I missed one. He crept up behind me and hit me over the head with a brick." She swallowed.

Glenn didn't push for more. He waited.

"I came to in the trunk of a car." She swallowed again, her throat dry. "Hot, dark, and cramped."

"Like this place."

Pretty freaking much. "They kept riding down bumpy dirt roads all day, trying to decide what to do with me. They didn't set out to kidnap an American soldier. It just happened, and they were feeling like big boys all of a sudden. They were having a grand old time congratulating each other."

His palm gently cupped her cheek, but his voice was tight with anger as he said, "While you were waiting in that trunk for hours for them to decide what they wanted to do with you."

"I figured I was as good as dead," she confessed with a twist of her lips.

"What happened?"

"They made the mistake of going home for some food. I banged on the trunk, and another family member heard me. The patriarch of the family let me out, beat those kids with a stick, literally, right in front of me. Then he personally drove me back to the base, even while he knew that those boys could be charged with being insurgents, tossed into prison, and never seen again."

She shook her head. "He could have been arrested or even shot the second he showed up with me outside the base." She was still as incredulous now as she'd been back then. "He did the right thing even if it put his entire family in jeopardy."

"What happened to the boys?"

"They were questioned, then handed over to local law enforcement. I think they were caned and released."

"You could have made a big stink over it. Demanded more."

"I didn't want more," she said. "I wasn't hurt."

"That's a matter of opinion." His whispered voice grew tighter with every word. Then he added a moment later, "I imagine you're not a fan of being stuffed in dark trunks."

"It wouldn't be my first choice for mode of transportation." Not that she would admit to being claustrophobic, exactly. She wouldn't let her discomfort stop her. The definition of bravery, as she'd learned in the army, was to feel the fear, but do whatever you needed to do anyway.

She rested her head on Glenn's chest, while he put his arm around her. She closed her eyes, and let his steady heartbeat comfort her. Her own heartbeat slowed to match. They lay together, practically fused together in the small space. But soon her hip was going numb and her toes were tingling. She tried to wiggle them.

"Here." Glenn rubbed her neck, her back, her arm that he could reach, her lower back, her buttocks, shifting so his long arm could reach lower.

The tingling numbness was soon replaced by a different kind of tingling altogether. The longer he worked on her, the heavier her breasts felt, the more heat pooled low in her belly. Then he shifted his hand to rub life back to her inner thighs.

Okay. We've clearly moved past the therapeutic massage thing. But she didn't have it in her to protest.

He worked on the muscles just above her knee. If he went even an inch higher . . . And then he did, his breathing growing heavier. He moved his long, kneading fingers up another inch. Her breathing was becoming erratic too. Soon his probing fingers were at mid-thigh. Then higher.

She knew only too well what those long fingers of his could do. Before they'd gone all the way, back in college, they'd spent weeks and weeks learning each other's bodies, learning to satisfy each other every way possible.

Engineering students liked to know how things worked. The human body and its responses to stimuli were no exception, no less fascinating than building a bridge. They'd learned each other's bodies with meticulous care.

Memories of those times pushed out the last memories of her terrifying day in captivity. With Glenn putting his mind to distracting her, resistance was futile.

As heat and need washed through her, she very nearly reached down to move his hand to the goal line, but ended up pushing him away instead. They couldn't do this. *Not now, not here.*

The tourists could be back any second. She couldn't even stand movies where the hero and heroine stopped to have sex in the middle of mortal danger. There was a name for characters like that: TSTL. *Too stupid to live.*

She waited until the rush of blood in her veins slowed to normal. Okay, she did feel a hundred percent better. Her body might have wanted more, but it got what it really needed: restored blood flow.

"My turn." If they had to leave their hiding place in a hurry, it'd be better not to fall on their faces with their first steps. She reached for Glenn, wanting to help his muscles regain circulation.

If she thought focusing on him was going to distract her from her own desires, she was sadly mistaken. Sweet heaven, the man had muscles.

She'd seen his back when he'd taken his shirt off at their campsite; she'd even snuggled against him. But having free rein to explore every impressive inch made the whole tactile experience very different. He had muscles like bridge cables. He swam. *How much could a man swim?*

She worked on his neck, back, lower back as far as she could reach. She moved her fingers along hills and valleys of muscles, over the thin ridges she knew to be scars. Until something hard poked against the V of her thighs as he shifted. She had a fair idea it wasn't a water canteen.

She snatched her hand back just as new voices sounded outside, excited chatter, some male, some female. The tourists were returning.

Moment of truth.

She'd been half on top of Glenn, but shifted now so she'd be on the outside, blocking his body with hers. Even as he growled his displeasure into her ear, she moved her hand toward the gun in the back of her waistband, held her breath as the voices reached closer and closer.

She didn't want a shootout. She didn't want any tourists hurt. But if she had to protect Glenn and herself from the guardsmen, she'd do what she had to. She waited.

If the driver opened the storage compartments for the backpacks . . .

But the bus dipped slightly as the tourists filed up the steps one by one. They never stopped talking. From the sound of it, the trek had been a wild success. In ten minutes or so, the engine started, rumbling, and they were on their way.

And the next second, with a ferocious growl as the only warning, Glenn shifted her under him, covered her with his well-built body, and crushed her lips under his.

Okay, then.

His soft beard, a few days' worth of growth, tickled her skin. The bus rattling over uneven ground and the hard metal beneath her took nothing away from the experience. She was too far gone to notice discomfort. She couldn't really complain with Glenn's tongue in her mouth, mastering her, whipping her need into fever pitch.

His large hand covered her breast, weighed it, measured it, caught her budding nipple between his thumb and index finger through the soft material of her shirt. Hot, liquid desire shot through her.

She moaned into his mouth. They no longer had to be silent. The people in the bus wouldn't hear them over the engine.

Glenn let go of her breast to slide a hand between them.

She felt a rush of tingles.

They were still in terrible danger, but they were safe for the moment and a moment was all she needed. Or maybe two, because he was taking his time, damn him.

He cupped her with his warm palm until everything he touched sang to life. Then slowly, oh ever so freaking slowly, he pressed his palm hard between her legs and rubbed her.

She arched her hips into the pleasure as tension built inside her.

Nobody but Glenn could ever do this to her, not this fast. She felt like a hormone-crazed teenager all over again. And had about as much self-control.

They were both fully clothed, for heaven's sake. They could barely touch each other, could barely even see each other.

But she'd learned from their long-ago experiments that when Glenn touched her body, she seemed to go to pieces with unfair ease. She was going to, soon now. She teetered on the edge. Right on the ragged edge . . . poised to tumble over when the bus stopped at the checkpoint.

Glenn froze.

She bit into his shoulder so she wouldn't moan in frustration.

This was so freaking unfair! Okay, okay. And dangerous. *Focus.* She inched her fingers toward her weapon.

The bus door creaked open, then soldiers talked with the driver. The bus rocked a little when one of them stepped up to look at the passengers. He took his damned time. But then he wished them a good visit at last, got the hell off the bus, and let them go on their way.

Relief flooded her, and then the heat and need were back, even as the bus chugged forward.

"Now. Please," she whispered.

"Tell me you missed me," Glenn demanded, his voice rough with need.

"I missed you."

But she couldn't think about that, or anything else, because he claimed her lips while he pressed his palm against her and kneaded her into the kind of oblivion only a prizewinning orgasm could offer.

Chapter 10

HIS BALLS HAD TO BE BLUER THAN THE TOUR BUS. GLENN MOVED OFF HER, making sure he was on the outside, protecting her, loving how she panted next to him, how she'd come for him, moaning his name.

He'd started out wanting to distract her, but the whole thing spiraled out of control pretty fast.

Miranda. She was a unique phenomenon entirely.

He wanted this. Not just more, not just to finish it, but he wanted her over and over again. Wanted Miranda back in his life.

He should have looked for her after she'd walked away from him. To hell with his injured pride and what his mother had wanted.

He should have gone after her ten years ago and done whatever it took to bring her back. In hindsight, it seemed pretty obvious. He felt like an idiot for not having seen the light sooner. It wasn't a feeling he experienced often. He frowned in the darkness.

The bus stopped, dropped the tourists off, then went on. Glenn stayed still in the cramped storage compartment with Miranda lying next to him. Another twenty minutes passed before the vehicle stopped once again. This time, the driver turned off the engine. They could hear his footsteps outside a moment later, his shoes crunching on gravel as he walked away.

Other engines rumbled on farther off, probably other buses coming and going. Glenn waited about five minutes to open the flip door to a crack and steal a glance of the outside world.

"Buses, buses, and more buses." Some new, some old, but they all stood empty. They were at some kind of a bus station, parked in the back.

"Can we get out?" Miranda whispered behind him.

He could see in only one direction, forward. A couple of men were going about their business at least two hundred yards away, wearing driver's uniforms. "I don't know."

"I have to pee."

He opened the door a little wider. Nobody looked their way. He slipped out, then nearly tripped, his legs stiff. His muscles needed a minute to find their strength after being cramped up for hours. He helped Miranda climb out behind him.

She glanced toward the squat building they could now see to their right, the people milling around, most of them tourists. "I bet they have a bathroom at the station."

Even as Glenn considered it, he spotted the National Guard under the awning by the front. They were scanning passengers.

He grabbed Miranda's hand and tugged her in the opposite direction. As the sky opened up in a soft drizzle, they ducked between empty buses and hurried to the chain-link fence in the back. A single-lane street waited on the other side and weather-worn row homes beyond that, definitely not the ritzy section of the city, but not exactly the slums either.

While he looked for a gap in the fence, she was checking the rest of their surroundings. *Bathroom. Right.*

"Go between the buses," he suggested, and once he assured himself that there was no way through the fence, he stepped away to give her a moment of privacy.

He waited a few minutes, then walked back to her. She was using a bus's mirror to pat down her short, dark hair. Her face was smudged with dirt, her cargo pants and khaki shirt wrinkled beyond hope.

"You look like hell," he said.

"Believe me, *GQ* wouldn't put you on the cover either."

He pulled his spine straight as he brushed off his worn T-shirt and canvas pants. "I'll have you know, I've been on the cover of *Scientific American*, which is way better."

She stuck out her tongue and blew him a raspberry.

And he wanted nothing more than to pull her into his arms and kiss her.

"We better clean up a little," he said instead, biting back a smile. They needed to look more like tourists and less like fugitives.

So, hidden by the buses, they used the rest of the water in their canteens to wash their hands and faces, combed their hair with the comb from the toiletry kit, and straightened their clothes as best they could. Then they followed the fence until they found a hole that let them through to the other side.

He took her hand as they crossed the street. He told himself he did it so they'd look a little more touristy. But as they walked through the quiet residential neighborhood, people still looked at them with curiosity.

"We're obviously not locals, and we don't look like the tourists," Miranda said under her breath.

"We need backpacks and better clothes." Of course, neither of them had money, or credit cards, or an ID for that matter. "Do you know which way the airport is?"

"Somewhere on the south edge of the city, I think."

At the first intersection, they chose the street that led that way. The rain kept coming down, but not too much, nothing they couldn't handle. The houses looked progressively smaller and poorer, until they reached an area where people openly slept in doorways.

Trash lined the streets. The homes were simple, one- or two-floor dwellings, the roofs ragged, a number of windows missing. They had to be close to the slums, he figured. When a police car rolled down the street, they ducked under the nearest doorway where a drunk snored. Crouching, they grabbed his blanket and threw it over their heads, pretending to be sleeping next to him.

The police rolled by.

Miranda gagged as she threw off the horse blanket that smelled of alcohol, sweat, and urine. She lay it back on the still sleeping man next to them, then stood and shook herself off. "Better not get lice, or fleas, or whatever."

"Lice won't kill you. The commander will."

They moved on and walked close to half an hour before they heard church bells in the distance, and saw the people in the doorways mobilize, get on their feet, and head in the same direction, some hurrying, others staggering.

"Let's check it out," Miranda said.

The homeless were heading south. Glenn shrugged. "We're going that way anyway."

They ended up at a simple wooden church barely taller than the hovels around it. *La Misión*, a sign advertised over the open wooden door, in front of which nearly a hundred people lined up. People filed into the church one by one on the right side of the door. Another row of them came out on the left, carrying food: bread, cheese, and an occasional banana.

Glenn's stomach growled at the same time as Miranda's. When she moved to the end of the line, he didn't try to hold her back.

But he did ask, "What if our pictures were on TV?" under his breath as he joined her.

"If anyone checks us out too closely, we take off. It'll take time for the police to get here even if someone calls us in."

The people around them didn't look like they owned a change of underwear, let alone a phone. And nobody was looking at anyone. They all kept to themselves. "Sounds like a plan."

The trail mix was a distant memory at this stage. Food and water would be nice. Things were looking up. Even the rain stopped, the clouds clearing.

An old woman shuffled around the corner and came to stand behind Glenn, leaning heavily on a cane. Various old men lined up behind her. Then a group of ruffians in their teens and twenties, loud, wearing mostly black, sporting metal-studded belts, joined the end of the line. They had scarves tied around their necks, backwards, like Old West train robbers. First they began shoving each other around, then shoving people out of the way one by one as they moved up the line.

Glenn glanced at Miranda, who looked like she was ready to put her army training to use and knock the jerks on their asses. Except starting a mass fight was probably not in their best interest. There was no telling how many buddies those kids had in the growing line farther up front, or in the back.

So before Miranda could do something they might regret, Glenn motioned the old woman to step ahead of them, then he turned to face down the young thugs. He squared his shoulders and let his body language spell out his disapproval.

The burliest of the idiots flashed a cocky grin and pulled his shirt up to show off a nasty looking knife with a nine-inch serrated blade.

Glenn could have pushed his own shirt aside to show the handgun stuck into his waistband. He didn't. He simply held the young thug's gaze, keeping his face completely expressionless.

Nobody moved. Tension sizzled through the air. Then Glenn nodded toward the end of the line with his head. One of the young men spit at his feet; another swore at him in Spanish, stepping closer. But Glenn stood his ground, and after a few more seconds, the boys sauntered back to the end of the line where they'd started.

In a little while, more people gathered behind them, until the line went around the corner.

"You handled that well," Miranda said.

Technically, he didn't need her approval, but he found that he liked having it. As the line moved forward, he nodded toward the church. "What if they ask who we are?"

She shook her head. "I don't think places like this ask a lot of questions."

The queue moved fairly quickly. Soon they were at the door, then stepping into the dim interior.

An altar stood up front, but no pews. Did people worship standing up? At the moment, most of the small church was taken up by a mismatched row of tables.

To the right, a water spigot stuck out of the wall, with a drain on the floor below it. Some of the people in front of them washed their hands, some drank right from the spigot.

When Miranda got up there, she washed her face again, then filled her canteens. Glenn followed her example.

They needn't have worried about being recognized by the staff. A hundred-year-old nun in a dusty black habit supervised the food distribution, her eyes overwhelmed by folds of skin and open only by the smallest of gaps.

She smiled a toothless smile every once in a while, nodding at the unfortunates who filed before her and raising her shaking hand in blessing at intervals, making the sign of the cross.

In front of her, one table held fist-size chunks of bread, another had much smaller chunks of cheese, and another served fruit: mangoes and bananas. Nobody took more than his share, and nearly everyone muttered a "*Gracias*" or "*Gracias, Madre*."

Glenn and Miranda did the same and kept moving.

On the way out, in the corner, piles of clothes waited in cardboard boxes, looking fresh off the Salvation Army truck. Most of the people passed right by them.

"You think that's free?" he asked Miranda. It would be nice to change out of the clothes he'd been wearing for several days. "Why doesn't anybody take anything?"

"When you're homeless, you can have only what you can carry with you wherever you go, which, for most, means the clothes on your back."

The swift sense of protectiveness hit him hard. "Were you ever—"

But she said, "I volunteer with homeless vets."

That didn't surprise him. The Miranda he knew always had her causes, had never been afraid to get herself dirty or lend a hand. In college she'd organized walks for multiple sclerosis, worked on Habitat for Humanity crews, and volunteered at the soup kitchen.

They stepped up to the pile and sorted through it, picked out clean shirts and clean pants. She even found a sisal bag, which she threw across her shoulder. He didn't find the backpack he hoped for, but came across a strap-on baby carrier. If he taped up the leg holes or put a shirt in there to block them, it could come in handy for carrying extra food if they came across another mission. For now, he jammed their new clothes inside and swung the baby carrier over his shoulder.

They put their food in Miranda's bag since it had no holes in it. Then as they turned to leave, Glenn kicked something on the floor, bent down to check what it was, and realized he'd found a pair of black horn-rimmed glasses.

He tried them on and the world turned into a dizzying blur. Okay, way too strong. But he shoved the glasses into his pocket anyway. Once they were away from the mission, a block or so down the road, he knocked out the glass and shoved the frame onto his nose. "Not much of a disguise, but hopefully better than nothing."

She grinned at him. "Hey, you can still look nerdy."

"Nerdy is the new sexy," he reassured her.

"You look like you did back in college. Okay, plus some muscles."

"You like the muscles. Admit it."

"I'm not against them." She grinned again.

He liked seeing her carefree for a second.

"With the clean clothes we'll be able to blend in somewhere in a better neighborhood. Even with tourists," she said as they walked. "We should be able to make our way over to the airport without drawing too much notice."

They pulled into the first abandoned alley they came across and changed.

"How do I look?" she asked as they reentered the street. She wore blue jeans and a tan T-shirt.

"Strong," he said. "Self-assured. All grown up. You look like an interesting woman."

She flashed a brilliant smile that reached all the way to his heart. "Smooth talker."

———

Oh, for love's sake. Miranda pushed forward. She remembered now why she'd fallen for him in the first place. Glenn never said what you'd expect from a guy. He was the type who'd keep a woman on her toes, and that was a good thing.

They kept walking south. When a police car turned onto the street, coming toward them, Glenn pulled her into the open courtyard of an abandoned house.

The ten-by-twenty-foot tiled space was strewn with dead potted plants and garbage. Two smaller doors opened from the courtyard, both of them boarded.

As the police car passed, Glenn threw her a questioning look. "We need someplace to spend the night."

She nodded. They'd spent more time hidden on the bus than she'd expected. A small town like this would probably have only one flight to Caracas per day. Chances were, they'd missed it today. Their best bet was to get off the streets for the night. The police might step up patrols after dark. She didn't want to run into them. She didn't want to run into the criminal element either.

The abandoned home looked like decent shelter. They had no guarantee that they'd find better.

She helped Glenn pry the boards off the nearest door. A little pushing, a little heaving, and they were soon in a narrow hallway, laid with the same white and blue tiles as the courtyard.

The masonry walls were peeling, a bare light bulb hung from the ceiling. She flipped on the light switch. Nothing happened. "No electricity."

For now, enough late-day sunlight filtered through the windows that they could see even when she pulled the door closed behind them. No sense in advertising that there were squatters here.

The downstairs consisted of only two rooms, one littered with broken furniture, the other—which might have been a kitchen before everything got ripped out—with more trash plus two dead pigeons. Way beyond the stage where they could be eaten, unfortunately.

Miranda ran up the stairs, taking them two at a time. "Looks better up here."

In the first room, an old mattress leaned against the far wall. Other than that, the room was empty and clean save for some dust. The single window looked to the street, its glass unbroken, a plus.

"At least we'll be able to see if the cops or the guardsmen are coming, doing a house-to-house search," she told Glenn when he came up behind her.

"I doubt they'll do that. I have a feeling they'd prefer to catch us quietly, without causing a scene inside the city." He opened the window a crack to let in fresh air. "There are too many tourists here. Must keep up appearances."

They walked across the hall to a smaller room, also empty, then to the bathroom in the back. She could have danced with joy at the sight of the single sink, beat-up cast-iron tub, and toilet.

"And now the moment of truth." She reached for the tap, turned it on. Nothing. "Oh well. It would have been too easy."

But even as she said the last word, the pipe began to creak. And, after a moment, water dripped from the faucet, dirty and rusty at first, but then the flow became better and the water cleaner.

She whipped around to look at Glenn, both of them grinning like idiots, from ear to ear. Who needed money to be happy?

She danced over to the tub and turned on the water there. "Oh my God, and we have soap!" She danced a little more. "We have soap!" She grinned wider, beyond-words happy for the pink little toiletry kit she'd lifted in the forest, possibly the best decision she'd made lately.

Glenn moved a few steps closer. "Wish the tub was bigger."

She put on her soldier look, eyes narrowed, chin out. "Step away from my bathtub."

"Oh, it's yours, all yours, is it?"

"I'm willing to arm wrestle for it." She rinsed the dirt out of the tub, then pushed the black rubber plug into place. She turned off the cold water and turned on the hot. She was so ready for this.

Nothing happened. No water.

She frowned. "This doesn't look promising."

He scoffed. "What's a faulty hot water heater against two engineer geniuses like us?"

"I'll make you a deal. You fix the hot water heater, you get first turn."

He headed for the door. "Prepare for a long wait while I soak my troubles away."

She turned off the water, checked the small window that opened to the back, and assessed how easy it'd be to climb out and get up on the roof if they needed to make a hasty exit. Not easy, but possible.

Up to the roof, over to the next house, down to the next court-yard. She planned for contingencies. She felt semi-comfortable with her emergency evacuation plan by the time Glenn returned.

The morose look on his face prepared her for the bad news. "Somebody ripped out the hot water heater."

"Cripes." She turned on the working tap again. "I suppose cold is better than nothing."

On the positive side, the water wasn't really any colder than the streams in the forest. On the negative side, it ran out before the tub filled even halfway.

The pipes groaned and moaned, but they wouldn't cough up another drop.

He rolled up his sleeves, a decidedly wicked gleam coming into his steel-gray eyes. "How about you stand in the tub, and I'll quickly wash you down?"

The visual the suggestion brought sent tingles through her. She fought back by glibly saying, "If you want to cop a feel again, say so."

He grinned. "I want to cop a feel."

His engineering brain worked as logically as a well-designed machine. He was straightforward, no subterfuge, which she'd always liked about him.

"I've already seen you naked," he pointed out.

"Not recently," she recounted.

"We already had sex in the bus."

She wouldn't have thought that at this stage of her life she could still blush, but she did. "I wouldn't count that as sex."

He held her gaze. "I apologize. I must have done something wrong. Next time, I'll try harder."

Heat punched through her. "There won't be a next time." This was pure insanity. They had to find their way back to the friend thing.

He shook his head, as if he didn't understand why she would even waste time and breath denying the obvious. "If you want to play it that way."

Yes, yes she did. She flashed him a look that she meant to be apologetic, but probably looked constipated.

With a slow nod, he turned on his heels and walked out with a couple of long-legged strides, closing the door behind him.

She let out a pent-up breath. *Okay, danger averted. Temptation faced, and resisted.* Yay for her.

She stripped, then kneeled by the tub and washed her face and hair first. In situations like this, having short hair was a definite advantage.

When she was done with her hair, she stepped into the tub. The water reached only about mid-calf. She washed herself quickly and couldn't shake the thought of how different this would feel with Glenn's hands on her, gliding over her body.

Glenn's long fingers on her nipples, drawing a slow trail downward, low on her belly—

"Are you sure I can't help?" His voice, coming from the other side of the door, made her jump.

"Almost done." She quickly finished rinsing off and stepped out of the tub.

The cleanest things she owned were the shirt and pants from the mission, so she put those back on. No underwear. She left her pile of dirty clothes by the tub, hoping to wash them later.

"Your turn." She opened the door and found him sitting in the hallway, his arms resting on his pulled-up knees, his head against the wall, his eyes closed.

He looked drained. Tonight would be the first night in a while that he would spend indoors, in relative safety and comfort. He'd been on the run for too long. And before that, the weeks of torture at Guri . . .

She wanted to sit down next to him and put her arms around him, but she was pretty sure she knew where physical contact would lead, so she didn't. She'd been sent to protect and return him. Her focus had to be on the job, not on the way he made her feel. She had to prove, to herself and to the general, that she could accomplish her mission without letting personal emotions get in the way. "Hey. Your bath is ready."

He opened his eyes and pushed to his feet, looked at her as she passed by him. "You can come in if you want to help."

She nearly choked on her own spit from the image that leaped into her mind. She hurried away without looking back. "I can hear the mattress calling my name."

He called a single word softly after her, "Chicken."

She preferred to think of herself as *smart*, and refused to rise to the bait.

He didn't take any longer with his bath than she had with hers. The water temperature didn't encourage lingering. By the time he appeared in the bedroom's doorway, she had most of the dust beaten out of the mattress and had it set up in the middle of the room.

"I washed the clothes," he said as he walked in, his dark hair glistening. "Hung everything on the staircase railing inside. Didn't want to hang it in the window and have someone who knows the apartment's supposed to be empty see it."

Uh . . . "Thanks."

"What?" Of course, he caught her momentary hesitation.

"I don't think I ever had a guy wash my underwear before."

"At the risk of sounding repetitive, I've already handled what's inside your underwear." A slow grin spread on his face.

"We accidentally rubbed against each other in the bus's storage compartment. Could have happened to anyone. Blame the insufficient space."

"Whatever you want to tell yourself." He humped down onto the mattress next to her and pulled over her sisal bag. "Dinner?"

"Rosemary chicken with roast potatoes and a glass of red wine, please. I'm thinking chocolate cheesecake for dessert."

"Yes, ma'am." He split the remaining stale bread and hard cheese between them. "I think you'll find the chicken especially tender tonight."

She bit into the cheese and made a show of enjoying it. "Seasoned to perfection."

"I'll pass on your compliments to the chef."

She swallowed the last bite of cheese and grinned at him. She hadn't goofed around like this in a long time. Back in the day, she'd let him take her out from time to time to some fancy restaurant. But only if he let her cook dinner for him in turn. Which mostly happened after hours in the engineering lab with a propane torch. She became an expert at shish kabobs.

"The marinade is simply sublime." He popped the last chunk of bread into his mouth.

"Secret family recipe?"

"So secret, it's forbidden to write it down." He meaningfully wiggled his eyebrows. "On his deathbed, the old chef passed it to the new chef."

He said the words with so much drama she laughed out loud. Abby would have liked him; the thought hit her out of the blue. Abby could be a total clown, or be completely serious when she wanted to be. She never wanted to play princess. She wanted to play Amelia Earhart, or Madame Curie, or Ann E. Dunwoody, the first female officer to be promoted to the rank of four-star general in the US military.

Abby would put on Miranda's uniform coat—the hem of which would reach the floor, stick star stickers on the shoulders—then march her mother and father up and down the living room with unbridled glee. The kid loved to be in charge. She probably *would* have ended up being a general or—

The staggering sense of grief and longing caught Miranda so hard it knocked the air out of her. She lay back on the mattress and stared at the ceiling, blinking back a sudden rush of tears.

Grief could be like that sometimes, a knife to the heart you didn't see coming.

"Hey. Are you okay?" Glenn bent closer to search her face, his eyes worried.

"Fine." Nothing anybody could fix.

"You don't look fine."

She scooted higher up on the mattress and lay down with her back to him.

He lay down next to her and, after a moment, pulled her into his arms. She let him, but she didn't turn.

The heat of his body soothed muscles she hadn't been aware were still tight. She accepted the comfort he offered, even if it made her feel guilty. She didn't deserve comfort. She wasn't a good person. Glenn just didn't know it.

Chapter 11

EVEN IN HIS SLEEP, GLENN KNEW THE WOMAN IN HIS ARMS. HE KEPT DREAM-
ing of her all night. In some of the dreams they were back in college, in others they were running through the jungle, then, just
before he woke up, he dreamt of making love to her. Over and over.

She was soft yet strong at the same time, no inhibitions, completely open, filled with curiosity. Back in college, she would pop
up on her elbow next to him in bed, narrow her eyes, and say, "Let's
try an experiment." And his body would be fully charged again
because he knew something mind-blowing was about to happen.

His dreams brought back the past in finely detailed Techni-
color images.

Predictably, he woke with an uncomfortable boner nestled
against her soft bottom.

The dim light of morning filtered through the window. Still
half-asleep, he nuzzled her neck.

She turned in his arms to lay her head on his shoulder.

"Good morning."

"Not yet," she protested.

All right. He stayed still so she could settle back into her dreams. He seriously hoped she was dreaming about him. He liked the idea of him swaggering around in her dreams like a stud muffin.

But she stirred a few minutes later. She blinked the sleep from her eyes. "Today's the day. We're going home."

"I'm glad you came for me," he admitted.

She got up and looked back at him, her gaze catching his raging hard-on before she quickly turned away.

He was a man. She was a hell of a woman. He wasn't going to apologize. He sat up instead. "How soon do you want to get going?"

"As soon as we can get ready. I want to be on the street around the time people go to work. It'll be easier to get lost in a crowd."

He nodded, impressed with her strategic thinking first thing in the morning, before coffee. His brain clamored for java as insistently as his body clamored for sex. He didn't expect either craving to be satisfied this morning. A terrible shame.

She grabbed the toiletry kit and headed out of the room, in the direction of the bathroom, returned a few minutes later and tossed him the pink bag. "We have water again."

So he cleaned up, brushed his teeth. By the time he came out, her clothes were gone from the staircase. He grabbed his own and went back to the bedroom, walked in on her as she was changing.

He stepped back. "Sorry."

But she didn't even look at him as she stared outside, her hands deathly still on the edges of her unbuttoned shirt, a stricken look on her face.

He hurried over and looked out, expecting soldiers. Instead, all he could see was a little girl, about six or seven, wearing a bright red dress, playing with a black puppy on the sidewalk. The game seemed to consist of who could love the other one more, the puppy wiggling to snuggle as close to her as possible and licking her face as the girl giggled and petted him.

"Abby wanted a dog," Miranda said quietly, her voice rusty. "God, she wanted a puppy so much. I promised to take her to the shelter for her birthday so she could pick one out."

Glenn silently drew her into his arms. He wanted to protect her from the pain he could hear in her voice, but he couldn't do a damn thing, not with all his power and all his millions and all the people at his disposal.

Being helpless sucked like a tornado, he decided. He hated feeling this way. He wanted to punch something, but that wasn't what she needed.

She turned in the circle of his arms, away from the window.

He kissed the top of her head. When she stayed where she was, without pulling away, he kissed her forehead. Then her left eyebrow, followed by the right.

And then she tilted her face up to his, blinked hard. Grief reflected in her eyes. He couldn't take that away. But he could distract her for a while. The streets were still empty. They had a little time.

So he kissed the tip of her nose, and then her mouth next. She only hesitated a moment before her hands slipped around his waist.

He didn't need more encouragement than that. He tasted her mouth from corner to corner, played with her full bottom lip. Then he moved over to her ear and did that little thing that used to make her go weak in the knees.

He grinned when she sagged against him.

God, he'd missed this. He scooped her up and carried her to the mattress, lay her down, and stretched out next to her.

She opened her eyes and looked into his. "Major déjà vu."

"Yeah." He placed a hand flat on her abdomen.

"What are you doing?"

"Distracting you."

She swallowed hard and closed her eyes. "Losing a child is not something a mother can be distracted from. Ever."

The pain in her voice cut him as effectively as a machete.

He wished he could invent a way to take her losses onto himself somehow. "What do you want me to do?"

"Try anyway."

He dipped his head to hers again, dragging his lips over hers as he ran a hand up her abdomen, pausing below her breast.

Her breath hitched. Her voice was a ragged whisper. "It can't possibly be as good as we remember, right?"

"Let's find out." But he held still.

Was he actually hesitating? He'd long grown out of his nerdy inhibitions. He hesitated about little these days, and certainly not about taking a beautiful woman to bed.

But Miranda was more than a beautiful woman. She was somebody to him. Part of his past. She meant something, maybe more than he cared to admit.

"I want you," he whispered against her full lips.

And she said, "Okay."

That was it. No games.

His fingers moved up until her breast filled his hand. Need raced through him, pushing him to hurry. But he wanted the moment to last. He took his time and let his hand explore the perfect globes of her breasts, even as his tongue explored her mouth.

She tasted like mint toothpaste, and felt like the very best memories of his youth.

He unbuttoned her shirt, pulled her no-nonsense cotton bra down until those dusky nipples lay bare before him. They drew his lips like magnets.

She moaned when he sucked on one while tugging on the other. *More.*

He alternated the pressure between gentle and demanding, teasing the hard nubs until she arched her back. Then he rose above her, straddled her legs, and kissed his way down her belly.

She snapped her hand over her belly button. She had an outie, which had always embarrassed her to no end. He loved it.

He drew her hand away, kissed her where he pleased, all the way down to the waistline of her pants. She'd lost weight in the last couple of days, maybe just a pound or two, but it was enough so he could pull her pants down without unbuttoning them.

He shoved them to her ankles, then went to work on her underwear, backing up so he could kiss her through the thin cotton. The gratifying sounds she made were enough for a moment or two, but then he wanted more.

He tugged the panties down to just above her knees. Then he bent to blow on her soft curls.

She writhed.

Yes. This was the only power he was interested in.

He looked up, over the flat planes of her stomach, her incredible breasts tipped with engorged nipples that strained toward the ceiling, and, beyond them, her graceful neck stretched, her head falling back.

She would have made a hell of a painting.

His body pounded with need.

But her body was still closed to his, her pants around her ankles holding her legs together. He drew a line with his index finger between her hipbones, then outlined the soft swell of the top of her vulva. When he drew his finger along the line in the middle, she shivered. Then he parted her flesh, revealing pink, the nub of her clitoris open to his hungry gaze.

He repositioned himself, bending so he could blow a puff of air over her. And when she squirmed again, he put one hand on her hip and held her down. Then he blew on her heated flesh one more time, this time from much closer, so she wouldn't experience a cool breeze, but his hot breath.

And then he licked her, because he wanted to, dammit.

He ran his tongue over the sensitive nub over and over, his own cock straining against his pants so hard he had to pause to unbutton them to give himself some relief.

He wanted to rip her pants and underwear from her legs so he could push her knees apart and bury himself deep inside her. He didn't. He forced the constraint on himself to have nothing but her pink, engorged clit available, even if the anticipation was killing him.

As he sucked her between his lips, she went still for a moment, then her back began to bow off the mattress. He slipped his hands under her bare buttocks to lift her to him. And then he feasted on her until she came with a helpless shudder, calling his name.

He preferred using his ordered, logical brain, thoughtful actions in all areas of his life above animal instinct. But the caveman part was taking over now, the ancient impulses deep inside him that said: *That's. My. Woman.*

He ripped off his pants, then tugged off hers. At least the pink bag with the condoms was within reach. He took care of protection, then pushed her knees up until she was wide open to him at last. Gloriously his. She was wet and ready, her opening glistening for him, the after-tremors of her orgasm squeezing his cock as he pushed inside her.

Slow.

Right. He had a hell of a time hanging on to control, especially when she wrapped her long legs around his ass and pulled him in even deeper. All the way to paradise.

She opened her eyes, held his gaze as she matched him thrust for thrust, her fingers splayed on his chest. She leaned up and bit his shoulder, a playful nibble that nearly sent him over the edge. "We still fit just right."

Not yet. Not yet, dammit. He wanted to prove to her that he had a little more staying power now than when he'd been twenty.

He supported himself on his left elbow while he reached down to caress her with his right hand, his hips pistoning. The pleasure and need inside him overpowered his brain. *No, no, no. Steady. Not yet . . .*

Oh, God. Yes, yes, yes.

As the tight fist of her body convulsed, it kept him coming and coming.

When he finally rolled off her, gasping for air on his back on the mattress next to her, he was an empty shell of a man. And yet, he felt more like himself than he had in a very long time.

She laid her head on his shoulder, and he put his arm around her to anchor her to him. He wasn't ready for her to move away, wanted to hold on to the sensation of them lying skin to skin, her breast pressed against him.

"Do you know what the difference is between men and women when it comes to sex?" he asked when he could form thoughts again.

"What?" she inquired weakly.

"Women want romance, eye contact, tenderness, a true soul-to-soul collection, the earth to shake, sparks to fly." He opened his eyes at last and looked at her beautiful, flushed face. "Men just want to last long enough not to embarrass themselves."

She laughed. "You have nothing to be embarrassed about. I swear."

"I aim to please." He grinned.

Once the rush of blood in his ears slowed, he could hear noises through the window, cars going by, people shouting. The morning traffic had started.

He reached up and traced her eyebrows with his index finger, then her nose, her mouth. He slipped his finger under her chin and tilted her head up. Her soft eyes met his. Held.

They were in their own little time bubble, but it wouldn't last much longer. Just a few more seconds.

Determined to make the most of it, he dipped his head and fit his lips against hers, took her mouth in a slow kiss. Neither of them knew what the day might bring, so he made the kiss count, made it last.

Then he kissed the tip of her nose, and her eyelids too, before he pulled away. "Let's clean up and get out of here."

They didn't take long. In ten minutes, they were downstairs. Miranda walked out of the courtyard first. He stepped out the open doorway behind her.

The little girl had left with her dog, for which he was grateful. He hated seeing Miranda in pain.

They headed down the street. She walked briskly next to him, a couple hurrying off to work. He liked the idea of it. He liked the idea of her. She wasn't tall and slim like the last couple of women he'd dated, or elflike and fragile, the type who brought out men's protective instincts and made them feel manlier. She wasn't lusciously curvaceous either, didn't fall into any of the male fantasy archetypes.

Yet her short-cropped hair fit her just as well as the long, tumbling locks of her college years. Her face reflected her no-nonsense attitude, her eyes always sharp, always working to make sure she didn't miss anything. She had a well-built body, and she carried herself with strength. She was nobody's damsel in distress. In fact, she looked like she could definitely kick a guy's ass if he was stupid enough to give her trouble.

He thought about it . . . giving her trouble. Or just letting her go when they got back to the States. She'd wreaked enough havoc in his life already.

Thing was, he wasn't the type to avoid trouble. He saw something he wanted, he went after it, both in his personal life and in business. And right now, he wanted Miranda. Again. So to hell with going their separate ways when they reached safety. This time, he was going to figure out how to make things work between them, he decided.

"I still wish you hadn't left back then. It would have been no big deal for me to pay for your tuition," he said as they crossed a side street.

"Because my dream was always to be some rich guy's charity case."

"I wasn't some rich guy. I was the guy who loved you."

She slowed and stared at him. "You never said that."

"Was I some awkward nerd or a smooth Casanova to the best of your recollection?"

"I wasn't looking for a smooth Casanova."

"My mother really scared you at Thanksgiving, didn't she?"

"I don't scare that easily." She hesitated, wouldn't look at him. "I missed my period."

He stopped in the middle of the sidewalk to stare at her.

She looked away, then back again. "I thought I was pregnant."

Incredulity and a strong sense of betrayal washed away the postcoital glow with the efficiency of a tsunami. His blood cooled. "So you decided not to tell me and take off with the kid?"

Her face twisted. "There was no kid." She drew a deep breath. "But I didn't know that for sure for a couple of days. And I did a lot of thinking during that time. I could see pretty clearly what would have happened if I had your baby. You would have proposed."

"What's wrong with that?" How could she still make him feel like a twenty-year-old nerd, clueless about what women wanted? He shook his head as he began walking again so they wouldn't draw attention. "The inner workings of a nuclear submarine are easier to figure out than the way a woman's mind works, you know that?"

"I didn't want you to marry me just because I was pregnant." She shoved her hands into her pockets. "Your mother would have demanded that I quit school and move to the family estate. I would have been installed in the east wing. The thought of living under her thumb . . ."

She rolled her shoulders. "Okay, not even that. The idea of being pressed into a mold of what your family expected your future wife to be. It scared the crap out of me, okay? That and knowing that even if I had let people trim away every bit of me that didn't fit what they wanted, if I let them twist me into the exact shape they wanted, I would still never belong in your world. Never."

He was fairly stiff with anger as he walked with that thought for a while. He and Gloria were going to have a talk when he got back home. He loved his family, loved his mother, but hurting Miranda wasn't okay, and they needed to know that.

"I so wanted to fit in someplace," she said quietly as she walked next to him.

He'd known that. His anger softened. Her father had left when she was young. Her mother remarried a minister and followed him to a mission post in Africa, leaving her stepsister to raise Miranda. But Miranda had always felt that she was the charity case her aunt's family couldn't really afford. She'd told him that during one of the many nights they'd lain in each other's arms. They used to stay up all night just to talk. *Okay,* not *just* to talk.

"You wanted a family where you felt you could fit in."

She nodded. "I did." She stayed silent for a beat or two as they walked. "I found it in the army. I was just another recruit, the same as all the others. For the first time in a long time, I wasn't some charity case like I'd been at home and at school."

"Going to college on a scholarship didn't make you a charity case."

"Yeah. But some of the mean girls rubbed it in every chance they got."

Now that she said it, he remembered that too, not that she ever complained. But she was the one who couldn't play tennis, or golf, the one who didn't know the rules for polo, or the rules of high society in general.

He'd tried to give her things that would have helped her fit in, but she refused anything expensive. She didn't wear designer clothes and carry designer purses, she didn't even know the brands, didn't know enough to fuss and fawn over the other girls' possessions, which they'd taken as an affront, snickering behind her back.

In the back of his mind, he'd known that. But he'd deluded himself into thinking that it didn't matter, since she had him, and he loved her, and that was all she needed.

Anger sparked alive again, this time directed more at himself than her. "I wanted to give you everything. I didn't understand why you couldn't accept it. I wanted to support you."

"I know," she said with a sad smile. "But I needed to create the kind of life where I could support myself." She shook her head. "Anyway, on the way back to the dorm from the campus doctor who confirmed that there was no pregnancy, I ran into an army recruiting officer handing out pamphlets. He told me about the Army Corps of Engineers. And I thought I better make a choice while I still had choices."

The old sense of betrayal bubbled up inside him. "I hated that you left," he admitted.

"You probably hated me." Her sad smile remained.

"I tried." But it was the one thing he could never succeed at.

Chapter 12

MIRANDA PULLED AWAY FROM GLENN A LITTLE, PUTTING ANOTHER INCH OR two between them as they walked. She wasn't comfortable with the emotions that tried to elbow their way to the surface inside her. Probably just shadow remnants of an old love, but still.

"Joining the army was the right thing for me. I grew up. I grew strong. I needed that." That was what she needed. Not him. He would have always been out of her reach, out of her league. She needed dependable and real.

Oh, but the new Glenn was tempting. Just as tempting as the old.

She didn't want to like him too much. She didn't want to get attached. She'd loved and she'd lost. More than once. She never wanted to be that vulnerable to anyone again.

"Or you could have given us a chance," he said mildly.

"I couldn't." Not the young girl, full of her insecurities about not belonging anywhere. She couldn't give them a chance then, and she couldn't give them a chance now. For different reasons.

She didn't have time for a relationship. And she had no use for love. You loved, and then the next thing you knew, your heart was broken into a thousand jagged pieces that sliced into you every way you moved.

Better that Glenn was mad at her. They could not revive their relationship. For one, she didn't want a relationship. With anyone. She wanted, needed, to lose herself in her new job. She wanted to find people and save them if possible, wanted the travel, the hard work, the long hours. She didn't want to have enough time to think.

She didn't want safety, either. If she got hurt, she got hurt—it'd be penance. Because she'd never be formally charged, tried, and convicted for her sins.

She couldn't go back to a normal life. And Glenn Danning, in particular, seemed like an exceedingly bad idea.

He raised an eyebrow, as if he could hear her thoughts.

"You do know that this gaping gorge between us is not really real, right?" said Glenn.

Ha! She was a murderer. He was a scion of industry.

His relationships were news in Maryland. And someday they'd be news on the national level, when he followed his senator grandfather's footsteps into politics. That was the family plan, the family path.

She couldn't be part of that, couldn't chance that the media would dig up her past. Someone like Glenn couldn't afford to associate with a murderer.

She wasn't a fan of politics or politicians, in general, but Glenn was a good guy. Maybe he could change things. If he could get into those circles, maybe he could make a difference for people. She wasn't going to ruin that for him.

"I'm not who you think I am." Even if suddenly she wished she could be. "I've done things."

"You were in a war."

"You don't understand."

"Then explain it to me. I'm quite capable of cognition." He was beginning to sound a tad irate.

She shook her head. She couldn't bear him knowing what she'd done. Judgment from anybody else would have been fine. In fact, she craved judgment. She'd done something terrible. She wanted her punishment. If she paid the price, then maybe some of the terrible dark weight would lift from her chest.

But she didn't want Glenn to think badly of her. The thought of him judging her and turning away hurt.

They walked in silence for a good while, going south. When they passed a souvenir shop, they stopped and looked at a map to figure out where they were, how far they had to go.

Glenn folded the map after a few minutes and returned it to the shelf. They had no money to buy it, but they both had pretty good spatial memory. "All right, so the airport is not exactly on the south edge of the city."

"But it's not far," she said as they left the shop.

According to the map, the airport was halfway between Santa Elena and the Brazilian border. Roughly half a dozen miles. Definitely doable.

When a cop car rolled down the street, they stepped into a bakery.

God, the bread smelled good.

They looked around, keeping their heads down in case photos of them had been on the local news, then walked outside as soon as the cops were gone. They had to repeat that evasive maneuver three times before they reached the edge of the city.

She didn't bring up the past again, and neither did he. Better this way.

She cast a longing glance at the bicycles lined up in front of what looked like a local dive.

Glenn followed her gaze. "It'd be nice if we could borrow two of them."

"Not worth it," she said. "If two bikes disappear, the owners will call the cops." She scanned the forest that lined both sides of

Route 10. "If we walk in the woods, we can stay out of sight until we reach the airport, but we'll be dirty and muddy so we'll stick out once we get there."

Glenn thought for a couple of moments. "If we walk down the side of the road, we'll be in full view of any law enforcement that drives by." He thought some more, then a slow smile spread on his face as he looked at her. "But the cops aren't looking for a couple with a baby. Let's switch." He handed her the baby carrier and took her sisal bag.

Okay. This could work. She shrugged into the baby carrier so it was hanging in the front, as intended. But, even from far away, it'd be pretty obvious that the carrier was empty. She raised an eyebrow at Glenn.

"Let's make a baby," he said with a grin and lunged into action, even as she had to catch her breath a little.

He used the canteens to create the bulk of the dummy, then his extra shirt to cover them up, the sleeves hanging out the bottom holes to look like legs, her old T-shirt balled up to create the head. Focused on the project, he was totally oblivious to how what he'd just said sounded.

She shook off the strange longing his words had brought to life inside her, and helped, considered the final product. "Not bad."

They weren't going to fool anyone who looked closely, but a police car driving by at fifty miles an hour would probably think that they had a baby with them. They wore different clothes than those that would be in their descriptions. Glenn had dark glasses.

They started out walking at a good pace, but had only walked a few hundred feet when a rusty pickup truck pulled over in front of them.

"*Aeropuerto?*" the driver, an older, local man, asked through the rolled-down window.

"Sí."

He gestured toward the back.

"Muchas gracias, señor," Glenn thanked him with a grin and they got in.

They sat on planks screwed to the metal frame, no tailgate, their feet just hanging over the edge. She put a hand protectively over her "baby," but the old guy wasn't driving fast, barely puffing along. Still, they were on their way. If they could get into the airport and sneak on a plane, they'd be halfway to safety.

Glenn kept an eye on the cars passing them. "How heavy do you think airport security is?"

"Nowhere near US levels. And this is a minor airport in the middle of nowhere. On the average day, I think we could sneak through without much trouble. But they'll be keeping an eye out for us."

He looked her over. "The baby helps, but we're still recognizable close up."

"Our best bet is to join a tourist group and get in with them."

They talked about that, and explored some other options on the drive there.

Once they reached the airport, the old man let them off at the turnoff to the main building, and they thanked him for his help. They walked the rest of the way to the parking lot and waited for the next tour bus to come in.

They didn't have to wait long. Two buses arrived at the same time, one carrying senior citizens, the other the same group of botanists they'd run into in the forest.

Neither group had kids.

She adjusted the carrier. "The baby's going to stick out." And even if it didn't, a single closer look at it would give them away. Anybody who came close enough would see that she just had a bunch of things stuffed in there.

As Miranda rounded one of the buses with Glenn, she shrugged off the baby carrier. "We need to get rid of our weapons too. Don't want to set off the metal detectors."

She shoved her gun and knife into the carrier. She waited for Glenn to do the same, then rolled the whole package under a bus when nobody was looking. Then they caught up to the tour group, as if hurrying to their flight.

"Excuse me." She pushed ahead, and people let her pass.

She was roughly in the middle of the group, Glenn still in the back. Better if they weren't right next to each other. They passed through the entrance—guards on both sides, looking at people, but the soldiers weren't checking papers at this stage. Miranda twisted backwards when she got in line with them, keeping her head down as if looking for her cell phone in her back pocket.

Two more steps and she was past the guards.

Okay. Don't stick out. Don't draw attention.

She stayed with the botanists until they began lining up for check-in at the counter. She had no papers. She couldn't check in, so she headed for the bathrooms. Glenn waited until she reached the door, then he strolled to the men's room.

"Four guards just in this area alone," he said under his breath once he caught up with her. He pretended to look at a tour company ad on the wall.

"I noticed." She bent to tie her boot without looking at him.

He didn't look at her either. "We need to find a way to the tarmac and hide on the plane."

She considered the possibilities as she straightened. If they could lift a pair of ground crew uniforms, they could get to the plane. Then maybe they could hide in a bathroom and not come out until the plane was in the air, stash the uniforms in the bathroom. Or . . . get into the luggage compartment. There had to be a way they could make this work.

She turned completely away from Glenn, then stepped inside the restroom, washed her hands, patted her hair down. She was out in two minutes, Glenn still reading the ad.

"I'll go and figure out when our flight is leaving. You go to the bathroom next," she whispered as she passed him. It was better for them not to be seen together.

She meandered over to the board and looked at the departing flights, barely a handful. A local airline was going to Caracas in two hours. She walked over to the airport map on the wall. The drawing showed a single runway. Okay, so finding the plane shouldn't be too difficult.

She went and sat in an out-of-the-way corner, inspecting every inch of the airport while trying to appear bored, staring around at nothing in particular. A door on the far wall to her left led to a restricted area. *Staff Only*, according to a bilingual, red-lettered sign.

That looked promising. Except for the armed soldier who stood guard.

She scanned him, his rifle, his build. She could probably take him, but she couldn't start a fight. They needed to reach the plane undetected. She turned back to the main area, hoping to spot an unsecured door.

Glenn returned from the bathroom and scanned the display at a small eatery tucked under the stairs that led to offices on the second level.

Miranda walked up next to him, looked through bags of packaged food as she said under her breath, "We should have gone to the service entrance instead of arrivals and departures. We can't go through check-in. The only door I can see that has potential is guarded. We have to find a way through it."

He nodded imperceptibly.

And then they went their separate ways. She returned to her bench, picked up a Spanish language newspaper somebody had discarded, and pretended to read it. At least she could use it to cover most of her face.

They needed a strategy. She settled in to analyze the situation.

Threat: Armed guard.

Opportunity: The door they had to get through didn't have a keycard. The airport as a whole didn't appear too high tech, in fact, which could work to their advantage.

Strategy: Move close enough to the door so if the guard was called away for a second or got otherwise distracted, they could slip through quickly.

To that end, she relocated to the very last bench, only fifteen feet or so from her target.

The guard looked decidedly bored, casting longing glances toward the coffee counter, and toward two of his buddies who were on duty outside, smoking and chatting in front of the wall of windows that looked to the parking lot.

Glenn understood her move, and strode up to the payphone on the wall on the guard's other side, pretending to be using it. Now they were both in position. If the guard went for that coffee, they'd be through the door before anyone could blink.

But the guard seemed to be resisting the siren call of caffeine rather admirably. He only stepped aside a foot as the door behind him opened and a cleaning lady came through, pushing her cart, heading for the bathrooms on the other end of the waiting area.

Possible plan B?

Even as she thought that, she caught Glenn eyeing the cart that held a gray plastic garbage can that could actually hide a small person. He raised an eyebrow at Miranda.

Let's see. For about half a minute she thought it might just work. But she shook her head as she ran through that scenario.

She could disable the woman in the bathroom, hide in the container; then, disguised as the woman, Glenn could push her through into the restricted area. Except Glenn was a full foot taller than the cleaning lady and only half as wide, missing melon-size boobs among other things. The soldier wouldn't mistake him for the cleaning lady in a million years, not even if Glenn had a Hollywood makeup expert to help.

She exchanged a disappointed look with him, then drew a deep breath. Back to plan A.

As the woman disappeared behind the door of the ladies' room, a family of six scrambled over and stormed the benches next to Miranda. Four kids under the age of ten. They were speaking some German-sounding language with English-like words thrown in. Maybe Dutch.

Their littlest girl, about two, ran around, checking everything out. She had the look of a kid who'd been cooped up in a car way too long. She stopped in front of the guard and flashed him an impish look, held out her stuffed horsie, and said something.

The guard smiled at her.

The little girl pulled a cracker out of her pocket and stepped closer to hold the treat out for the man. He laughed out loud at that, nodded to the parents, then back to the girl, "Muchas gracias, señorita."

He was friendly, maybe had a kid that age at home, Miranda thought. The girl ran another couple of circles, but then dashed back to talk to the guard. She seemed to be very taken with him. They didn't speak the same language, but that didn't seem to bother them any.

The kid ran out into the open area again, arms stretched to the side, making airplane sounds. And then she tripped.

She went down hard, head first into the tile floor, blood squirting from her nose the next second. Her parents ran toward her, and so did the guard.

While all attention was on them, Miranda and Glenn darted for the door. A few steps and they were through, in a long hallway.

She hurried forward. "Let's find the locker room where the ground crew gets dressed. We need uniforms."

Glenn caught up, grinned at her. "Hey, we're almost there. We did it."

They were about three quarters of the way when the door at the other end opened and Roberto stepped through, four guards coming in behind him.

Shit. Miranda didn't have time to so much as blink before the men aimed their weapons at Glenn and her.

———

They had nowhere to run, and certainly no place to hide in the hallway. For a split second, Glenn considered charging the men. Even certain death would be better than being dragged back to the torture chamber.

But reason won over his animal instinct of flee or fight. *Game theory.* When one opponent was overwhelmingly superior in strength, the weaker player's best option was to complicate the game. You added some twists and turns, some variables. The more complicated the game, the more luck came into play. Luck could even the odds, favor the weaker player.

So playing for time was their best option here. Drag it out. Give luck a chance to come into play. Glenn stepped in front of Miranda and raised his hands into the air. "We surrender."

"Take them out back," Roberto snapped. All civility gone from his face, his eyes were hard, his body language aggressive, head forward, shoulders up. His prisoners' escape from the transport truck had obviously pissed him off.

His jaw stiff, he gave a sharp nod, and two guardsmen rushed forward to grab Glenn to drag him toward the back door that led to the tarmac. Glenn didn't fight them. Better save his energy for a time when it would make a difference. He glanced back to Miranda just as the other two guardsmen grabbed her by the arms.

He hated that part the most, assholes putting their hands on her, being rough. She didn't let them intimidate her, though: chin up, she ignored them as if they were nothing.

In a few steps, they were all outside, squinting against the bright sun. The plane sat at the end of the runway. Right there. Within reach, dammit. Frustration punched into Glenn as he scanned the half-dozen mechanics servicing the plane, other workers loading luggage. Given the right uniforms, Miranda and he could have made it on board.

To be caught this close to the goal line was beyond maddening.

But disappointment and frustration were unproductive emotions that weren't going to win the day here, so he let go of their failed plan. No going back. He had to move forward, come up with something else. *Complicate the game.*

"We're United States citizens," he called back to Roberto. "I demand that the United States embassy is notified of our arrest. I have rights."

Roberto sneered as he passed the prisoners. "You will find, Mr. Danning, that capitalist spies have very few rights in my country."

"The US government will be looking for us," Miranda warned, sounding calm and reasonable. "You don't want to create an international incident."

Roberto shrugged. "If someone else comes, I'll happily assist with the investigation. Of course, such investigations are rarely fruitful. Do you have any idea how many people disappear in Latin America without a trace every year? My report will show that Mr. Danning mixed himself up in drug trafficking. I'll document that I advised you of that fact and warned you not to travel into dangerous areas and approach the criminal element. Unfortunately, you ignored that advice. Americans are very stubborn. They think they know everything better. They think they're invincible."

Glenn kept the rising fury inside him bottled, to be used at a more opportune moment.

They were marched to a loading bay where a canvas-backed army truck waited for them, the kind they were already familiar with. Once again, they were loaded into the back, but this time, the guardsmen cuffed the prisoners to the bench and kept their guns in hand, ready and aimed.

"Shoot them if they so much as sneeze," Roberto ordered dispassionately before closing the flap himself.

Glenn scanned the interior of the truck. The trick they'd used last time wouldn't work. One step forward, two steps back.

Complicate the game. Sounded good in theory. What in hell could they complicate in the back of a moving truck, handcuffed in place?

He examined every inch of the interior, looking for an idea. If the truck held anything that could help them escape, he'd missed it. He returned his gaze to Miranda. "I'm sorry. You're only here because of me."

"If I wasn't here for you, I'd be somewhere else for someone else. I signed up for this mission knowing full well what it entailed." She turned to the soldier next to her and spoke in broken Spanish, "Could you please tell me where we are going?"

The young man didn't respond, just kept his rifle aimed and steady.

What if the soldiers were taking them back to Guri?

Glenn turned toward the canvas flap that closed them in, but couldn't see out through the narrow gap. He had no idea what direction they were going.

Cold dread spread in his chest. *All right. Don't think about the commander. Think about the opportunity.* Guri would be several hours away. A lot could happen on a long ride. He or Miranda could come up with a brilliant plan between now and then.

But they spent less than twenty minutes on the main highway. The truck turned onto a dirt road and kept going, rattling over the uneven ground. Soon the narrow crack in the canvas flap showed green outside. They were heading into the forest.

To be summarily executed?

Glenn's gaze cut to Miranda, but she didn't look worried.

"Where are you taking us?" she demanded of the guardsmen. "We are innocent. We are US citizens."

None of the men blinked an eye. Maybe they didn't speak English.

Glenn tested the cuffs. Tight. No slipping out of those. But maybe Miranda's slim wrists . . . He checked her hands. Maybe not. Her cuffs looked equally snug.

The idea of her coming to harm was unbearable.

He wanted to grab one of the bastards in the back of the truck and . . . All right. They couldn't grab. But they could kick. He tried to catch Miranda's eye, but she sat deep in thought. "Why are you so calm?"

"Panicking isn't going to help." She glanced up. "They're not going to kill us yet."

"How do you know?"

"From what you told me, the commander is a sadistic tyrant. He'll want his pound of flesh. He'll want revenge. You made him lose face in front of his men when you escaped. He's going to want retribution for that."

"There's a thought to make a man feel all warm and fuzzy inside." *More torture.* Every muscle in Glenn's back tensed. "So this is the good news?"

"The good news is that we'll get a little time after we're uncuffed from these benches. Better than instant execution. Although, I'd prefer a weekend in Vienna." She smiled at him.

She was trying to cheer him up, a valiant, selfless effort. This was his Miranda. His heart turned over in his chest. No, he wasn't going to let her go again. Now that he had her back in his life, he'd be damned if they were going to die in the middle of some godforsaken rainforest.

"I'm going to take you to Vienna," he promised. Then refocused on what they had to do before that could happen. "Do you think the commander is around here somewhere?"

She thought about that for a few seconds. "He sent his guardsmen to assist Roberto. He's definitely in the loop. So once he hears that you've been recaptured, will he shrug and go on with his business?"

Images from the Guri torture chamber flashed into Glenn's mind. The way hate had boiled in the commander's eyes, his immense enjoyment from dominating and torturing another human being . . . No way the commander would give up a chance to personally punish him for the escape. "If he's not here already, he's on his way."

Miranda scanned the truck, the soldiers and their weapons, tested her handcuffs. When she looked at Glenn, the determined angle of her chin said she wasn't giving up. She fully believed that another escape was possible.

Hopefully, before they reached wherever they were going. Currently they were on the road with just a handful of guardsmen in a truck that had canvas for sides. Chances were, at their final destination there'd be a larger force and a prison with cement walls and steel bars.

Glenn tested his own cuffs again, looked from man to man, trying to figure out if any of them had the key. With his hands immobilized, he couldn't reach even the nearest guy. If he could get one to move closer . . . A headbutt? But then what? Assuming he could knock one out and Miranda could knock one out, that still left two more, and with rifles.

Chapter 13

GLENN CLOSED HIS EYES. IN HIS MIND, HE MOVED THE COMPONENTS OF their situation like chess pieces on a board. If he did this, then Miranda did that, and the guards responded a certain way . . . He discarded one idea after the other, hoping to hit on something viable in short order.

But he still had nothing workable when the truck stopped two hours later. They were at some kind of a jungle camp. The guards wasted no time dragging their prisoners to one of a hundred or so square huts that sat on stilts off the ground.

The men tied Glenn and Miranda to opposite corner poles inside, then left. A bar slid in place to lock the door from the outside.

Glenn scanned their ten-by-ten-foot prison. Bamboo floor, bamboo walls, a palm thatch roof, one small window in the back without glass, maybe a foot wide and a foot tall, definitely too narrow for his shoulders.

"What do you think this is?" He looked at Miranda who was conducting her own assessment, examining the small space.

"A training facility for the army for jungle warfare."

He tested his ropes, pulling against them. The bamboo beam moved. "We could probably shake this place apart."

Who knew how long the construction had been sitting out here, exposed to the elements, the ends of the supporting beams dug into soft jungle soil instead of resting in a solid cement foundation.

But Miranda shook her head. "Don't count on it. Bamboo is flexible. It's stronger than you think. And even if we could move a pole enough to create a gap, we couldn't do it without anyone noticing. We're surrounded by armed men."

Okay, there was that. What else? He turned his attention to the walls.

Since the bamboo logs didn't all fit flush against each other, he could see through the cracks.

At least three-dozen guardsmen were going about their business outside, some collecting wood, others preparing food over an open fire, several men standing on guard duty. The camp didn't appear to be at full capacity, but enough men were stationed here at the moment to make an escape difficult if not impossible.

The scent from the stew cooking over the fire made Glenn's stomach growl. Miranda's responded. They exchanged a glance. A little nourishment, for energy, would have been nice. They hadn't eaten since breakfast. But when the food was ready, the soldiers didn't bring the prisoners any.

Glenn rolled his shoulders, trying not to feel disappointed. "How are you holding up?"

"Fine." She lowered herself to sit on the floor. Their ropes allowed for some movement, although not enough for them to reach each other or the door. "Remember the shish kabobs in the engineer lab?" A half smile twitched at the corner of her lips.

How could he forget? "My favorite." He sat too. He watched her for a minute as she rested her head against the wall, eyes closed. "Do you ever regret leaving MIT?"

He definitely regretted not going after her when she'd left. *If it was meant to be, she'll come back*, Gloria had advised. *A Danning doesn't beg.* And Glenn's pride had been injured enough so that he'd agreed. Miranda had walked out on him. She was the one who had to realize her mistake and come back.

She opened her eyes to look at him. "If I hadn't left, I would have never met Matthew, and then I would have never had Abby."

"Sorry. Stupid question." Of course, a mother would never regret her child. He tried to imagine her life, what she'd had and lost. "What was Abby like?"

She waited a long time before she responded, blowing the air from her lungs, then refilling them again. "She was the best little six-year-old who ever lived. Sunshine in a bottle."

A sad smile crossed her face. "She didn't have one bad day, that kid. And she wasn't scared of anything. She put the worms on the hook to fish with Matthew. She'd make friends with strange dogs in the park. Climb every tree she came across. She had endless energy and an endless need to discover the world."

Sounded like the Miranda Glenn had known back in college. "A special kid."

"She was. I'm not just saying that as her mother. She would give her toys away to the neighbor kids. The first egg hunt I took her to at the VFW hall at Easter, one family came late, and there weren't any eggs left. When Abby saw those kids cry, she ran over with her bucket. She didn't keep a single egg for herself. She said she already had her fun finding them." Miranda looked away.

He pictured a child with Miranda's eyes. For a man who'd always been ruled by reason instead of emotion, the storm of feelings swirling inside him took him by surprise. He felt the sharp grief, the scalding fury that someone would hurt that little girl. He wanted to ask about the kidnapping, but didn't want to cause Miranda pain.

She folded her arms around her knees. He'd never seen her look fragile until now. Her body seemed to shrink as she said,

"About a month after the egg hunt, she was invited to a birthday party at one of those indoor playgrounds where they have a million bouncing castles, and a warren of tubes to crawl through, games and prizes. There are two or three hundred kids in there at a time, and you hear nothing but screaming, everybody all sugared up and going wild, everything padded so the kids could bounce around."

The pain in her voice was so sharp he could feel himself bleed.

She drew a long breath. "Abby went into the tube maze. She'd been in it before. She loved it. It's like a rabbit warren. You can come out up high and go down on a slide, or into a bouncy castle, or into a pen of balls, other stuff." She shook her head. "I didn't think anything when she didn't come out right where I waited. She had a bunch of her friends at the place. All the parents were standing around, everybody watching everybody's kids to make sure nobody got hurt."

His jumble of emotions coagulated into a sick feeling in his stomach as she talked, a cold tightness a hundred times worse than the hunger.

"I went over to the ball pen." Swallowed. "Abby wasn't there either. The place was huge. I figured she'd run off to play another game. I walked around for about ten minutes, looking for her. Then I started asking other parents if they'd seen her. Nobody had, so I asked the staff. They helped me look for another ten or fifteen minutes, quietly first, since they didn't want to upset everybody over nothing. We were all so sure she was either playing inside one of the tubes or moving around from game to game and we just kept missing her."

She swallowed hard.

When she continued at last, her eyes haunted, she said, "Then they shut the place down and every child was accounted for, separated into the party rooms in the back where they normally serve cake for the various birthday groups. Abby wasn't there."

His hands fisted. He was a pretty cool person, the need for violence that coursed through him foreign. He'd never felt murderous rage like this before, not even toward the commander. But he'd never wanted anything as much as he wanted to kill the bastard who'd put his hands on that little girl. "I'm sorry."

She nodded, her face wooden, her voice brittle as she said, "Her body was found three weeks later, twenty miles from where she disappeared, a few hundred feet off a hiking trail. She'd been strangled." She drew a shuddering breath.

A hell of a thing, watching as someone's heart broke in half. Watching it happen to the woman he was falling in love with was nearly unbearable. Frustration pushed Glenn to his feet, and he stepped as close as he could to her, ropes straining. He wished he could reach her and put his arms around her. "Did they catch the bastard?"

If they hadn't, he was going to personally make sure that the full resources of Danning Enterprises would be put behind hiring private investigators, pressuring the police, FBI, whatever it took. He *was* going to see to it.

She closed her eyes. "They caught him with the help of DNA evidence. He's in federal prison."

Not enough. Glenn paced back to his corner and kicked the post as hard as he could, rattling the walls and the roof.

"*Alto!*" One of the soldiers outside shouted at him to stop.

Fuck them. His chest heaved with fury. He wanted to kick the stupid hut to shit. But pissing off the soldiers and getting beaten up wasn't going to help Miranda.

His anger wasn't what she needed.

He drew a deep, long breath as he turned back to her. "I'm sorry that you had to go through that." He moved as close to her as he could and sat down, every cell of his body aching for contact, even if just the tip of their fingers, anything. "I'm so sorry."

Her face was a study in controlled pain as she nodded, her skin drawn tight over her cheekbones, her eyes lined with misery. "I try to be grateful and celebrate the years we had. We had some really good times. Those are the memories I go back to. She was so much more than just the police reports at the end."

When he nodded, his eyes burning as he watched her, she went on. "After Matthew died, I didn't reenlist with the army. I'm so grateful for those years Abby and I spent together."

He watched her, his heart breaking for her. "How did you end up an investigator?" Maybe a change of subject would help.

She breathed in and out slowly a couple of times, visibly struggling to put away the worst parts of her past. Eyes downcast, she rubbed her hands on her lap.

"After Abby was gone, I couldn't stand being in the house, so I reenlisted. I went back to the Army Corps of Engineers. But everybody there knew about Matthew and Abby. I didn't want the pity on people's faces when they looked at me. I asked for a transfer, and I was offered a chance at Personnel Recovery."

She hesitated. "Eventually, I left the army. A couple of weeks ago, I was recruited by a new government agency that's trying to find US citizens who disappear overseas. You're my first case."

"I'm the practice run?" He tried to look appalled and scandalized, hoping to lighten the mood. He ached to comfort her. "Two brilliant minds collaborating—who can stand against us? We'll get out of here. Don't worry about it."

Her face softened. "I think I'm the one who's supposed to be telling you that."

Before he could respond, the door opened and two men strode in. They untied her and dragged her to her feet. She shot Glenn an encouraging smile, showing no fear—chin up, shoulders squared.

"Hey." He scrambled to his feet. "Where are you taking her?" He lunged forward, but his ropes held him back. "Hey!"

The men paid no attention to him as they escorted Miranda away, while Glenn could do nothing but watch and curse them out in his limited Spanish.

If they hurt her, so help him God . . .

He stepped to the wall and pressed his face against the largest gap in the bamboo. The soldiers were shoving Miranda down the path to another hut at the far end of the training camp. Up the steps. Inside. The door closed behind them. Not a minute passed before the soldiers came back out and took up their position at the top of the steps.

Glenn strained his ears, every muscle tense, trying to listen for her if she cried out, but she was too far. And even if she hadn't been, the soldiers in camp, the popping fire, and the sounds of the jungle around them drowned out everything else. He hadn't known what fear was until this moment.

Fury filled him all over again. *If anybody lays a hand on her . . .*

But he fought back the blind anger. He needed to do better than that, something more productive. He checked over his ropes, tried to untie them, fought against them until his fingertips bled. The damn rope wouldn't give.

By the time half an hour passed, he was half out of his mind with rage again, then with worry. He couldn't find his way back to his cool, rational mindset.

What if they don't bring her back?

He couldn't stay still. He paced. At least, he hadn't heard gunshots. He tried to tell himself that was good. Encouraging. He refused to think of the dozen ways someone could be hurt or killed in silence.

———

The hut, larger than where Miranda and Glenn were kept, held three beds plus a desk and chair in the corner, probably the officers' quarters for the camp.

Roberto sat behind the desk while Miranda stood in the middle of the open space. A loaded handgun lay on the table in front of Roberto, out of her reach, even if her hands weren't tied.

He watched her with a thoughtful look on his face, his eyes cold and calculating. "As one investigator to the other, I have to admit, I do admire your intellect, Miranda. The plan was to let you lead me to your countryman. We were sure you've been in communication. Once I realized you weren't in contact with him and didn't know where he was"—he shook his head—"I didn't think you'd be of much use. But you surprised me at every turn. Well done."

She said nothing. She certainly wasn't going to thank the murderous bastard for the compliment.

Roberto leaned back in his chair. "Give me Danning."

"You already have him."

"Give me the truth about Danning. Why is he really in Venezuela? Who are his contacts? What kind of information is he looking for? How much has he gotten and transmitted back to the US? What are his plans? What plot is the US government hatching against my country?" He smiled, but the smile didn't reach his eyes. "You can't blame me for wanting to know. I am a patriot, as I'm sure you are."

He kept repeating the same questions, same themes, hoping she'd give up and crack. He didn't know her very well. Which could work to her advantage.

"Glenn didn't come to Caracas with ill intent," she said.

Roberto's smile turned superior. "But you see, we already have confirmation that he had. Do you think we would risk kidnapping a US citizen off the street without cause? It wouldn't be worth the diplomatic headache."

She stared at him, her mind switching into higher gear. "What cause?"

"Not everybody thinks that the USA should rule the world. A lot of people think sovereign countries should remain sovereign countries, without US pressure and influence in their politics and commerce. Not everybody likes a bully."

"What do you call this here? Kidnapping me, holding me captive, interrogating me without charges, without a lawyer, convicting me without a court. Isn't this bullying? An abuse of power?"

"You're right." He kept his smile. "We should be more like your country. Since you're such a shining example, with your secret CIA prisons all around the world. Even the inmates at Guantanamo, they get lawyers and due process and speedy trials . . ."

He trailed off, the smile sliding off his face. "Wait. No they don't. Your country holds prisoners against all the rules of the Geneva Convention, does it not? Remind me how waterboarding isn't an abuse of power."

She stayed silent. It didn't matter what she said, whether she was right or not. The bottom line was Roberto held all the power in the present situation. No amount of talking was going to change that.

"I wish it could be different," he continued, more pensively, after a moment. "I would love to try this case in open court. But the second you were publicly charged, the US would exercise diplomatic pressure to have you released. So this is all I have, if I want to protect my country."

"Glenn and I are not spies."

"I'm sure all the occupants of secret and not-so-secret CIA prisons say the same. Do you think your CIA takes their word for it?"

"This is ridiculous."

"Is it?" He leaned forward and folded his hands on top of the desk, his knuckles brushing his weapon. "We have credible information that Mr. Danning came to Venezuela to undermine our oil and natural gas businesses, which are critical to Venezuela's economy and national security."

Information from where?

This was different from getting picked up on suspicion, out of sheer paranoia. No, someone had deliberately reported Glenn as a spy to the Venezuelan government, made up the charge, knowing what would happen to him. Someone had informed on Glenn, had set him up.

"How do you know you can trust your informant? Who is it?"

Roberto smiled mysteriously and said nothing.

He had all the advantage. She needed to find his weak point. He certainly hadn't shown any so far. But he did resent that his investigation had to be conducted behind the scenes. He couldn't very well receive recognition for his work here, could he? No promotion, no raise. No acknowledgment, which would bug a man if he had any vanity.

And judging by Roberto's car and clothes, he had plenty.

She tilted her head. "So you'll execute us here, without ever having to prove in a court of law that you're right about anything. That doesn't require an exceptional investigator, does it? You don't have to make your case. You don't have to prove anything to anyone. Can't say I'm impressed."

The muscles in his jaw tightened. "Getting me angry isn't going to bring you any advantage. I'm your only friend here, Miranda."

Right, because they were BFFs for sure. But she played along. "And what's that going to get me?"

"Give me Danning, and I'll see to it that you're not harmed."

Impossible, even if she were willing to consider it. "You can't let me go back to the US. You can't afford to let me file a report on this case."

He assessed her for a long moment before he responded. "I do enjoy intelligent women." He unfolded his hands, picked up a pen, and tapped it against the desk. "Consider this. What if you go back and don't make your report?"

"Why would I cover for you?"

"You've seen Venezuela. It's a great country. The people are good, but they're poor. A big reason for that is economic pressure. Western countries want to get their hands on our oil and gas, take all the profits out and let all our people starve. What do they care? We don't wish to become a colony again. Is that such a crime?"

She wracked her brain for a way out of this maze, some kind of a strategic move that could set both her and Glenn free.

"You are American," Roberto went on in the meanwhile. "You believe in freedom, yes? Are you like some Americans who believe in freedom only for themselves? Or do you believe in freedom for every human being?"

Again, she remained silent.

"You could go back home and help us from there. Let us know when more spies are sent. Let us know about the never-ending plots to gain control of our natural resources. If you believe that freedom is a human right, then help to keep Venezuela free."

She would say whatever she needed to say to get out of the jungle alive, but she wasn't going to sacrifice Glenn. "I can't give you Danning. Let us both go."

He smiled a knowing smile, as if he'd expected that answer. "I'm sorry, Miranda, I can't do that. But I'll give you some time to think. When you realize that helping us is the right thing to do, call for the guards and ask them to bring you to me." He turned toward the door. "José! Antonio!"

The two men hurried in and grabbed her by the arms. They were pulling her down the handful of wooden steps when Roberto called after her, making her turn.

"Don't take long." He was standing behind his desk, his dark gaze following her. "Do remember that this is a National Guard camp. I'm not the highest authority here. My ability to help you, the window of time, is not unlimited."

———

Glenn could see the men bringing her back. She was walking on her own. No bruises on her face. No bleeding. Some of the knotted muscles in his shoulders relaxed.

"What did they want?" he asked as soon as they brought her in, tied her up, and left again.

"Roberto is convinced that you're a spy. He thinks I full well know it. He wanted to know how many other spies the US has here."

"Did he hurt you?" Although she had no visible marks on her, there were other ways to hurt a woman.

"Maybe he's saving physical violence for later. For the first round, he just wanted to show me how intimidating he can be." She shook her head. "I don't know. I got the feeling that he's the type to leave the torture to others. He's a cold son of a bitch, but I don't think he'd enjoy beating up a woman. Yet, I don't think he'd be bothered if someone did it for him, as long as he got the results he wanted."

Glenn considered that piece of insight. She was probably right. But over his dead body would the bastard, or anyone else, put their hands on Miranda. "We're leaving tonight, as soon as it gets dark and the soldiers pull back into their huts. Time to complicate the game a little more. We're going to break out, whatever it takes."

To his relief, she didn't insist that they should wait for the right opportunity, to obtain a weapon first or food, or the keys to one of the vehicles. Instead, she said, "Someone reported you. Someone informed the authorities that you're a spy. That's why they grabbed you on the street."

The idea that someone he knew would deliberately set him up required a moment to digest, the betrayal difficult to accept. "Who?"

"I thought maybe one of the businessmen you've come here to meet."

He considered that for only a second. "They are at bigger risk than I am. I met with them. If the government found out about those meetings, they'd be labeled traitors and probably executed." They seemed to be decent men. He hoped they hadn't been caught up in this witch hunt.

But Miranda said, "Your brother told me he called them after you disappeared to see if they knew where you'd gone. That means they were still okay well after the National Guard picked you up."

Glenn rolled that new piece of information around in his head. "If the National Guard didn't know about my meetings, then they weren't following me from the moment I got off the plane."

"Maybe whoever reported you didn't call in the trip ahead of time. Maybe he or she only contacted the authorities on March first. The National Guard tracked you down and picked you up after dinner." She paused. Narrowed her eyes. "Was it Cesar's idea that you should come to Venezuela?"

"No. Mine. Cesar objected. He doesn't trust the Venezuelan government not to interfere with whatever private agreements we make with businesses here."

"And you do?"

"Probably not. Knowing what I know now. But it's a huge market. I didn't want to discount it out of hand. I thought it was worth at least checking into, putting out some feelers."

And those feelers led here. Somebody had fed false information about him to the Venezuelan government, knowing very well what would happen.

Somebody wanted to kill him.

He rolled his shoulders, considering the new piece of information from every angle. "Not that many people knew that I was coming here. Gloria, Tyler, and Cesar." He trusted all three. He couldn't see any possible angle for any of them to want him out of the picture. Then he remembered something else. "The secretary who made the travel arrangements, Nina."

"Does she hate you?"

"Not that I know of. Unless she's an excellent actress. She's been with us forever. She seems happy with her job. And if she wasn't, she could just quit. I don't see her going to this length just because I don't keep my travel receipts straight."

"Personal enemies? Outside of work."

"I don't live a life that exciting. Running the company takes too much time."

"Does the company have enemies? Business rivals who want to grab your market share?"

"Every business has that. But even if I disappeared forever, Tyler and Cesar are more than able to lead the company." He thought for a minute. "Although a transition could be disruptive."

"Long enough to lose a key customer?"

He nodded. An angle worth checking out when he got back home. As soon as he had his full resources back, he meant to get to the bottom of this. Industrial espionage was certainly a factor in the oil business. His computer could have been hacked, his travel information ending up in the hands of the wrong people.

But before he could tell Miranda that, new trucks rolled into camp.

The sight of the man who stepped out of the first truck filled Glenn's stomach with cold dread, snapping his full attention to the here and now.

The commander from Guri stretched his legs and looked around, like an emperor surveying his domain.

Chapter 14

AS RAIN DRUMMED ON THE ROOF, MIRANDA LOOKED OUT THROUGH THE nearest gap in the wall. The commander remained ensconced in the officer's hut with Roberto. They'd been in there for at least three hours now.

What were they talking about? How to best get rid of their prisoners?

Then the commander appeared in the doorway at last and strode to another hut some distance away. Two soldiers immediately grabbed a wooden crate from his truck and carried it after him. The commander's new quarters?

"He's pretty rough," Glenn warned. "He's here for me, but he might want to question you too. If he wants you to confirm that I'm really a spy, just tell him what he wants to hear. He has that in his head already. He won't accept any other answer. At this stage, I don't think it matters. The most important thing is for you not to get hurt, so we can run tonight."

She nodded, accepting his logic, even if she hated what that logic required. She hated the idea of Glenn being tortured. She'd never wished that she had a weapon as badly as at this moment.

They sat in silence, waiting for the commander to send someone for Glenn. But the two soldiers who came hours later wanted her. Once again, they left her hands tied as they escorted her out, and took her into the wet woods.

What? Why? Her heart lurched into a race.

She desperately scanned the undergrowth. Which was the best way to run? Expecting a bullet in the back of her head, she lurched forward, but even as she did, one of the soldiers said in Spanish, "Go ahead. Relieve yourself."

She stumbled, glanced back, eyes wide, her heart in her throat. *What?* She'd expected a rapid execution. They were giving her a bathroom break?

"Hurry up!" the soldier snapped.

So she moved toward the bushes. *A favor from Roberto in his quest to turn her into a traitor?*

"Far enough."

Not nearly. But she wasn't going to argue. She turned her back to the men, dragged her pants down the best she could with her hands tied, and squatted to pee.

They laughed behind her, made remarks about her ass. She ignored them, her mind on escape. Could she take them? The element of surprise would be on her side. They had probably no idea who she was, that she had military training. They wouldn't expect her to know how to fight.

She straightened, hurrying to pull up her pants.

If she could somehow overpower these two and run . . . But what about Glenn?

"*Alto!*"

She froze when the barrel of a rifle touched the back of her head.

While one of the soldiers held the gun on her, the other walked around, leering at her. Her pants were halfway up her thighs. She held still as the man touched the top of his rifle against the bottom edge of her shirt, slid it along her skin, up and up, bunching the material until her breasts popped into his view.

He clicked his tongue, then winked at his buddy, said something she didn't understand, probably dirty slang.

She stood still. Nothing she could do would be faster than a bullet.

The man moved the rifle back down, scraping the barrel against her skin, all the way, the metal parting her pubic hair. He grabbed himself between the legs with his free hand and flashed his buddy a bragging look, then a leering grin to her.

She held his gaze. She wasn't going to cower.

But before she could do more, something furry dropped out of the tree above her, screeching like a banshee. The soldiers jumped back, as startled as she.

They aimed their guns at the monkey, but Winky had already darted into the bushes, gone as fast as he'd appeared.

Her heart clamored from the sudden fright, but she was grinning as she yanked up her pants while the men cursed after the monkey.

Then the guard who'd been messing with her turned back to her, looked her over. "No time now," he said. "Big man wants you." He flashed a dark smile. "Time later."

Miranda buttoned her pants, refusing to let them see her fingers tremble. And when the men shoved her forward, back toward camp, she went. Glenn was right. They needed to leave here as soon as possible. Tonight. As soon as Roberto sent her back to the hut again.

He'd said he would give her time to think. How much time? Was this it? Would he expect a response right now? Her heart sank.

The rainy season was on top of them. She doubted the soldiers would spend it at the training site. They'd want to be back in their well-built, dry barracks before a torrential downpour began. Which meant that Roberto and the commander planned to end the problem of the two foreign spies here in short order.

Some questioning mixed with torture, then a speedy execution. The jungle would consume the bodies. By the time the rainy season ended, there'd be scant evidence left.

Thoughts about how to avoid that fate occupied her mind on their way to Roberto's hut.

He sat behind the desk like the last time, bread, cheese, and two boiled eggs on a plate in front of him, along with a cup of black coffee.

He gestured toward the food. "Hungry?"

Pride pushed her to tell him to go to hell. Common sense nudged her forward and had her saying, "Thank you."

She needed energy if they were to break out of camp.

"Have you thought about my offer?"

She started with an egg, eating slowly. "Yes."

"And did you decide freedom was for all people, not just Americans?" He had a way of turning his words to make them sound so right.

"I do believe in freedom," she said around the food in her mouth. "But I don't believe in spying on my own country. That's treason."

"Yet, you believe in spying on my country and you think there should be no consequences."

She shook her head. "Glenn Danning isn't a spy. Why would he be? He has everything a man could want. Do you understand how wealthy he is? Why would he risk his life?"

"Maybe you should ask him."

"The information you have on him is incorrect. Someone set him up."

"Who?"

"Someone who wants him dead."

"The men he'd met with in Caracas?"

"I don't know who he met with." She didn't want anyone else to end up in the situation she was in.

"I do," Roberto said easily. "We took those traitorous businessmen into custody yesterday. I have their confessions. Multiple sources corroborate the charge that Mr. Danning had come to Venezuela to gather information on the inner workings of our oil and gas industry, pay off the key players, and sabotage the production and distribution of our most valuable national resources, thereby undermining our country's national security."

"Corroborated under circumstances like this?" She gestured at the camp outside. "Or in torture chambers? People will say whatever you want them to say under torture. It's not a very reliable method of intelligence gathering."

"Yet your own country seems so fond of waterboarding." He sneered.

She kept eating. He could send her away at any second. She needed those calories inside her. "Danning is innocent."

"So you say."

"Who told you that he was a spy? That's the guy who's setting him up, for whatever reason."

"Every one of the traitor businessmen he'd met in Caracas confirmed."

"At gunpoint, no doubt," she said. "Before that. Someone had to have given false information on him or you wouldn't have tracked him to his business meetings in the first place." She finished the second egg and drank the coffee, which had gone cold, but she so didn't care at this stage.

Roberto shrugged. "Maybe you're right. Maybe Mr. Danning has enemies who set him up. Or maybe I'm right, and he's a spy.

Maybe you know that, maybe you don't. I'm leaning toward the latter."

"If you think I'm telling the truth, then let us go."

His gaze hesitated on her for a while. "I'm sorry. That has never been an option."

The food stuck in her throat. She swallowed painfully. "You knew from day one that you would kill us?"

He looked at her with faint regret, but his jaw was set at a determined angle. "If you didn't find Danning, I would have let you return to your country. No harm done."

"But once we found Glenn . . ."

"At that point, your fates were decided." He paused. "Unless I can persuade you to work with me. In which case, I'm authorized to offer not only protection, but also financial compensation."

She shoved the last of the bread into her mouth since she had a feeling her response was going to end the interview. "No thanks."

She had nothing but the cheese left, she grabbed that and shoved it into her pocket, hoping to take the chunk of food back to Glenn.

She looked toward the door, but Roberto didn't call the guards. Instead, he pointed toward one of the empty beds. "You'll spend the night here."

She stiffened.

He shook his head and offered a wry smile. "I'm not that much of a bastard."

"Then let us go."

He held her gaze. "Even I report to other people, Miranda. That decision was never mine to make. I'm leaving in the morning. All I can offer you is one last night of protection." He paused. "You are a remarkable woman. I do wish we'd met under different circumstances."

She pulled her spine straight and met his gaze in full. "I wish you choked on your own spit."

He smiled at that. "I can't say I blame you, all things considered." He opened his laptop. "I need to type up my report. You should get some rest."

She sat on the bed farthest from him. He didn't look up again, busy with his work.

After a while, she lay back on the bed and closed her eyes, pretended to sleep while cataloguing the vehicles, the camp, the soldiers, trying to find the weakest point.

She'd come to Venezuela to take Glenn home. She refused to fail her very first assignment.

—

The commander didn't bring his electroshock therapy machine with him. Three hurrahs for the fact that the camp had no electricity, Glenn thought as the bamboo cane came down on his naked back again.

Holy mechanical engineering, that hurt.

"Give. Me. Names," the commander growled. He'd sent for Glenn minutes after Miranda had been taken to Roberto. He'd wasted no time on niceties.

Glenn gritted his teeth. He needed a moment to conquer the pain before he could speak. "François Englert, Peter W. Higgs, Martin Karplus, Michael Levitt, and Arieh Warshel."

The cane paused in the air.

"Who are they?" the commander demanded.

"Last year's Nobel Prize winners in physics and chemistry. If you want to chat about people, we might as well pick someone worth talking about."

Wham! The cane came down hard across Glenn's shoulder and split the skin. Warm blood trickled down his back. Stars danced in his vision.

The interrogation continued.

If he gave an answer the commander didn't want to hear, he was beaten. If he stayed silent, he was beaten. Yet those were his only choices. If he gave the commander what the man wanted—admission of guilt—he would have been taken out and shot in the head.

Goal #1: Stay alive long enough to escape.

Goal #2: . . . He didn't have energy for more than one goal.

The questions continued and so did the pain, his back drenched in blood, his skin flayed. The commander didn't stop until Glenn fell over, sometime around midnight. Only then did the man call for two guards to drag him back to the prison hut.

Every little move hurt like a sonofabitch. But Glenn had a secret that kept him going. The commander had made a mistake right at the very end. The sliver of bamboo the man hadn't seen when the cane busted at last was now tucked into Glenn's pants, hidden. He had a weapon.

Miranda was going to be proud of him.

The soldiers shoved him up the steps roughly, kicked the door open, then pushed him in.

Nothing but darkness inside.

He whipped around, his stomach clenching. "Where is she?"

The pain in his back was nothing compared to his panic that they'd done something to her. With a growl, he charged at the guards, trying to knock them out of the way, but they shoved him back, onto his back, the agony enough to nearly make him black out.

While he struggled for breath, they tied him up, then slammed the door closed and locked it.

"Miranda!" he howled her name, but the only response was the guard outside the door telling him to shut up before they came back in and made him.

Miranda.

He dragged his battered body to the wall and lined up his eyes with the nearest gap, but it was too dark to see Roberto's hut. Was she still there? What was Roberto doing to her?

Glenn grit his teeth, fighting back thoughts as dark and heavy as the night. Fury and worry churned in his empty stomach.

He stayed where he was, lying on his side, and watched that hut all night. He didn't draw a full breath until Miranda appeared in the doorway at dawn.

Every cell in his brain was awake in a blink of an eye.

Her clothes weren't torn. She didn't walk with a limp as the guards escorted her forward.

Glenn struggled to sit, his back on fire.

The door opened and she stepped in, eyes snapping wide as she stared at him. But she said nothing while the guardsmen tied her up. Only when the men left did she move as close to Glenn as the rope would allow. Still out of reach. He wished he could see her face better.

She went down on her knees. "How badly are you hurt?"

He reached for a joke, something glib, something to reassure her. But it seemed he'd run out tonight. He filled his lungs with cool dawn air. "I don't think anything's broken. You?"

"I'm all right." She lowered her voice to a whisper. "The next time they untie either of us, we break free."

He nodded. He couldn't take another beating.

Since her voice had been thick with worry, he found a joke after all. He kept his voice low. "Hey, I have a gift for you in my pocket."

"Yeah?"

He could see enough to know that the corner of her mouth turned up a little. He moved carefully and pulled the inch-thick, six-inch-long bamboo sliver from his waistband. He kicked it over to her. "Courtesy of the commander."

"Broke the stick he beat you with?"

"They don't make instruments of torture like they used to."

"I always said you were hardheaded." She picked up the stick, then turned it around in her hand. "Would be nice if we could sharpen the end enough to stab with it."

That wasn't going to happen without a knife. "We use the tools we have." A basic tenet of engineering and innovation—using what you had to solve the problem at hand. "Worst comes to worst, go for the eye."

She paused mid-motion and raised an eyebrow. "I'm in charge all of a sudden?"

"You had hand-to-hand combat training. I didn't. You're the better person to have our only weapon."

She held still. "All right. Now you're really starting to worry me. Are you sure you don't have brain swelling?"

He managed a grin. "Sure. Mock a man when he's down."

"Best time to mock him." She dropped back into a sitting position. "I have a gift for you in my pocket too."

She tossed something to him that turned out to be a chunk of cheese, and he fell on the food, the best thing he'd ever tasted.

She watched him with a smile. "Do you think you're up for a mad dash through the woods?"

He sure as hell was going to try. He swallowed the last of the cheese. "Listen." He tried to hold her gaze, difficult in the dark. "If I fall behind, you keep going. There's no sense in both of us dying in this godforsaken place."

"Nobody's dying."

"Because you said so?"

"Damn right."

"I like it when you turn dominatrix." The corner of his lips twitched. Picturing her in a little leather outfit made the pain cursing through his body dull a little. So he did it again.

She shoved the sliver of bamboo up her right sleeve. "Watch for my signal."

"Yes, ma'am."

He lay on his side, the least agonizing position, hoping to catch a few minutes of sleep. She scooted back to the wall so she could lean against it as she sat.

Dawn was lightening the sky outside at last. Glenn closed his eyes, but the sounds of a motor starting had him opening them again.

Miranda said, "Roberto is going back to Caracas."

That meant that their treatment had been left in the commander's sadistic hands. "Shit."

"Try to rest up. Let me know if you feel faint, or dizzy. Jokes aside, a drop in blood pressure could mean internal bleeding."

He licked his dry, split lip, wishing for water. "He's beaten me worse before. The bastard's just warming up."

Maybe the commander wanted to pace himself, Glenn thought when two guardsmen showed up a couple of hours later to take him back for more torture. They were both young, one stocky, the other one a regular beanpole.

"Hey, amigos. Just let me piss first, okay?" Glenn asked in his friendliest, most reasonable voice. "It'll only take a second."

The tall one, the one with red pimples on his chin, flashed a bored, dispassionate look. Guard duty in the woods clearly wasn't the highlight of his life.

Miranda came to her feet. "I have to go too."

The two guards exchanged flat glances that suddenly made Glenn uneasy. Then, finally, the heavyset one said, "Sí."

The prisoners were untied, then led to the jungle at gunpoint. But when they arrived at a suitable spot, the guards didn't step back. The stocky boy escorting Glenn stepped close enough to press his gun barrel to the back of Glenn's head. The other one shoved Miranda roughly against a tree, face first.

Beanpole grinned at his buddy, his eyes lively all of a sudden.

Gun at her back with one hand, he tore her pants down with the other, then shoved her legs apart with his knee and went to undo his own clothes.

Everything happened so fast, Glenn could barely catch up with what was happening. "No!"

He twisted to attack, but the guard behind him smacked the barrel into the back of his head so hard it made his brain rattle. Apparently, with Roberto gone, all restrictions on the treatment of the prisoners had been lifted.

"No!" Glenn tried to turn again, but was shoved roughly forward, went down hard onto his knees. The cold barrel of the rifle pressed into the back of his neck hard enough to break the skin. "Miranda!"

The other bastard was touching her.

She didn't protest. Her gaze cutting to Glenn, she didn't so much as curse out her attacker.

She had a weapon up her sleeve. *Use it!* Glenn begged with his eyes. But maybe she was worried about the rifle pointed at him.

"Use it!" he shouted.

"Don't do anything stupid," she begged him instead. "It's not worth it." She swallowed hard as the man grabbed her hip with his free hand. Her gaze clung to Glenn's. "Look away."

———

She made the same decision she'd made in the trunk of that car when those Iraqi hoodlums had kidnapped her. She would endure whatever she had to endure. She was going to survive whatever she had to survive so she could escape later.

But a dark rage filled Glenn's face, every muscle in his body tightening. "Like hell," he spat the words with uncontrolled fury.

Then he turned with a roar and went for the bastard behind him.

Glenn jackknifed his body and threw his weight forward, knocking the surprised guard to the ground. The second guard swung his gun from Miranda to Glenn, and that was when she finally went for the bamboo pike. Elbow to the bastard's chin first, knocking it up, then she shoved the pike up into the soft skin below his chin, up all the way until blood poured out, his tongue pierced through so he couldn't even scream.

A monkey screeched in the tree above them. The ruckus he was making masked the sounds of fighting below.

"Forgot to tell you," Miranda said as she grabbed for the nearest gun. "Winky's here."

She disarmed the man who'd attacked her, then knocked him out with his own rifle. By the time Glenn disabled his own opponent, choking him to oblivion, she was already undressing the man on the ground in front of her. "We need to blend in. Clothes. Hurry."

In less than three minutes, they were dressed in camouflage, rifles over their shoulders. They rolled the men into the bushes.

Winky jumped to a lower branch. Winked at Miranda.

Glenn grunted. "Listen to me, you two-trick monkey. Get your own woman."

Next the monkey winked at Glenn.

Miranda grinned. "He's an equal opportunity flirt."

"We need to go." Glenn half limped, half darted toward the path that led deeper into the forest.

Too slow. Disappointment slammed through Miranda as her brain reevaluated their situation.

She grabbed after him. "Wait!"

"Come on!" He pulled forward.

But she shook her head. He wasn't going to make it on foot, and she wasn't going to leave him behind. That left one option. "Go back into camp and duck under our hut. Wait there for me."

The huts sat about a foot off the ground, the gap obstructed by greenery, the best hiding place she could think of at a moment's notice.

They had no time to argue, and he didn't. He took her at her word that she knew what she was doing. He hurried off toward camp.

Winky looked after him.

"We'll be leaving," she told the monkey. "Thanks for the help. Watch out for snakes and harpy eagles. I'll have to make some noise now."

Winky gave Miranda one last wink, then climbed high up the tree. She fired a couple of shots in the opposite direction, then ran off parallel to the camp's perimeter.

She stopped in the cover of the bushes when she reached the edge of the clearing, watched as guardsmen ran off in the direction of the gunshots. Then she stepped out and headed toward the middle, passed by the prison hut with her hat pulled deep into her face, hurrying like anyone else.

"Get to the trucks when you can," she told Glenn without slowing and headed toward the vehicles.

The commander was yelling at two hapless guardsmen in front of his hut. Miranda hurried by them as if on a mission, straight to the trucks. She headed for the one closest to the road and jumped in.

No key.

She searched above the visor, under the seat, urgency drumming in her blood, her fingers frantic. Nothing. Okay, hotwire. Basic electrical engineering.

Then Glenn was there, glancing behind him as he opened the door.

She sorted through the wires, trying to remember how to do this. "I don't have the key."

"Move over."

"You think now is the time to reassert your masculinity?"

"You're the better shot. I drive, you take care of any shooting if we need it."

She slid over to the passenger side, and half a minute later the engine came to life.

He flashed her a grin.

Then the commander appeared in front of the truck out of nowhere, holding a gun at Glenn's head through the windshield.

"*Alto!*" His face was twisted, his features distorted with rage.

Glenn raised his hands into the air. Miranda tightened her fingers on the weapon in her lap.

But before she could do anything, Glenn slammed his foot on the gas and bounced that sucker right off the hood. The man's startled face was pressed against the windshield for a moment; then, as Glenn gave the truck more gas, the commander slid off to the side, his broken nose leaving a smear of blood behind.

The truck rattled as the tires rolled over something. Could have been a hole in the dirt road. Or—

She whipped her head back, but couldn't see anything. "Did you just run him over?"

Glenn focused on the road, his lips flattened. "Ask me if I care."

Miracle of miracles, nobody called out, nobody came after them as they flew down the dirt road. Hopefully everybody was busy rushing in the opposite direction, where the prisoners had been last seen.

The road turned and dipped, but Glenn handled the terrain well. "How long do you think before they figure out that we took the truck?"

She looked at the side-view mirror. "If the commander is dead or knocked out, then ten or fifteen minutes. If he's all right, he's probably sounded the alarm already."

He glanced at her. "Airport?"

She nodded, holding on to hope.

The truck flew down the dirt road at twice the speed than was safe, but Glenn kept control. The soldiers still caught up with them long before they reached anywhere near the city.

"Hold on," Glenn said between his teeth.

They reached a section of the road where it turned and twisted to follow a creek. Glenn slammed on the gas and put some distance between them and their pursuers, then after a particularly sharp turn, he drove straight into a gap in a stand of leafy bushes.

A few seconds later, half a dozen trucks zoomed by behind them without slowing.

In full daylight, the tracks on the ground and the broken branches would have been seen, but in the dim light of dawn, the soldiers, certain the escaped prisoners were ahead of them just around the bend, missed the signs.

Once they passed, Glenn backed out of the bushes, catching up to the train of National Guard trucks and joining the line from behind as they roared toward Santa Elena de Uairén at full speed.

Nobody thought to look back. And even if they glanced in the rearview mirror, they'd just see one of their own trucks. Miranda and Glenn were in uniform, the trucks rattling so hard that catching a good look at their faces through the windshield would be impossible.

Glenn flashed her a satisfied look. Yeah, he was handy to have around. Miranda grinned.

At the edge of the city, the trucks slowed and separated, each taking a different road as turnoffs became available. Glenn headed toward Route 10, then south toward the airport. Nobody thought to follow them.

They were at their destination in minutes, and pulled into the parking lot without anyone giving them a second glance.

He parked as near the entrance as he could. "This is it." He shut off the engine and reached for the door handle. "Can we take our guns?"

"We don't know if they allow them inside the airport for people who are off duty," she reasoned. "And we don't know if it's the right time for a change of guards so we can pretend to be the next shift. I say we pretend to be guardsmen on leave, heading home. I doubt even the National Guard fly with their rifles on a commercial airplane." She laid her weapon on the floor by her feet.

After a moment of consideration, Glenn nodded and did the same.

Raindrops splashed onto the windshield, one after the other.

They got out and straightened their clothes. She checked Glenn's back. "You have some bloodstains on your shirt."

"How bad?"

"A couple of dark spots. They mostly blend into the camo pattern. Let's hope nobody looks too closely."

They headed for the front doors, pretending to be soldiers who looked forward to leave and seeing their families, happy and excited. At the entry, the guards waved them through without a second look, one busy lighting his cigarette, the other one looking at his cell phone.

The waiting area was nearly empty, only a handful of people milling around. Miranda glanced at the board.

The morning plane to Caracas was leaving in twenty minutes. The passengers were probably at the gate already.

They had no money, so they didn't go to the ticket counter. They walked straight toward the door that was marked "staff only." The guard let them through with a bored expression, saying something about the rain.

Miranda gave a sympathizing nod. This time, they didn't meet anyone in the long walkway as they hurried out. The plane stood on the tarmac, with the stairs up against it.

She scanned the windows for movement. "Do you think they already loaded the passengers?"

Even as the last word left her mouth, sliding doors opened on the side of the building and people stepped from the gate to walk toward the plane. Miranda exchanged a glance with Glenn, then headed toward them.

Some of the tourists looked uncertain and reached for their papers, thinking this was a last-second check, but Miranda waved them along magnanimously and joined the end of the line, Glenn behind her.

They had nothing. No ID, no tickets. But hopefully all the checkpoints and security were behind them. If the flight attendants asked for their boarding passes, they were screwed. All the way to the plane, she prayed.

Down the tarmac, up the stairs.

One flight attendant stood in the door. She greeted them with a smile and a sincere "*Bienvenidos.*"

"*Gracias.*" They passed by her and simply took two empty seats in the last row.

The small plane had only two flight attendants. They went about their business. In the US, there'd be a headcount check. But maybe that wasn't the standard operating procedure here, since the country didn't have issues with terrorism. Or maybe the women did check, but didn't feel brave enough to harass two National Guard members. Either way, nobody came back to ask any questions.

The passengers settled in for the flight, but as minutes ticked by, the plane didn't begin to taxi down the runway.

"Do you think the commander called in and had the flight grounded?" Miranda asked under her breath, then glanced around for an escape route should they need one. The only open entry was in the front. In the tail, a parked beverage cart blocked the emergency exit.

She and Glenn were sitting ducks in the back. *Great.*

Her muscles tensed as minute after minute ticked by. Sweat beaded above her upper lip. They'd come too far to fail. She couldn't even imagine what the commander would do to them if they were recaptured.

But when a tall form appeared in the open front door, it wasn't the commander or one of his goons. Roberto filled the narrow walkway, dragging his carry-on and smiling at the young flight attendant, showing all his blinding-white teeth.

Chapter 15

GLENN SLID DOWN IN HIS SEAT AND LEANED HIS HEAD AGAINST THE HEAD-rest, bracing his weight to keep his raw back from touching the seat as much as possible. He pulled his hat over his face as if sleeping. Next to him, in the window seat, Miranda did the same.

Still, if Roberto sat anywhere near, there was no way he wouldn't turn around at least once during the flight and recognize them.

Glenn waited, watching from under the brim of his hat. Miranda's breath hitched as Roberto looked down the length of the plane and started toward them. But he stopped at the fifth row and settled into his aisle seat.

As soon as the flight attendant closed the door, the plane began taxiing down the runway.

Glenn tuned out the captain's greeting and the emergency information. He pushed back his seat once they reached altitude so he could get even lower, kept his hat on his face.

"What do we do once we reach Caracas?" he asked under his breath. The plane was only half-full; nobody sat in the seats in front of them to overhear.

"Get off the plane last. Make sure he's way in front of us. We'll cut out of the airport, then head straight to the US embassy."

Sounded like a plan. They had to have their passports replaced, for starters. Then what? Security could still stop them at the airport when they tried to fly back to the States. They were probably on some kind of a watch list.

He'd worry about that when they got there, Glenn decided. Complicated problems were best solved one step at a time. They had plenty to worry about right now, right here.

He pulled out the in-flight magazine so he could use it to hide behind in case Roberto walked around to stretch his legs or use the bathroom in the back of the plane. An ad for Curaçao dominated the front cover.

Tropical paradise, just twenty miles off the coast of Venezuela, with the convenience of an international airport right in Willemstad.

Curaçao was a small island, its own country, no connection to Venezuela. All they'd need was a boat and a deserted beach. He nudged Miranda and showed her the page.

"We'll see," she whispered.

She trusted the US government, counted on making the call from the embassy and being extracted. He was more of a do-it-yourself guy. He'd learned that in the business world. The government could lift you up, hand you a juicy government contract. But the next second, it could smack you down, cancel the contract because of budget restraints, increase regulations, pile on more corporate taxes. What one administration gave, the next could easily take away. He'd learned to run Danning Enterprises without counting on the government being helpful. Or even sane.

The younger of the two flight attendants brought around food and drinks, handing the passengers plastic-wrapped packages. He had to work at not falling on the sandwich like a starved wolf. The chunk of cheese had been barely enough to blunt his appetite.

While the woman bent to serve the other side, he reached into the cart and grabbed two extra packages, dropped them on his lap and covered them with the in-flight magazine.

Once the flight attendant moved on, Glenn offered half the loot to Miranda.

"I'm good." She pushed the food back to him. "I had more to eat at camp than you did."

He tried again.

But again, she resisted. "We'll have more food in a couple of hours at the embassy. I want you to eat."

"You're reasserting that you're the official in this rescue op, and I'm the target or what you called it."

"You have a problem with a woman in a leadership position?"

"Why would I?" Some men preferred a weak woman so they could feel strong next to her by comparison. He never understood that. "Any structure, including a partnership, is only as strong as its weakest link. Two strong people make the strongest team. To any man of reason, the strongest available woman should always be the most desirable."

She patted his knee. "I do like that logical brain of yours."

And he liked everything about her. More than liked. He ate the food and drank every bit of the water.

After their garbage was cleared away and the trays turned up, he took Miranda's hand. "I'd like to see you once we return to the US."

He'd been stupid to let her go in the first place. Luck or fate had brought her into his path again. He wanted to think that he was smarter than he'd been at twenty, that he knew a good thing when he saw it.

But instead of smiling and saying she felt the same, she pulled away. "I don't think that's a good idea."

Like hell it wasn't. He narrowed his eyes at her. "Why?"

"We're not a good match that way. Weren't back then, aren't now."

"Are you saying we don't make a great team? After what we've just been through? You don't think we work well together?"

She shook her head, as if she didn't want to consider his words, or as if his reasoning didn't matter. "That's not enough."

"What part exactly didn't work for you?" he asked under his breath. "The morning at the abandoned house?"

Just thinking about that morning, him sinking into her tight, wet heat had his cock twitching. He wanted her. Again. And again, and again. He wanted her in his bed, but that wasn't nearly all of it.

Why didn't she want the same?

Was she still in love with the man she'd married?

His mood darkened at the thought. Matthew had been killed in action. He was a hero. How was an ordinary guy supposed to compete with that?

He spent a few seconds smarting from her latest rejection, then set that aside to look at things from her point of view. She had had losses. Terrible, inconceivable losses. She didn't need him pushing her, demanding things she wasn't ready to give.

Yet he couldn't accept the idea of never seeing her again. Fine. If she needed more time, he'd wait. If she wasn't ready for another man in her life, he'd be whatever she needed.

"Friends?" he asked.

And then, finally, she smiled. "Always."

Good. Better. "How long have you lived in D.C.?" He gave friendly conversation a try.

"A few weeks. I just started the job."

He grinned at her. "Congratulations on successfully completing your first mission."

"Let's wait with the champagne until we're back in US airspace." This time, her smile was a little less strained. "We should grab some sleep before the plane lands. We could use some rest."

No kidding. "You first. I'll keep an eye on Roberto, in case he starts looking around or walks back this way."

"You didn't get much rest last night."

"I'm not going to get any in an airline seat. I can't put my full weight on my back." His skin was flayed. Putting pressure on it was killing him. He had a feeling he was going to sleep on his stomach for the foreseeable future.

She conceded after a moment and pushed her chair in the reclining position, closed her eyes, and pulled her hat back over her face. Her breathing evened in a few minutes. As if on command, she was asleep, probably a skill she'd learned in the military.

When the plane hit a patch of turbulence, she shifted against him, her head on his shoulder. He held still so she wouldn't move away.

Even though he knew he'd catch hell for it, he didn't wake her up halfway through the flight so they could switch. He let her sleep until the captain announced that they'd be landing in ten minutes.

She blinked awake. Sat up. Shot him a dark look. She was about to chew him out for letting her sleep that long, but up ahead in row five, Roberto stood and stepped out into the aisle. He stretched his legs, rolled his shoulders, then he began walking toward the tail.

Both flight attendants were up front, working their way slowly down the plane, taking trash and telling people to straighten their seats and fasten their seatbelts. Roberto hurried back for a quick bathroom visit.

Miranda pulled her hat as deep into her face as she could and slumped against the window, pretending to be sleeping.

Glenn wished he still had a knife.

Roberto was ten feet away. Eight. Six. Four. Then he was right in line with them, slowing.

Glenn had his head down, his chin to his chest, his hat covering most of his face, watching through one eye opened to a slit, seeing nothing but the man's shoes.

Why did he stop? Did he recognize them? What would he do?

He couldn't use his cell phone in the middle of the plane preparing for landing—a few minutes of advantage.

Roberto moved on, into the bathroom, and then Glenn was on his feet the next second, grabbing the door before Roberto could lock it behind him. No room for the two of them, but Glenn squeezed in anyway, closing the door with one hand to shield them from view, his other hand grabbing Roberto's wrist as the man went for his weapon with a startled curse. Before Roberto could call out, Glenn delivered a crushing blow to the man's chin, knocking him out cold.

His back hurt from the movement, his shredded skin burning, but he barely felt it. Adrenaline pumped through him as he emptied the man's gun and dumped the bullets into the garbage receptacle, hid the gun under his shirt. Then he opened the door, finding Miranda outside, ready to assist.

She glanced past him, at Roberto crumpled on the toilet.

"Do you have a problem with that?" Glenn closed the door behind him, hoping nobody would go in there now, since the plane had already begun descending.

"Two strong people make the strongest team." She went back to her seat.

He dropped down next to Miranda and snapped on his seatbelt, fished the gun out, and shoved it to the bottom of the seat pocket in front of him. Caracas was an international airport. They'd have to go through more security before they were allowed to leave it. He didn't want to set off any machines.

—

Miranda padded down the hallway on her way from the shower back to her room, wrapped in a luxurious bathrobe, her short hair still wet. The US embassy at Caracas had facilities in the basement, in case the staff got barricaded inside in an emergency.

Upon arrival, she and Glenn had been whisked off for debriefing, hours of questioning, phone conferences with General Roberts, with the FBI, the CIA. But then they were finally given rooms. They were to remain on embassy grounds while their release from the country was negotiated.

She knocked on Glenn's door. "Bathroom's all yours." She didn't go in. She retreated to her own quarters.

God, it was nice to be safe, to be able to relax for a change. To be able to sleep in a bed again. To be able to eat and go to the bathroom whenever she wanted. She grabbed a banana from the fruit bowl on the table just because she could, and smiled as she ate it.

When the phone rang, she wasn't sure if she should pick up the call, but it kept ringing so, after another moment of hesitation, she did.

"I have some good news for you," General Roberts said on the other end. "Under pressure from the US, the Venezuelan government agreed to grant both of you safe passage out of the country."

Relief rushed through her. "When?"

"Tomorrow morning."

"Thank you, sir." She could only imagine the kind of strings the man had to pull.

"I sent you in. I'm going to get you out. That's a promise."

"I'm sorry about the mess."

"Most extractions are messy. You found the target and you got him to safety. Job well done."

She thanked him before they hung up. The general's acknowledgement made her feel like she might just have a future someplace. She was once again part of a team. This could be a way to move forward. Matthew would want that for her.

He'd been the quintessential soldier. Whatever he did, he gave everything he had, and when he succeeded, he pushed on to the next mission objective. If something didn't go well, he didn't dwell on it. He tackled life like he'd tackled the obstacle course in basic training.

You simply didn't walk off, no matter what happened. You pushed through to the finish.

He'd always been about forward movement. He'd want her to move on. But she wasn't sure if she was ready.

A knock on the door jolted her out of her memories.

Glenn stuck his head in, scanned her face. "What's wrong?" He stepped inside, hair wet, face cleanly shaved, his white robe identical to Miranda's.

She rubbed a hand over her eyes. "I was thinking about Matthew."

"I see." He stopped where he was and didn't come any closer, watchful, looking as if he meant to say something, but in the end he didn't.

She stood and smoothed down her robe. "My boss called. We're leaving here tomorrow." The thought that she might not ever see Glenn again once they arrived in the US and parted ways stole the enthusiasm from her voice as she said, "The Venezuelan government agreed to our release."

He covered the distance between them with an ear-to-ear grin, picked her up, and twirled her around. "Hey, we did it!"

His infectious smile, being in his arms, the way their bodies pressed together . . . A jolt of reckless desire shot through her.

He must have misinterpreted the expression on her face because he set her down and took a reluctant step back. "Sorry."

To hell with it. She stepped forward, slipped her hands inside his robe, and pressed her lips to his.

To his credit, he got with the program in a heartbeat. His mouth slanted over hers, and the next second she was pressed so closely to his hard body she could have no doubt how much he wanted this.

One last time. She opened herself to his kisses. *One last time,* so she would have at least some good memories to take back with her to her lonely apartment in D.C.

She would never see him again save on TV when he began his political campaign. Someday, when she was watching him with the right wife by his side, at least she would have the memory of the night they'd spent at the embassy.

She tugged the bathrobe off his shoulders, revealing his scarred body.

"How's the back?"

He'd received first aid when they'd arrived.

"It'll heal."

He looked nothing like the preppy trust-fund nerd she'd once thought him to be. He'd survived trial by fire. He was as tough as any soldier. He was the type of man who fought for what he wanted, who protected what was his.

He was all that, and kind, funny, brilliant. Thank God she was smart enough not to fall in love with him. That would have been a disaster.

Her fingers slid up his chest, along the ripples of muscles under his warm skin.

His eyes darkened, focused on her face. He reached up and his long fingers slowly pushed her robe down her shoulders, the soft glide of the material over her naked breasts a tantalizing torture. He bared her upper torso to his hungry gaze, then he hooked a finger into her belt and tugged. And then she stood naked before him.

He looked at her as if she was the most beautiful woman on earth, as if she was the *only* woman on earth. She fell for it, of course. How could she not? Who could resist the need that boiled in his gaze?

She untied his belt and sent the robe pooling at his feet.

He had the body of a warrior, lean and scarred.

His erection strained toward her belly, the tip blue-red with blood, more than ready. A thrill shot through her at the obvious proof of how much he wanted her.

His hands caressed a tingling path up her arms. She moved toward the bed, but his fingers curled around her shoulders and held her in place. He kissed her mouth one more time before bending to her nipples to tease them into aching buds. Then he dropped to his knees in front of her and grabbed her by the hips, pulling her closer.

She couldn't put her hands on his scarred shoulders, so she placed them on his head, shoved her seeking fingers into his thick, wet hair, even as liquid need filled her limbs, making her legs unsteady.

He held on to her right hip with his left hand while nudging her thighs apart with the other. Then he parted her flesh with his fingers and found the nub that ached for his touch.

He leaned forward and sealed his warm lips around her clitoris, sucked it gently while she hung on to him for support. She might have protested, but speech was beyond her at this point.

Need grew and swirled, mixed with heat, with naked desire as she watched his dark hair against the white skin of her belly. Her breath hitched when he removed his hand from her hip and ran his fingers up her inner thigh.

"I want you," he said, his voice raspy, as he dipped a finger into her opening, then rubbed his moist fingertip up and down. A second finger joined the first before she could catch her breath, teasing her entry.

She let her head drop back, her eyes squeezing shut. She held on tight. She wasn't going to be able to take much more of this.

One long finger entered her first, then another, his mouth keeping up its gentle suckling the whole time, only pulling back now and then to let the teasing tip of his tongue torment her.

Inside her, his fingers curled against the backside of her clitoris, and he massaged the sensitive bundle of nerves, sending a mad pleasure through her.

She remembered how back in college he'd have her naked and spread eagle on the bed, experimenting and constantly surveying. "How does this feel?" "What about this depth?" "What about this angle?" "I think applying heat would increase blood flow and make it feel even better."

He'd have her mindlessly lost in pleasure with ridiculous ease. And he had never tired of her body. It'd been a miracle that they ever made it to class.

She'd blocked out a lot of those memories over the years. She'd made herself forget the incredible way he could make her feel, so she wouldn't miss him.

But there was no denying the here and now. Pleasure spiraled out of control inside her, waves and waves washing over her until her legs folded.

He caught her, held her in his arms with a satisfied look on his face.

"It's not polite to gloat." But as she turned her face to his warm skin to inhale his scent, she grinned into his shoulder. He probably thought he won. He probably thought he proved something. He liked reducing her to a puddle, did he? Two could play this game.

"You're going to have to pull me up. I don't think I can stand on my own," she said weakly as she sat back on her heels.

But when he pushed to his feet, instead of reaching for his hands, she leaned forward, grabbed him by the hips, and closed her mouth around the tip of his erection.

Air hissed from between his teeth. He went utterly still, a fierce concentration on his face. "Give a man some warning. You'll give me a heart attack."

She pulled back long enough to say, "I think you're safe from that. All the blood is down here." Then she tasted him again, slowly, carefully drawing him into her mouth. One hand went to wrap around the base of his cock, the other cupped his testicles.

A deep groan of pleasure escaped him. "We could have had more fun, but if you're determined to end this in the next two seconds—"

She sucked on him softly at first, then harder.

His hand came to rest on the top of her head. "Miranda, honey . . . you're killing me."

Who was the boss now? Her lips curved into a grin around him. She used the pressure of her tongue and her lips simultaneously.

Until he reached down and lifted her up, tossed her on the bed. He grabbed for his robe and produced a foil packet with a grin. "We have a fully stocked bathroom cabinet."

He rolled on the condom in one smooth move, then covered her with his body. He pushed her knees up as he plunged his hard cock inside her all the way, filling her.

Her private parts were still sensitized from her orgasm, all the blood still oh so close to the surface. The sensation of him stretching her nearly undid her all over again. One more move and . . .

But he wasn't moving. He held himself motionless inside her.

His burning gaze held hers. "Don't you dare move. Give me a minute. That's an order." His lips flattened, his face tightening with concentration.

"You're not the boss of me." She wrapped her legs around him, tilted her pelvis, and drew him in even deeper.

He swore between his teeth, pulled back, then plunged in again, hard, unrestrained.

And then she realized her tactical mistake. Giving him a minute to cool off would have given her a minute to cool off too. As it was, the hot, heavy pleasure built deep inside her again with alarming speed.

She was so going to lose it. He was right. They weren't going to last another minute.

Her back arched. She felt her eyes roll back in her head. She was at the peak, on the edge of the precipice. And then she tumbled over, into the sea of warm pleasure that closed in over her.

She barely registered as Glenn groaned her name, convulsing inside her.

———

Okay. Wow. Okay.

Glenn tried to catch his breath as he lay on his side next to her, watching her relax in post-orgasmic glow. His heart beat so hard against his ribcage, he thought it might crack a rib. If he was to talk her back into his life, he was going to have to up the time he spent at the pool. Or she *was* going to give him a heart attack.

She was everything he'd remembered and more. So much more, dammit. She might have thought that there was no room in her heart next to Matthew's memories, but she was going to have to make room. He needed to prove to her that it was possible.

"I want to see you when we get back home," he told her again. He'd keep asking until she agreed.

She drew a deep breath, her gaze becoming shuttered. In the space of a split second, it was as if an invisible barrier had been dropped into place between them.

"No. I'm sorry. The sex doesn't change anything." She pulled the sheet up to cover herself. Yet another barrier. "We've been locked together for the last couple of days in a life-threatening situation. The adrenaline rush got the better of us. It would have happened with anyone."

She was trying to explain away what they had. She'd left him before, and now she was preparing to leave him again.

"Because of Matthew?" Jealousy hit swiftly, making his shoulders tense. "Because you're still in love with him?"

"No."

He relaxed his muscles. Okay. As long as she wasn't in love with anyone else, there was a chance she could love him again. "Because I have more money? It means nothing. It's a tool to use.

I'm a successful businessman. You're a successful investigator. One comes with money, the other doesn't. It's a minor detail."

Her eyes said he was full of BS. But she didn't argue with him. "I don't care about your money."

"Then what? I think what we have here is special."

She was a reasonable person, logical, in every other aspect but this. He would make her see the truth this time, the elemental truth that they belonged together.

But she stubbornly said, "We're not right for each other."

"Don't pretend that there's nothing between us. Give me some credit."

"Your life path is different from my life path." She moved back from him.

He lifted himself to his elbow. "That's bullshit."

She yanked the entire sheet to her side and sat up, wrapping herself in the white expanse of cotton, then went to sit in the chair that faced the bed. Her face held a mix of emotions, none of them resembling the love and devotion he wanted. Instead, she looked torn, desperate, in pain. He didn't understand any of that, even as her obvious misery tugged at his heartstrings.

"What's wrong?"

"You are someone in the public eye." She clasped her hands on her lap. "You'll be even more in the public eye once you enter politics."

"So what? You're camera shy now?"

She pressed her lips together. Her voice dropped. "My past won't stand up to scrutiny."

"What are you talking about? You served our country. You're a hero. Look at what you're doing now. Saving lives. You just saved mine." His voice held more snap than he'd meant, impatience pushing him. He wanted her back in bed with him instead of arguing.

"I killed someone," she snapped back.

"You were a soldier. That was your job. I'm pretty sure I killed a guardsmen and probably the commander as we were escaping, but I'll be damned if I feel guilty about it."

She watched him with big brown eyes, all spunk draining from her face. She wrapped her arms around herself and somehow seemed to shrink, her expression becoming haunted as shadows filled her face.

She swallowed. Shook her head. "I killed someone outside of combat. An unarmed man. My superior officer. I received a dishonorable discharge from the army." She gave him a very small, incredibly sad smile. "I'm not politician-wife material."

The pain in her voice twisted his heart.

He stared at her for a moment. What was he supposed to say to that?

He pulled the blanket up to his waist and sat up in bed, a million questions flying through his stunned brain. "Can you tell me what happened?"

She rubbed her hand over her face, then dropped it back to her lap. Watching her in so much misery killed him. He wanted to go to her, but everything in her closed body language said to stay away. She didn't want him to comfort her, which added more layers of emotion to the already emotionally charged conversation.

As a guy, and an engineer, emotions weren't his specialty. He preferred problems to be of a mathematical nature. He liked it when he was in control of a situation. He liked it when he had solutions. Preferably, solutions he could personally implement.

He was all the way out to sea here. "Miranda?"

"I was with Personnel Recovery." Her voice turned wooden, her gaze moving to a spot on the wall behind him as she withdrew even more. "Two soldiers went AWOL from a Southeast Asian army base. Thailand. My CO and I were sent to find them. All signs pointed toward them just walking off base and getting lost in the red-light district."

Her lips flattened, as if from physical pain, as if just saying the words hurt.

But she continued. "My commanding officer and I split up, looking for them. The pleasure strip was a pretty grim place. I couldn't wait to get the hell out. I found the soldiers, escorted them back to base for discipline. I couldn't find my CO. He didn't answer his cell. I went back to make sure nobody jumped him. Places like that, they don't like outsiders who go around asking questions. I found him inside one of the seediest brothels on the far edge."

She paused. Closed her eyes. "He was with a little girl, six or seven years old. I saw her pass out"—Miranda's voice broke—"while he was laboring above her." Quick breath. "I told him to stop. He said, 'When I'm done.' He kept on going. 'Stand down, soldier. That's an order.'"

She drew another ragged breath. "I told him he was done. And when he didn't stop, I pulled my service revolver and shot him in the head." Her shoulders collapsed with the last word. She looked spent, broken, shattered.

Holy shit.

Disjointed thoughts pinged around in Glenn's head like atoms in a nuclear fission chain reaction, one thing pushing its way to the forefront: the knowledge of what had happened to Miranda's daughter.

What that moment at the brothel must have been like for her. Just . . . *Jesus.*

Sympathy coursed through him, and anger, frustration. He wanted to kill the bastard all over again. He wanted to go back in time. He wanted whatever supernatural powers it would take to free Miranda from the crushing pain that clearly had her in chains.

He wrapped the blanket around his waist and went to her, dropped to his knees in front of her, tried to put his arms around her, but she pushed him away, drew back from him.

"I should be in military prison." She pressed her lips together, her eyes begging him to understand. "But the army didn't want a scandal. They released a cover story that the CO was attacked and killed by local criminals while on duty. He got a posthumous medal. His widow and his kids don't know the truth to this day. As far as they know, the man was a true hero. His hometown named a playground after him." Sheer misery crept across her face. "So I can't even apologize to anyone."

He took her hands, needing the contact. Her fingertips were ice cold. "What can I do to help?"

"Nothing." She pulled her hands back and held herself rigid, as far from him as the chair allowed. "I want to take my punishment, but nobody will give it to me. I want to pay the price for my action, so maybe someday I can get absolution."

At last, he understood the times when she'd withdrawn, the times when he'd caught that hollow look in her eyes. She'd lost her husband, then she'd lost her daughter, then she was put in a situation where her worst nightmare played out right in front of her eyes. Too much. It would have broken anyone.

He could see the cracks now, and they scared him to death. He didn't want her to break, he couldn't stand the thought of it, the thought of the enormous pain she was holding in.

"You did nothing wrong," he said, in a harsher tone than he'd meant. He tempered his voice as he continued. "The bastard deserved to die. If you ask me, he died too easily."

He would have done anything to take the burden of guilt from her. He refused to move away. "You did nothing wrong," he repeated. "Do you hear me?"

But she shook her head. "I had no right to be judge, jury, and executioner."

"You saved that little girl's life."

"I don't know if I did. I was put on a plane back to the States the same day. Nobody would tell me anything about her."

Her face etched with agony, he could see now what she carried, day after day, could finally understand what tremendous energy it took to keep everything bottled up, secured behind walls, and still keep functioning, going about her work.

"Then you saved the bastard's next victim. And the next. He was a predator. He would have done it again."

Nobody should witness the rape of a child; nobody should have to make a decision in the heat of such a horrible, desperate moment. And sure as hell nobody should be blamed if she did what Miranda had done.

She stood, turning from his arms when he tried to hug her. She kept moving away, putting distance between them. "Would you mind going back to your room? I'd like some time alone. I want to get dressed. I need a moment of privacy."

Leaving her alone went against every instinct he had. But she had asked, so he would go. He needed her in his arms. Regardless, he would give her what *she* needed.

But they were far from done talking about this.

He strode to the door. Looked back. Tried to think up something to help her.

Her smile was heartbreakingly sad as she spoke. "Quit thinking determined thoughts. This is not a geometric problem you can solve with the right tools and the right equation. You are going to high places. I have a past that can't go there with you."

"Engineers don't believe in unsolvable problems," he warned her.

Chapter 16

MIRANDA WOVE THROUGH RUSH-HOUR D.C. TRAFFIC AS SHE HEADED INTO work, trying not to think of Glenn. She hoped he was all right, that he'd hired the best private detective money could buy to figure out who'd set him up. She hadn't seen him since they'd returned to the US. She'd barely gotten back to the office before she'd been sent to Mexico to look for a pair of missing teenagers.

She'd tracked them to Tijuana. They'd decided to give up college and stay down there to party for the rest of their lives. To their parents' relief, she was able to convince them to return home and rethink their life strategies.

Back to work, she was ready for her next case. She parked in the underground parking garage. Michael, the homeless vet she'd met weeks ago on the corner, no longer sat on the grass. He was working at the veterans' assistance agency and living in a group home. She loved seeing his spot empty. Made her feel like progress was being made. She crossed the street, went through security, and took the elevator down to the basement.

General Roberts was in, she registered as she walked through the doors. He waved at her as soon as he saw her, gesturing for her to come into his office. He'd been overseas when she'd returned from Caracas. Since she'd only had the phone interview, she'd never seen him in person before.

"Sir."

The man, tall and lean, stood and greeted her, sharp eyes, unreserved smile. "Karin says you're shaping up to be an excellent investigator. I had no doubt." The overhead light glinted off his closely shaved head.

"Thank you, sir."

"If there's anything you need, you just let me know."

"Yes, sir."

The man nodded. She took that as a dismissal and stepped toward the door.

But he said, "I'm glad that you came on board. I was impressed with your service record. I knew you'd be a great addition to the team."

Did he know the full truth of why she'd left the army? She didn't want to live a lie. So she filled her lungs and said, "There's something you should probably know about me, sir."

He lifted a bushy eyebrow. "Are you going to do your best in this job?"

"Yes, sir."

"That's all I need to know."

She hesitated.

He cleared his throat. Measured her up. Then he seemed to come to some sort of decision. "Close the door and take a seat." He waited until she did so. "A decade or so ago, when I was a colonel, I had a young officer under my supervision. Lieutenant Lester."

She stiffened at the mention of the name.

"I had a complaint from a female soldier about Lieutenant Lester behaving inappropriately. No proof, no witnesses, a her-word-against-his type of thing, and there were rumors that the two had a relationship that ended badly, giving way to hard feelings. The lieutenant had a spotless record up to that point, something I was reluctant to destroy. Instead of charging him officially for conduct unbecoming, I transferred him."

He paused as her mind reeled. But he went on after a moment. "I made a mistake. The way he ended up is just as much my fault as anybody else's."

"You're not responsible for what he did, sir."

"Then what happened wasn't your fault either." He folded his knobby hands on the desk in front of him. "No explanation of your past conduct is necessary. I'm sorry you were put in a situation where you had to deal with him. As far as I'm concerned, the incident needs no further discussion."

The unconditional absolution left her stunned. "Yes, sir. Thank you, sir."

She blinked hard as she stood and walked out of the man's office.

The general's words were nothing like the army saying, nothing happened because we can't publicly admit what happened. She couldn't fully accept this sudden absolution, not yet, but it loosened some of the old tightness inside her. There were people she respected, the general and Glenn, who knew what she'd done and accepted her with that knowledge.

She felt twenty pounds lighter as she walked back to her desk, but before she had a chance to think more about the general's words, Karin forwarded her a call from another investigator in the field.

Paul Mitchard needed passenger logs for a flight from Moscow to Calcutta. He was trying to track down a human rights activist who'd gone missing a week ago. Miranda tackled the task, working through the maze of bureaucracy to receive the necessary permissions.

By the time she finished, mid-afternoon, a new case came in. The nephew of the state attorney general disappeared in Hong

Kong, where he was studying marine biology. Miranda accepted the case, downloaded the files, and asked Elaine to make the travel arrangements.

"There's a flight tonight. Might as well go home to pack," Elaine called back from her desk a few minutes later.

Miranda finished up some emails, then headed home. She was packing her suitcase when her phone rang. She glanced at the display and her heart skipped a beat.

"I thought I'd check on you," Glenn said as she took the call, the sound of his voice sending tingles down her spine. "How have you been?"

Missing you. "Busy with work. How are things on your end?"

She winced as the words left her mouth. Weren't they polite? She hated that they sounded like distant friends, but nothing else was possible.

"I was thinking about coming down to D.C. tonight. I'm heading over to our R & D lab right now. Then there's a really late meeting. I was going to skip that, but Cesar just tipped me off that it's a surprise party, the managers putting something together to commemorate my recent adventures and officially celebrate my return. But after that, I want to drive down and see you. I need to talk to you."

"I'm leaving for Hong Kong. I'm working a new case." She wanted to see him, desperately, but what would be the point? To keep meeting with him would be like picking at a wound, never letting it heal. They had no future. She could bring him nothing but trouble.

"Bad timing," he said after a long pause.

She forced herself to sound steady as she asked, "Any new clues on who set you up?" Being back at work while knowing that someone in his immediate surroundings had betrayed him, wanted him dead, had to be difficult. She'd been thinking about that, about him, a lot this past week.

"The investigators I hired cleared the secretarial staff. And our industry rivals. Right now we're looking at a vocal environmentalist group that might have hacked our server. They published some confidential memos to throw dirt on us in the media. If they had that, they might have had my travel arrangements and meeting schedule."

"Sounds like a promising lead." She wished she could be part of the investigation, but that wasn't how her job worked. She was strictly retrieval, and that part of the job had been accomplished.

"I want to see you when you come back," he said.

"My schedule is pretty crazy."

She couldn't see him. There could never be anything serious between them. It hurt to stay away from him, but to have him in her life while knowing that there could never be more than the most superficial friendship, would kill her. What was it her mother used to say? *A painful end is better than endless pain.*

Miranda swallowed hard. Bad enough that she'd stupidly fallen in love with him all over again. The first time around, she'd given him up for her own sake, to make a life of her own without the influence and limitations of his powerful family. Now, the second time around, she was going to give him up for his sake. So her past wouldn't hold back the success story that he could be.

"I need to focus on my new job right now," she told him.

The pause on the other end was even longer this time. "I'm coming down," he said at last, the words coming slowly, carefully. "You can give me half an hour."

He hung up before she could protest.

She clenched her jaw. She had to make him understand that a relationship between them couldn't work. She braced herself for the conversation, knowing she'd have to say whatever it took to make him walk away. Even if it'd kill her.

She packed her clothes, shoes in one outer pocket, toiletries in the other, fleeting thoughts nagging in the back of her mind.

She was done with packing and in the shower when the disjointed thoughts that barely floated on the surface of her consciousness suddenly snapped into place as she looked at the clothespins that held her shower curtain. The glass door had no glass, and the super was slow having it installed. She used what she had on hand to make the shower functional in the meanwhile.

We use the tools we have.

One of the cardinal rules of engineering and innovation. Take something that you have and make it work.

How many times had she done that in her life? How many times had they done that while trying to escape?

So someone wanted Glenn out of the way. And that someone had Venezuela in his tool box. He used what he had. He knew the system enough to know who to call. He knew what would happen to Glenn.

She could think of only one person in Glenn's immediate circle who had a working knowledge of Venezuela, who was from Venezuela in fact. *Cesar Montilla.*

She'd discounted him for two reasons: the Venezuelan government was his enemy, and she couldn't think of anything he'd gain by Glenn's death. And yet . . . If he did want Glenn out of the way for some reason . . . *We use the tools we have.*

Her heart raced suddenly. Glenn was on his way to meet the man, at the company, after hours. Did anyone else know about that welcome back party?

She jumped from the shower and, dripping on the carpet, tried to call Glenn. He didn't pick up. He was probably in his car, driving to the meeting.

She rubbed a towel over her body and hair in a rush, jumped into her clothes, then ran like hell for her car. She could be in Maryland in under an hour.

But would that be fast enough?

Cesar was making his move to remedy the fact that Glenn had returned from Venezuela in one piece. If she was right, Glenn was on his way to be murdered.

———

Glenn's first clue that something was off was that the roof was empty of people. No roof party. Instead of tables, the helicopter stood on the helipad, the rotors in motion.

He glanced at his cell phone as he let the elevator door close behind him. He had a couple of missed calls from Miranda. Probably calling to tell him not to come to D.C.

He dropped the phone back into his pocket. He was driving down and they were going to talk. She was going to hear him out. He didn't care about her past, and he wasn't leaving her tonight until he found a way to make her understand that.

Plus, he had news for her. News she would want to hear. He'd been working on a little surprise for her.

Cesar walked from behind the chopper, keeping his head down. "You're here."

"Are we going somewhere?" Glenn asked. Both of them had their pilot licenses. Maybe the party was on a boat, part of the surprise. Cesar was a boat guy. He owned a hundred-footer, albeit without a helipad.

But instead of responding to his question, once Cesar was far enough away from the helicopter to straighten, he reached into his suit and pulled out a handgun. He pointed it at Glenn without hesitation.

"Toss the phone. Walk toward the chopper." Cesar moved to the side.

Glenn threw his cell phone a couple of feet and took a few steps forward. The rotors weren't going at full speed, but spun fast enough to produce a wind that flapped his suit jacket and blew his hair back from his face. He kept his eyes on his old friend, feeling confused and betrayed. "Why?"

The man scowled. "You left Victoria."

"She asked for the divorce." Glenn tried to inject some reason into the conversation that had his mind reeling.

"Because you couldn't love her. My daughter wasn't good enough for you." Cesar's expression darkened.

"She wasn't in love with me either."

"She would have done as I told her," Cesar snapped. "But you couldn't be a decent husband."

"And what does killing me solve?"

"I'm marrying Gloria."

The news knocked Glenn back. But in an instant, he could see the whole plot. The way Cesar had always been there for Gloria. Gloria coming to depend on him more and more over the years, increasingly leaning on his advice.

At company functions where she was the hostess, Cesar had been the host since Oscar Danning's death. He'd been the other founding member, Oscar Danning's best friend and business partner, the vice president of Danning Enterprises.

But he wanted more.

Understanding dawned on Glenn at last. He'd been too focused on growing the business, taking the core team for granted. If he'd paid more attention back at home instead of looking outside the borders . . . He should have seen this coming.

His hands fisted at his side. "You want the whole company."

Cesar's eyes glinted with a cold gleam. "It should be mine. The idea was mine."

"Yours and my father's."

"Mine first." The man shrugged. "But he did expand on it."

"And provided financing."

"He had family money. I was just starting out. We should have had equal ownership, but your grandfather wouldn't commit the money unless I agreed to a twenty-five, seventy-five percent split. I was a minority stockholder from the beginning. All the power, all the big decisions were his."

"Not anymore." Oscar Danning's seventy-five percent controlling interest had been equally divided between his two sons and his widow after his death, each receiving twenty-five percent. Cesar's own twenty-five percent was now equal to all the others. "You're an equal partner."

"In a company that should be mine." His jaw tightened. "Don't do me any favors." He practically spit the words.

Glenn stared. If he died, his shares would be split between his mother and brother. When Cesar married Gloria, he would assume control of her and her vote handily. She'd follow his advice even more than she did now. Tyler would be the only one to stand against him, but by controlling Gloria's shares, Cesar would effectively have majority control. All decisions would be his.

"You had your chance." Cesar motioned for him to step back even farther.

Glenn did, bending to avoid the propellers. If he could get into the helicopter, he could lift off, maybe, before a bullet hit him.

"You brought this upon yourself." Cesar put his other hand on the gun and spread his feet, took aim. "If you'd stayed with Victoria, your shares, along with mine, would have gone to the son you would have had. Fifty percent in the hands of a Montilla. I would have been satisfied with that."

Glenn took another step back. Cesar meant to shoot him, then escape in the chopper. Maybe take his body and drop it into the ocean. It'd take time, but eventually Glenn would be declared dead. Then Cesar would gain the power he craved.

But instead of squeezing the trigger, Cesar said, "Get in."

Did he plan on carrying out the murder over water? The bullet hole in the chopper would point the finger at him. Maybe he'd just push his victim out over the open water, too far from shore to swim back.

Yet there was a flaw in the plan. In the close quarters of the chopper, Glenn could overpower him. Hope reared its stubborn head.

He opened the door and stepped up, waiting for Cesar to get behind the controls.

But the man stayed on the ground. "Go!" he shouted. "In a couple of hundred yards, the chopper will lose power and you go down. Whether you are over a populated area at that point or over water is your choice. Don't bother trying to call for help. The radio is disabled."

Cold sweat rolled down Glenn's back. "And if I refuse to fly?"

"I shoot you right here. I'll make sure it'll look like the work of environmentalist extremists."

"They wouldn't. I cancelled the Florida oil rig contract."

"I reinstated it this afternoon and issued a press release to go public tomorrow morning. Florida is good for our bottom line."

"But that's not the direction the company is going." They'd agreed to diversify into renewable energy.

"It is now." Cesar's expression stayed somber.

He had a weapon. Glenn had nothing.

Or . . . He was sitting in a potential weapon, actually. He closed the door and went through the preflight check, registered the alarms that told him everything wasn't as it should have been. But Cesar had told him he had a few hundred yards in the air. He only needed a couple of feet.

He lifted the bird into the air, but instead of banking to the left and taking off towards the harbor, he stayed low and drifted toward Cesar, turned so he could get between the traitor and the door to the staircase, then he herded the bastard toward the edge of the roof.

The first bullet hit the windshield but missed him. So did the second. Glenn pushed forward. If a bullet hit the fuel tank, the game would be over in a hurry. The chopper was an imprecise weapon, while the handgun wasn't.

But as Cesar dropped on his stomach and aimed again, his arm jerked, red spreading on his shoulder.

Glenn glanced back, just in time to catch sight of Miranda dashing forward from the elevator, head down, her weapon aimed. He set the bird down a safe distance from her, then ran to help because Cesar was now shooting at her.

Chapter 17

MIRANDA STOOD AT THE EDGE OF THE ROOF, LOOKING OVER THE LIGHTS OF Baltimore and the harbor, while Glenn talked to the last remaining police officer by the elevator. They'd taken Cesar away in handcuffs, but her body was still buzzing with adrenaline. The scene that had greeted her when she'd opened the door to the roof had about stopped her heart.

She'd pushed aside all emotion to enter the combat situation, but now those emotions were rushing back and stealing her breath.

She was in love with Glenn. She was no longer the clueless young woman, a fish out of water, insecure, like she'd been in college. She hadn't known her own mind. Hell, she hadn't known herself. And still, giving him up hurt like hell.

But this time around . . . The thought of giving him up again felt as if she was trying to rip her own heart out of her chest. She wasn't sure she could do what she had to do here.

Glenn came up behind her, put his arms around her, and pulled her against his chest, holding her tightly against him. "They're all gone. Cesar will be officially charged in the morning."

She sagged against him, soaking up his presence.

"How did you know?" he asked next to her ear.

"We use the tools we have. Cesar had Venezuela."

He pressed a kiss against her temple. "God, I love your brain."

Her heart leapt.

"You saved my life again," he said.

"We all have some bad habits. I'll try to quit this one. I didn't mean to hover."

"I want you in my life."

"You're just saying that because you think I'm cheaper than a full-time bodyguard. Which you seem to need, by the way."

"I'm serious."

She turned to face him, wishing that things could be different between them. "You know why that's not possible."

"I don't care about your past."

"But the media and your future constituents will."

"I want you more than I want future constituents."

"Don't ever say that in front of Gloria," she advised. "She'll have a heart attack."

"I love my mother." He flashed her a level look. "But my entire life can't be about pleasing her, or about the company, or about a possible future in politics."

"You could help a lot of people."

"I can help a lot of people without becoming a politician. The way Washington is gridlocked these days, I can probably do more from the outside than from the inside."

"Your grandfather was a senator."

"I'm proud of him. I'm pretty sure he'd be proud of me no matter what I decide. He was big on common sense. And nothing makes more sense than to marry the woman I love."

Her heart thumped against her ribcage. His words made her dizzy. "I have to go to Hong Kong. I should be getting to the airport."

"We'll take the corporate jet."

"You have to stay here." She gestured vaguely. "You have to talk to your mother and your brother. Victoria." She still didn't know how she felt about his ex-wife. "Cesar is going to be big news. You have to be here to deal with the press, the board of directors, and the rest."

"The one thing I learned in Venezuela is that Tyler can manage pretty well without me. My absence forced him to step up to the plate."

"I don't know how long I'll need to stay in Hong Kong."

"We'll make further plans once we know. If I have to fly back, I'll fly back. But right now, I intend to spend a couple of uninterrupted hours with you, even if I can only get them over the Atlantic."

He had his determined face on. She was too emotionally exhausted to argue with him. "I need to go back to D.C., finish packing, grab my laptop."

"I need to file flight plans." He kissed her forehead. "We'll take the jet down to the airport in D.C. I'll meet you there in two hours?"

She nodded.

The rest—the ride back home, the packing—passed in a blur. She was on the Danning Enterprises corporate jet before she knew it, sitting on a comfortable white leather sofa across from Glenn, a bottle of red wine on the table between them.

"Do you like it?" he asked, his eyes serious, as if her response was important to him.

"Not that different from military transport," she said bland-faced. But then she grinned. "It's seriously over the top, you know that, right?"

He was silent. Worried that she wouldn't approve?

"Of course I love it," she said. "Good grief, I could live on this plane and I don't even like flying."

And then he smiled at her.

Which she ruined by saying, "I still don't think I could ever get comfortable with your lifestyle. How do you end up with a private jet?"

He frowned. "One thing leads to another."

She couldn't help a small laugh. "Most people say things like that about doughnuts or Girl Scout cookies."

"I'm not most people." Now he sounded displeased.

"I noticed that."

"We're not that different."

God, this was hopeless. He refused to acknowledge the gorge between them. Desperation mixed with exhaustion inside her. It had to be past midnight. She stifled a yawn.

He pushed to his feet, then sat down at the end of her couch and drew her into his arms. "Sleep. You need to work in the morning. I'll wake you when we stop in Vienna to refuel."

She hesitated only for a moment. Sleep was easier than trying to come up with ways to convince him that they didn't have a future, especially when she so desperately wanted things to be different.

She put her feet up and curled up with her head on his thigh. She was not going to be the reason he gave up the political future he'd spent his life working for. They'd finish their talk in Vienna. Then they'd go their separate ways. The only sensible course of action. She told herself that a couple of times to push back against the misery that descended on her.

He reached down and brushed the hair out of her face, then left his arm draped around her. She fell asleep like that, enveloped in his comfort and his scent, his warmth surrounding her.

She slept all the way to Vienna, where they stopped for refueling.

"Want to go out into the city?" he asked, and she wondered if he'd slept at all. If he had, it couldn't have been too comfortable.

"I've never been to Vienna," she confessed. "How much longer to Hong Kong?"

"Eight hours."

She glanced at her clothes, all wrinkled. "I should probably change if we're going out in public." She could brush her teeth in the bathroom, but what she really wanted was a shower.

He must have read her mind because he said, "While you were sleeping, I called ahead and got us a hotel room. In case you wanted to spend a few hours here. There's something I'd like you to see."

He was being all mysterious. She raised an eyebrow.

"It's an engineering thing."

"I don't like it when people try to use my weaknesses against me." But she was smiling. "Okay. Show me this Viennese engineering wonder."

A quick phone call and a hired car, a gleaming black Mercedes-Benz, came for them to the airport. The chauffeur drove them to the Empress Hotel, a luxury hotel decorated in gold and white marble inside and out, the lobby all palm trees, mirrors, and crystal chandeliers.

The manager greeted Glenn by name, and the porter just about bowed as he escorted them up the elevator.

They went straight to the top, into the Empress Suite that stole her breath away. "Wow. Seriously?"

The suite occupied at least half of the top floor, had glass walls on three sides, the city of Vienna sprawling before them, the Danube River a blue ribbon through it. Palaces, churches, bridges. She could only gape at the beauty of the architecture.

"Glenn, this is . . ." She turned.

"Over the top? Like the jet?"

"Way over."

He sighed dramatically, mischief glinting in his eyes. "Then you're really not going to like what I want to show you next."

Something more elaborate than this? She couldn't imagine.

But he enfolded her hand in his and drew her to a different, smaller elevator door at the other end of the suite. The door opened at the push of the button. They went up one more level.

"The roof?" She wasn't keen on roofs at the moment. She'd almost lost Glenn on a roof in Baltimore just hours ago. But when the doors opened, the sight that greeted her rendered her speechless.

A smile teased Glenn's masculine lips as he drew her forward, into the glass-and-steel conservatory. The shape resembled the scaled-down version of a European cathedral, except the walls and ceiling were all glass.

In the middle, what looked like a natural pond—the size of an Olympic pool—reflected the rising sun. The incredible blue of the water played off the lush greens of the palm trees that edged the walls. A stone shower stood at one end next to a shelf filled with white bath towels. A wrought-iron table sat in the other corner with a couple of chairs, a fancy cappuccino machine on the shelf behind it.

"The pool house goes with the Empress Suite," he said. "It's ours. The regular hotel elevators don't come this high."

"I thought we were just going someplace to shower and change, have a light breakfast."

"We did. We came here."

"I don't even want to know what you're paying for this."

His smile widened. "I get a discount. Don't worry about it."

She narrowed her eyes at him. "Why do you get a discount?"

"Because I designed this." A proud grin sat on his face. "One hundred percent energy neutral. Solar power runs the heating, cooling, pool pumps, everything. Recycled steel frame. Green building concepts. Before my father died, I was thinking about making these and starting my own business. Then I had to take on more responsibility at the company, so I sold the design. This is the prototype. The hotel bought it from me."

She kept staring around. "It's incredible." Then a faint memory tugged in the back of her mind. "Wait a minute." Excitement shot through her. "It's the palm house!" Except way more elaborate.

When they'd been at MIT, they participated in a contest to design a palm house for the Boston Public Garden. Their design had been very similar to this, except Glenn seemed to have solved some problems that they didn't have the right technology for back then.

"I named it the Miranda." He watched for her reaction.

Her heart twirled in a pirouette inside her chest.

She moved forward, drank it all in, tried to remember the exact details of the blueprint and small-scale prototype they'd put together. They hadn't won the contest, but they'd spent a ton of time together during the project and became lovers.

The palm trees were just like the plastic model ones she'd used, except much bigger and beautiful. The banana palms even had bananas growing on them.

"It reminds me of the rainforest in Venezuela." The soft sounds of the water circulating in the pool sounded like the creeks they'd come across. "All it's missing is our bamboo sleeping platform."

He grinned and led her to a stand of trees at the far end. An antique fainting couch, made of bamboo and upholstered in a traditional print, stood in the middle, looking like it came from some British colony a hundred years ago. The perfect place for a nap.

"What do you think?"

She oohed at the sight of the lush greenery around her, then turned back to the pool, the city in the background. "It's magnificent."

He looked pretty magnificent himself, his wide shoulders emphasized by dappled sunlight, his brown hair tousled. He was his healthy self again, looked nothing like the gaunt fugitive she'd found in Santa Elena.

She wanted to throw herself into his arms. Instead, she turned from him to walk back toward the water.

He followed after her. "Stay here with me. Just for a day and a night."

"I can't."

He stepped forward and turned her toward him. "Stay with me forever."

"Don't you ever give up?"

"Not on you. Not ever again." His long fingers slid down her arms to take her hands. "Tell me that you have no feelings for me."

She closed her eyes for a second. "My feelings don't matter."

"They matter to me. If you don't think what we have is worth fighting for, if this is not what you want, I'll let you walk away. I'll hate it, but I'll step back. But if you're turning your back on what we could be from some sense of nobility, wanting to give me what you think I should have . . ." He pulled her against his chest and reached under her chin with a finger to tilt her face up to his. "That's bullshit."

The heat in his eyes fogged up her brain. She needed to make a logical, convincing argument here, but her thoughts wouldn't line up. "I want you to be all that you can be."

"I appreciate that. But we're talking about the rest of our lives. It's a little more complicated than an army recruiting slogan."

"What do you want?" She turned the tables on him. Maybe if he spoke his plans for his future out loud, he would see, at last, how incompatible they were with her.

"I want you. Above all. I want to spend today in the city with you and tonight here under the stars. And then I want to spend the rest of our lives together, as many days and nights as our work will let us have. Unless you're ready to retire with me right now and spend the rest of our lives in bed. I can hand the company off to my brother."

Ha! Like he would ever give up the company.

Would he?

She wouldn't want him to, she realized. The family company was part of who he was. She liked who he was. And she didn't want to give up her work either.

"I like my new job." Not that his idea didn't sound incredibly tempting. But she couldn't see herself as a kept woman. It wasn't who she was.

"All right. You marry me and you can keep your job." He brushed his warm lips against hers, then pulled back far enough so he could look into her eyes. "But you're not allowed to fall in love with any other man that you go off to save. I want to be clear about that."

She smiled. Her heart was so full of him, she didn't think there could be room for anyone else. "You're not the boss of me," she said, just so he wouldn't get a fat head.

"Oh, yeah?"

"I'm an independent woman. I don't need a man to complete me."

"How about to pull you out of the water?"

She was in the pool before she could ask what water. She plunged under, all the way to the bottom, pushed away, barely able to believe that he'd shove her in.

She broke the surface, shook water out of her face, and glared at him.

"I'd help you out, but on second thought, I'm pretty sure you'd pull me in."

He was right about that.

She swam toward the steps and walked out of the water, plotting how to get back at him, glaring all the way.

Hands in his pockets, a glint in his eyes, he didn't look as if he felt threatened. "Is there a wet T-shirt contest somewhere?"

"Very funny."

"Not really. It's more on the sexy side." He moved toward her. His voice dipped. "Very sexy."

She stood where she was by the pool and waited until he reached her.

"You should take your clothes off and let them dry."

"Ever the helpful one."

"I do what I can." He reached for the bottom of her T-shirt.

She caught him by the wrists, flipped him sideways in a move she'd learned in hand-to-hand combat training, and tossed him into the water. And then, as he splashed, grinning, she jumped in after him. *Oh, what the hell.*

"Payback sucks, doesn't it?" She tried to push him under.

He put her arms around her, plastering her against his wide chest. "Maybe I'm exactly where I want to be." He flashed an evil grin.

And before she had time to think about whether he'd planned the whole thing, he was already peeling off her T-shirt. And her pants. And her bra, and her panties.

His own clothes were gone just as fast as hers. Then they were pressed together skin to skin. "I'm not letting you walk out of my life again without a fight," he murmured against her lips.

"This could be the beginning of a terrible mistake," she warned.

"Engineers don't make mistakes. On our way to resounding success, we identify methods that don't work."

He reached down to wrap her legs around his waist. "I don't know about you, but from where I'm standing, this method is working pretty well."

She laced her arms around his neck. His steel-hard erection was pressed against her, but not inside her.

"D.C. is just an hour's drive from Baltimore," he said, his voice strained. "It's not a bad commute. I could drive to work from your place."

She stilled. "You'd be willing to move to my one-bedroom apartment?"

He turned serious. "I'd be willing to do pretty much anything for you."

Her heart smiled. "I'm not going to be home a lot with this job."

"How about we'll start with being together when you're home, and go from there?"

"My job wouldn't bother you?"

"The truth? I'd rather that you quit work and live with me. In between meetings, I could run home and make mad love to you."

"Sure. And I could just cook and clean for you while I was waiting."

His eyes lit up with approval.

She snorted and placed a hand on his forehead. "I think you might have come home with some kind of jungle fever. I've never known you to be this delusional."

Since she was using her legs and arms to anchor herself to him, he could let go to rub his fingers across her nipples, roll them as they swelled into hard peaks. "I think you boggle my mind."

He sure boggled hers. Her breath caught as arousal flushed her body with heat.

She could never forget the family she'd had. They'd been front and center of her broken heart all this time and that was where they'd remain. But somehow in the past two weeks, her heart had healed up around them, and that was Glenn's doing.

He didn't take Matthew's place. He added something extra to her life, something wonderful that tasted like love and smelled like hope. Something she'd desperately needed even if she'd been too busy to admit it.

He dipped his head to hers and took her lips in a rough kiss, possessive, urgent. Then, before she could recover, he grabbed her behind and strode out of the water holding her, snatching up his pants that floated on top of the water.

He carried her straight to the large divan in the circle of palm trees and lay her down, pulling back, worshipping her body with his gaze, his eyes dark with need. He reached into his pants pocket, came up with a foil square.

She was ridiculously grateful for his forethought. But she teased him anyway. "Aren't you just prepared for everything?"

"I happen to be an engineer."

He sheathed his erection before he joined her on the divan.

Only the sound of their breathing and the water lapping the side of the pool broke the silence. Sunlight filtered through the palms. They could have been the first two people in paradise.

"When is the plane leaving?" she asked, not that she wanted to think about anything else but him right now.

"Whenever we get back to it."

Okay, she could begin to see why living this way would be convenient.

He rubbed his lips against hers, nibbled the bottom lip, licked the corners first, then the seam, then he swept inside and she forgot all about schedules. His long fingers dragged across her abdomen, up to her breasts, caressing, outlining. He rolled her nipple, and need swirled through her. Then he pinched, applying gentle pressure at first, then increasing it, tugging, even as his tongue made love to her mouth. She grew damp between her legs.

She was ready for him. Now. She arched her hips. He moved his mouth from her lips to her free nipple.

She moaned. The tugging and the suckling together were too much. An electric charge ran straight from her nipples to her clitoris. "Please."

He lifted his head and flashed a devilish grin. "I like it when you're so subdued."

"Don't get used to it."

He positioned himself between her legs, on his knees, and sat back on his heels. For a moment, it occurred to her that they were in a building made of glass. Then she told herself that nobody could see them up here. She didn't have it in her to worry. She couldn't think of anything else but his hard length entering her at last.

He took his time, the bastard. He grabbed her under her knees and slid her bottom up his knees, pushed her thighs apart and spread her wide. His breath quickened. He watched her body grow even more moist for him as he caressed her inner thighs, played with her pubic hair, outlined the opening of her vagina in a circular motion, over and over again, flicked his thumb over her clitoris, all the while, his cock just inches away from where she wanted him.

"I'm so going to torture you back for this," she threatened.

He grinned a slow grin that was full of sex. "I'm counting on it."

And then he moved forward, touching the tip of his penis against her opening, holding her in place with his hands on her thighs so she couldn't move. She could only arch her back, blindly seeking release, but he would have none of it.

He pushed in an inch, stretching her opening, then pulled back again. One hand slid up her thigh and found her clitoris. He circled his finger around it, then pushed in again. Circled. Pulled out.

Her heart raced, her breath hitched. Was he trying to kill her?

Circled. Pushed in. This time two inches. Circled. Pulled out. Then he pushed in again, but instead of circling his finger around her clit, he left his fingertip on her engorged nub, and pressed down. He kept that pressure as he pushed into her all the way.

That was the thing about engineers. They always knew what button to push, she thought hazily, her body focused on pleasure. A hot wave built inside her as he moved in and out of her body, a wave that rose to towering heights, then crashed, crashed, crashed, her body convulsing around him as she called his name.

Only then did he grab for her hips with both hands to pump himself inside her hard, allowing his own release at last.

Later, as they lay next to each other, looking up at the palm fronds and the sky, she thought: *I could stay like this forever.*

So as they went down the elevator, even later, naked, with an armful of soppy, wet clothes, she said, "Maybe."

He raised an eyebrow as they stepped out into their opulent suite.

"Maybe we could give it a try," she said. "While I'm in Hong Kong, I'll think about it."

He dumped the clothes and picked her up, carried her to the antique Persian rug in front of the fireplace, laid her down, paused to turn on the fireplace with the remote before covering her with his body, and took her mouth in a kiss that she felt to her toes.

"Again?" she asked weakly when they came up for air, his renewed excitement, trapped between their bodies, unmistakable.

"It's been a long time since the embassy in Caracas," he said as he nibbled on her lip. "I've been saving up. Basic fluid dynamics."

Freaking engineers.

Chapter 18

ON THE FLIGHT TO HONG KONG, MIRANDA READ THROUGH HER CASE FILE, while Glenn slept a little. The couches were larger than a bed in first class on any given airline, so he looked comfortable as he slept.

He woke tense, as if from a bad dream, then looked at her, and slowly relaxed. Did he dream about the torture?

She was never going to forget the sight of the welts on his back or the burn marks on his collarbones. She knew he'd never forget how he got his scars.

He sat up. "Come here."

She pushed her work aside and walked over. He pulled her onto his lap. She laid her head in the crook of his neck. He smelled like sleep, and leather, and Glenn.

He pressed a kiss against her temple. "Hungry?"

Her stomach growled as soon as he said the word. Their breakfast at the Empress Hotel seemed like a lifetime ago.

He ordered food and they were served immediately, so they moved to sit at the table. In a jet that was worth millions, somehow he made her as relaxed as if she were sitting across her kitchen table from him.

He glanced at his watch as they finished the salmon with rice and steamed vegetables. "I'm going to have to work a little." His voice held plenty of reluctance.

After what had happened with Cesar . . . she imagined there'd be a lot of damage control to do.

"I wanted to check out the entertainment system anyway." She didn't want him to feel like he had to babysit her every second. She couldn't believe all the time he was taking from the company at a crucial moment like this, for her.

So, like an old married couple, he worked on his laptop while she watched a movie, then picked up her case file again, planning out her day, which people she wanted to talk to first after her arrival.

They were less than an hour from landing when an email came in from Karin.

Target located. Mission cancelled.

She told Glenn. "I'm sorry you came all this way with me for nothing."

"Not for nothing. Actually, I meant to show you something around here." He stood and hurried to the cockpit, talked to the captain.

From the few words she was able to catch, he was asking the man to file a change to the flight plan. Then she caught the word "Thailand," and her stomach clenched.

The last time she'd been to Thailand . . . She never wanted to go back there. Ever again. Did he think the trip would be therapeutic? She was pretty sure it'd be the exact opposite.

Nervous energy pushed her to her feet. "Why are we going to Thailand?" she asked as soon as he came back.

He took her hand and pulled her closer, then reached up to smooth the furrows on her forehead. "I have a surprise for you. I meant to take you over once you solved your case, or when you had a couple of hours free."

Her entire body was tense. "I don't want to go there."

He took both of her hands into his, his gaze searching her face. "Do you trust me?"

She stood there, even as part of her wanted to flee. She'd known him forever. He'd been her first lover. He'd saved her life in the jungle and she saved his. They were bound by so many threads already.

He'd asked her to marry him.

She'd told him she would think about it.

She swallowed, held his steel-gray gaze. "I trust you. Yes."

His instant, pleased smile sent delicious tingles down her spine. He pulled her closer, tucked her against his chest, then lifted her chin with a finger and claimed her lips in a kiss so tender it made her heart ache.

When they came up for air, he dropped to the leather couch behind him and pulled her onto his lap, and for the rest of the flight they made out like teenagers.

He only let her go to sit in her own place and strap in as they were landing.

"We had this plane configured for corporate travel. It's a work-horse. If passengers need a nap, they can stretch out on one of the couches," he told her with a rueful smile.

"It's fantastic."

"As soon as we get home, I'm ordering a remodel."

"Why?"

"I'm having a bedroom put in the back. We'll be traveling a lot when we're married. I want to show you the world, Miranda."

The word *bedroom* coming out of his mouth made her even more hot and bothered, and their kissing marathon on the couch already had her entire body aching for him.

Suspicion reared its ugly head. "Are you trying to seduce me so I'll marry you?"

"Is it working?" he asked with so much boyish enthusiasm that she couldn't help but laugh.

"Maybe."

"I'm learning to hate that word," he murmured. "I'd like to progress to an unqualified yes."

They landed without a hitch and had a hired car waiting for them, like in Vienna. Despite the very excellent memories their Vienna stopover brought to mind, Miranda's entire body was taut with nerves as they traveled to their destination.

Glenn enfolded her hand in his, his thumb caressing the back of hers.

How strange, she thought. They used to hold hands in college, always touching one way or the other. But she hadn't really done that with anyone else. Kind of thought she'd grown out of it, that handholding was a juvenile thing, not for grownups. Yet holding Glenn's hand felt both comfortable and comforting. He kept her grounded.

Until he said, "Gloria wants you to come to dinner."

That threw her off balance all over again. "What? Why?"

"To thank you. The fact that you brought me back when all the other hired investigators couldn't left a big impression."

"No thanks necessary."

He squeezed her hand. "My family isn't perfect. But maybe you could get used to them. I think you'll find their attitude improved the next time you meet."

Before she could figure out what to say to that, the car stopped in front of a square building, the signs not only in a different language, but a different alphabet, swirling curls flowing into each other. Kids played outside, around two dozen of them, a variety of ages. All girls.

Once again, Glenn claimed her hand as they walked up the steps. An elderly nun waited for them at the door and introduced herself as Sister Maria Isabella, greeting them with an Eastern

European accent. She knew Glenn by name and seemed to be expecting them.

They went down a long hallway, passing classrooms, children studying in the local language, some classes taught by nuns, others by civilians. Their guide led them to the open door of a classroom in the back where an English lesson was in progress. A woman and a man stood in the front of the class, their clothes simple, matching blue shirts and khaki pants. They wore necklaces with crosses around their necks. A missionary couple?

Miranda glanced at Glenn. Did he donate to the school? Was he supporting children here? Orphans? Was this what he wanted to show her, that he was a good guy who also did good things in the world and not just flew around in his private jet?

The gesture was completely unnecessary. She already knew what was in his heart. Knew it and liked it. She smiled at him.

The woman at the front of the room pointed at herself and said, "Mrs." then pointed at her husband and said, "Mr." Then she pointed at herself again. "Lady." And she pointed at her husband. "Gentleman." Then she repeated it again. And after a few encouraging smiles, the children repeated the words after her, in a chorus of timid voices.

Twenty little girls sat on pillows on the floor, ranging in age from six to twelve or so, wearing colorful, if faded, clothing, all very somber, looking eager to please. Nobody was whispering with her neighbor. Not one of them was smiling.

Then Miranda's gaze caught one of the younger girls in the back. She sat away from the others, her arms wound tightly around her skinny little body. She presented such a lonely, solitary figure, the sight of her twisted Miranda's heart.

She narrowed her eyes. *Wait a minute—*

Was she? Miranda took an involuntary step forward, the rest of the world disappearing from around her. Blood rushed in her ears. She'd only seen the little girl in the brothel for a very short time.

And this girl's hair was shorter. She was a year older. But Miranda was almost sure . . .

Then the girl turned, her gaze locking with Miranda's. Her little brown eyes went wide, huge in her thin face. As if in a trance, she scrambled to her feet and stared at Miranda, her mouth opening and closing, opening and closing again.

Then she began to run through the back of the classroom, and she was shouting all of a sudden. "Mrs. Lady, Mrs. Lady." Then more words in her own language. Then, "Mrs. Lady!" again and the other words, until she was out of the classroom and threw herself at Miranda, clutching Miranda's legs in her skinny little arms, pressing her face against Miranda's.

"This is the first time Mai has said a word since she's come to us," the nun said next to them, her expression stunned and joyful at the same time.

Miranda knelt to put herself on the child's level. "What is she saying?" she asked without taking her eyes off the child, her oversize eyes, the badly cut dark hair, the arms that were so slim the sight of them nearly broke Miranda's heart.

"She's saying, 'Mrs. Lady, you saved me,'" the nun translated.

When Miranda opened her arms, the child burrowed against her breast as if she wanted to hide herself inside Miranda, as if she wanted to climb inside her. Miranda stood with her, holding Mai tightly to her chest. Hard to say who was holding on tighter.

"Hello, Mai. I'm Miranda." She smiled at the little girl, then glanced back at Glenn, who'd taken a few steps back. Because Mai might be scared of men. If Miranda wasn't already hopelessly in love with him, she would have fallen for him right then and there.

"Is this an orphanage?" she asked.

"Kind of," he answered carefully.

"It's a children's home." The nun provided the information. "We raise them and educate them, teach them sewing before they leave us at eighteen."

"Are they eligible for adoption?" Miranda asked without having to think about it.

The nun hesitated. "We don't normally receive requests. This is a rescue home for girls recovered from child prostitution."

"All of them?" Miranda felt the blood drain out of her face as she looked around at all the innocent faces. The lack of smiles suddenly made sense. "I'd like to adopt Mai."

Glenn moved a little closer. "I can take care of the paperwork and the lawyers, if you'd like."

Another gift. She didn't even think about refusing it. His company probably had an entire legal department, and a lot of those lawyers would know international law like the back of their hand. Glenn had contacts in politics, possibly even in foreign countries where his company held interests. If he could shorten the wait time by even a single day, she would be grateful beyond words. "Thank you, Glenn."

The female English teacher came from the room at last. "Is everything all right here?" she asked in a British accent, then smiled at the little girl. "Mai doesn't normally let anyone touch her. Do you know her?" she asked Miranda.

And Miranda said, her heart swelling with so much emotion she could barely contain it, "I'm her mother."

She turned to Glenn, smiling her gratitude and her love. The love brimming in his eyes took her breath away.

She had so much to tell him, but she said only a single word. "Yes."

Acknowledgments

My most sincere gratitude to JoVon Sotak, Melody Guy, Lauren Kennedy, and the brilliant staff at Montlake for their wonderful help. Huge thanks to Sarah Jordan and Diane Flindt. I'm lucky to have you all on my team.

About the Author

Tunde Tucsek, 2011

New York Times and *USA Today* bestselling author Dana Marton has thrilled and entertained millions of readers around the globe with her fast-paced stories about strong women and honorable men who fight side by side for justice and survival.

Kirkus Reviews calls her writing "compelling and honest." *RT Book Review Magazine* says, "Marton knows what makes a hero . . . her characters are sure to become reader favorites." Her writing has been acclaimed by critics, called "gripping," "intense and chilling," "full of action," "a thrilling adventure," and wholeheartedly recommended to readers. Dana is the winner of the Daphne du Maurier Award for Excellence in Mystery/Suspense, the Readers' Choice Award, and Best Intrigue, among other awards.

Her book *Tall, Dark and Lethal* was nominated for the prestigious RITA Award. *Deathscape* reached the number one spot on Amazon's Romantic Suspense Bestseller list.

Dana has a master's degree in writing popular fiction, and is continuously studying the art and craft of writing, attending several workshops, seminars, and conferences each year. Her number one goal is to bring the best books she possibly can to her readers.

Keeping in touch with readers is Dana's favorite part of being an author. Please connect with her via www.danamarton.com or her Facebook page (www.facebook.com/danamarton).

Having lived around the world, Dana currently creates her compelling stories in a small and lovely little town in Pennsylvania. The fictional town in her bestselling Broslin Creek series is based on her real-life home, where she fights her addictions to reading, garage sales, coffee, and chocolate. If you know a good twelve-step program to help her with any of that, she'd be interested in hearing about it!